clever girl

Tania Glyde is twenty-nine. She lives in London.
Clever Girl is her first novel

tania glyde

clever girl

PICADOR

First published in Great Britai

This edition published 1996 by
an imprint of Macmillan General Books
25 Eccleston Place, London SW1W 9NF
and Basingstoke

Associated companies throughout the world

ISBN 0 330 34260 6

This novel is a work of fiction. Names, characters, places and incidents are either the product of the author's imagination or are used fictitiously. Any resemblance to actual events or places or persons, living or dead, is entirely coincidental.

9 8 7 6 5 4 3 2 1

A CIP catalogue record for this book is available from the British Library

Typeset by CentraCet Limited, Cambridge
Printed and bound in Great Britain by Mackays of Chatham plc, Chatham, Kent

For Katrina Farrell

Acknowledgements

Many, many thanks to Rachel Calder at Tessa Sayle, and to Georgia Garrett at Picador. Thanks also to Katrina Farrell, who died suddenly and tragically in March 1995. She was the best employer a writer could ever wish for.

'. . . for everybody must now move in a circle, to the prevalence of which rotatory motion, is perhaps to be attributed the giddiness and false steps of many.'

Jane Austen

I CLAMPED MY HAND over my mouth, every finger dug deep into the surrounding flesh. Breathing shallowly through my nose I sat, unblinking, for over an hour.

'Jesus loves you, you've got to remember that.'

The woman leaned across to me and touched my hair, steadying herself with her other hand as the train rocked. We passed under a bridge. Her black skin shone like silver in the flashing darkness. She was smartly dressed in a fuchsia and white suit with a nipped-in waist and matching hat. Her face was so kind. I felt the familiar well of tears, as always when a stranger punctures the membrane of private misery.

She had a child with her, about five years old, an adorable little girl, her hair braided in tiny acorns all over her head. She wore a red coat with a bright orange sweater underneath, and held out a shiny little book with thick cardboard pages depicting hungry caterpillars and beneficent lions. She was turning and turning the book, her hands like leaves as they twisted back and forth. The train passed through a field of Friesian cows pushing their moist black noses through the skinny hedge. The little girl let out a shrieking cry of delight. I reached over and slapped her so hard she fell sideways against the window and remained there, staring at me with huge terrified eyes. The mother leapt up and began screaming in my face. The old man next to me grabbed my arm and shouted as he shook it. People craned over the backs of their seats, their faces striped by the bars of suitcase rests as if I were in a cage, or they were. I sprang to my feet, heaved open the carriage door and jumped.

Everything went dark. I flew and flew. I did not land. I could not open my eyes against the strobing light or close my ears against the screaming in them. I seemed to disintegrate and then to disperse. The sound and movement stopped. I had no breath. I was bathed in silence.

I opened my eyes. A huge translucent creature was edging coyly towards me out of the darkness, its face pulsing with the circulation of its luminous blood, all mouth and the huge bulbous eyes of the deep-sea dweller. I fled upwards, the dank waters parting in a mist of light. I reached the surface. I felt a catch in my throat as I absorbed the new atmosphere on shore.

There was not a living creature anywhere, nothing but grey rocks and dull, foolish vegetation. I blinked, and I was back at the office, from where I had been sacked two weeks before.

the vigilante within

one

Fascinated, I watched Billy's quivering robotic charge towards my limbs. He swung over me and sank his teeth gently into my hand, nibbling quickly, not deeply. His breath stank.

'Little bastard!'

No matter how hard I resisted him, he clung to me, his movements barely thrown off course by the flinging action that nudged him further and further down my body. I threw my head back and laughed, my legs twisted round each other like toffee. I offered him Toby, and he willingly mounted him in a hail of thrusts, lips wobbling.

The sun smoothed its mandala over the hall wall. I rolled on to my stomach and swilled cool milky tea from a white mug that depicted a fat pink bull with flowers twined in its horns. Billy shoved his nose in my crotch and inhaled deeply.

'Piss off, Billy! Piss off, flare-wearer!'

I pushed him so hard that he tipped over backwards on to the floor with a hollow thud. He shot me one last look, one ear tucked back, before trotting out of the room. I jumped up to wash the cheesy tang off my hand. Toby remained in a headstand between my pillows.

'Billy wears flares!' I shouted, as I ran to get a Penguin.

Nineteen eighty. Me. Sarah Clevtoe. Thirteen. Tall For My Age. Cleverer Than You Twats. Hair a shining mouse-brown basin, afflicted with occasional bouts of dandruff that fell, when my long, heavy fringe was agitated with sufficient fingers, in a gritty shower on to the pages of *Cosmo* and *She*. Sculptor, scientist, loved Thatcher, only just done Hitler, currently working on, among other things, a scale model of a grebo in metal, childhood cast-offs and surplus bottle trimmings from a school trip to a plastics factory.

I refilled my mug and went back to what was really my studio, except that thirteen-year-olds don't get studios we get the *utility room*. The ceiling was a merciful mud-brown which partly concealed the spiders and their egg sacs that squatted above me. Trying not to look up, I picked up an old leather gardening glove and a sanding block and set to work on some shelves. An hour and a half later I stopped, took off the glove and swore. Between my thumb and forefinger was a blister, a hard capsule in a sea of chafed red. I teased it with my teeth until the rich fluid burst forth and ran down my hand in a gleaming rivulet.

In the next room, my parents were perusing the *Radio Times* and discussing the increasingly puzzling wealth of their brash but decent next-door neighbours the Batesons. Their speculation was, as usual, accompanied by theatrical scorn at the growing number of extensions on the Batesons' home, and assertions that such additions to their own were not necessary. An additional source of irritation was that the Batesons were big-hearted in an almost *foreign* way. Mrs B. took in crippled cats, and my mother would return from her duty visits particularly irritated by her neighbour's benign rule over these needy, collapsing beasts. Even from our house we could hear the tap of spoon on dish, and soon after, as if from nowhere, a chorus of strangled mews would announce the arrival of a host of balding, limping, lopsided pets. I would watch from high up in the branches of our tree as one, a Douglas Bader among cats, was always first to reach the food. It hurled itself over the pink geometric paving stones, the stumps of its hind legs leaving a dewy trail.

The sun entered its autumnal equinox; the leaves untensed and yellowed. My parents basked in a nirvana of parochial surmise and accompanying rancour from which they were always reluctant to return.

Five o'clock. I picked up an old radio and tried to yank its back off. I sat spread on an old sunchair, the radio's sharp, laminated corner digging into my thighs. It had lain untouched for over a year, and a soft grey nest of old spider's web rolled into a tight ball against me as I tugged. Pink brick dust striped my lap. I didn't want to shout for Dad but it was driving me crazy, that one bit I couldn't unscrew. I bit hard at an apple.

My hands were permanently stained with paint or dye or oil, but my legs felt long. I wanted a shorter skirt than the new school A-line hanging upstairs but my hair was still in the style of Henry the Fifth. The hairdresser had assured me this cut was very suitable for a girl my age, as she teased out a dreadlock of six months' standing, and I screamed for an anaesthetic.

As the sun set, my dad stared out at the garden and the three things which adorned his lawn. It was high time they were removed, as they were starting to rust from the late summer rains. The oldest of them was starting to leave a stain. Up to now Dad had mown around it, but I sensed he had had enough, although he had not yet tackled me on the subject. My sculpting had become a bit public for his liking.

'Large family avyer?' the new postman had suggested, stretching out to hand him *Which?* over my latest pile of tin cans awaiting regeneration. There was a permanent smell of old coffee grounds and egg-waste. Dad gave him a watery smile.

The Times lay open on the table. A survey declared that only 18 per cent of the population thought class distinction lay at the root of Britain's problems. The only things right with the country, it went on, were the police and the monarchy.

'Look, two-thirds of the population want to abolish private education. That's so ridiculous. They're just jealous.'

My mother had always firmly believed in fee-paying schools, even though she had had to go without new clothes for several years so that I could attend the place in the next town as a day pupil.

I galloped into the room. 'I can't open this radio. Can I have a biscuit?'

I took a handful and ran back to my bedroom, where I began tearing up old magazines to stick on the walls.

Sex Progress Workshop, Mondays 7–9 p.m. Meet Bethnal Green Tube. All pre-orgasmic women welcome.

Small ads like these reduced me to giggling hysteria. A little later, however, I caught sight of an article that put me in a rage, which I vented on my nodding parents.

'God how absolutely disgusting I just read how this woman

left her husband and two-year-old child and went off to live in a horrible sort of communal tent place with other women all because of nuclear bombs. I mean we need nuclear bombs don't we? I can't believe anyone would do anything like that God typical lefties making a filthy mess what's it for anyway how selfish. She's a disgrace to the name of woman! I mean who needs feminism anyway? I know I don't, and look at Mrs Thatcher!'

'Quite right, dear. Now, about those things of yours.'

I reluctantly agreed to move them next to the big tree at the bottom of the garden.

Sunday. I awoke early. It had rained heavily in the night but now the sun shone through a soft mist. I pulled on my cords and went outside to move the things. Feeling that something was being disrupted, I turned the process into a ritual, taking the oldest one first. It was a peacock, its tail the cut halves of fruit tins coloured and varnished to let the light reflect on to the metal. It had rusted deeply and was hanging sideways on its post, the reddish taint seeping down like blood. It stood as high as my waist. I bent over the stake and pulled it with both hands. The old damp wood splintered against my fingers and left them smeared green with lichen. The bird rattled cheaply as I walked it towards the tree. I looked down at it, dripping and browned, the head sagging, the colours obscured by birdshit. Defiantly I pushed the stake into the earth. As I bent to drive it further into the thick, meaty grass I saw them. Cigarette ends, split and faded after a summer outside. I looked harder and found more, maybe even a hundred, clustered down by the roots.

Half an hour later the things were arranged round the tree as if in worship. The most recent was the largest, the blue one.

I had never been sure what it was. It had almost built itself. It was nearly as tall as I was. It had arms that curved up and then round, as if it were not sure whether to menace or embrace. Blue made it stand out from the garden. I ran to fetch my Instamatic before the sun moved.

There was a rumble of large engines not far away. The School was coming back to life.

two

SEDGEBOURNE; POPULATION twelve thousand, its heart a bundle of cute cottages milling at the feet of a large private boarding school for boys. Along its main arterial roads were council houses, and estates of privately owned dwellings, whose small windows indicated a developer who knew the value of heat-saving. From the sky, Sedgebourne had the appearance of a skeletal hand, the heel well dug in, the fingers featherlight but growing swiftly, steadily. The country was not pretty, the landscape nearly flat. One of its long sides bordered on a small, jaded stretch of northern sea.

Along the back gardens in our road, beyond the thin, shivering hedges and flimsy gates, was a path. Lined in summer with thrusting nettles, it was trodden mostly by dog-walkers and the Boys who used it as a shortcut from the village square. On the other side of this path was a high brick wall, and behind the wall was Kangaroo Court, one of the boarding houses that served the School, with its outbuildings and smallish Quad.

From a young age, I had been given to understand that Sedgebourne was a very important school, certainly the most important in the county. This was partly due to a dog-eared booklet, bearing the School's crest, that lived among the old copies of the *Radio Times* by our loo. I had perused this short history with interest many times, and many of its images had imprinted themselves on my mind.

Sedgebourne School, apparently, had been quite insignificant until early in the last century when a man called Thomas Gennifer appeared with his money and took charge. There followed a drawing of a group of smiling slaves carrying enormous boxes on their heads.

Gennifer transformed the status of the school. Homes grew larger; culture and heritage arrived in the town. One drawing had a row of erect masters presiding over some celebration with an unpronounceable Latin name. It all looked so *respectable*, and yet I had heard elsewhere that, at schools like this, a newcomer might have marmalade smeared on his testicles, and be made to kiss scalding taps.

The next picture showed local people merrily chipping in during Gennifer's rebuild. The villagers looked only too cheered to serve him, gardening, cooking, cleaning, polishing, saddling, supplying. I imagined them frantically shovelling horseshit, as carriage after carriage rolled away.

Sedgebourne School had a strong sporting history. Certainly, every garden in our vicinity was a convenient catchment area for the tennis balls thrown regularly into them from Kangaroo Court's Quad.

There followed a dark sepia print of the School's Grand Hall. I loved this old photograph. I would stare and stare at it until I felt I could walk inside it, my skin fawn and red-gold against the soft sorrel stone. I strained to hear sounds too, burnished and muffled like the scenery before me. Once, after a long appeal for which the entire village had been enlisted, the outer walls of the Grand Hall were cleaned up. Increased traffic, while improving local business, had blackened them considerably. My parents had walked around the renovated building, admiring its blaring brightness in the winter sun. I had lagged behind, listening to two elderly ladies snivelling with irritation. *Surely it can never have looked like that!* they shuddered. *Looks like some Sheikh Abdullah's going to shove a plaque on it!*

The last picture in the booklet was of a group of recent parents, smiling proudly at an award ceremony. Perhaps I had read too much for a thirteen-year-old, but it seemed to me that there was an agony of effort in their smirks, as if they were straining to live up to whatever it was they had bought.

It was to my school, Whaley, that I now returned for the first day of the new school year. I always loved this day, that going-back feeling, a new folder, a new pen, the clean white tops of pages, other people's suntans. I queued for class, looking over the swirl of heads, the bleach-fronted blondes with whitened eyebrows, the newly shaved backs of necks, the urinous smell of disinfectant. A boy pushed past me in the crowd. His shoe scraped my ankle which was protected only by a red sock. The pressure left a shiny black patch against the little hill of bone.

I sat down with Dido, to whom I had just offered my last piece of doughnut and then skipped away, leaving the bag on her hand. I sucked the remaining sugar from my fingers. The new English teacher caught my eye as I did so, but got only a reptilian flicker in return.

Before roll-call he requested three spellings, *diarrhoea, embarrass* and *liaison.* Giggles, writing sounds. I stared round the room. My skirt was scratchy. I drew a cube while waiting for the others to finish.

'Emma Brown, Mark Carnell, Sarah Clevtoe—'

There was a universal groan at the mention of my name. I had spent most of the previous year in trouble. But this was not trendy trouble, no snogs, substances, escapes, or even thefts. No sins that would later earn me a tousle and fond smirk from raffish older relations, had I any.

I had spent a large part of the year inventing and then promulgating a secret language. Dido, MT, Lorna and another girl called Sally, whose parents had subsequently removed her from the school, had taken to it in earnest. It followed a structure similar to that of Morse code, except that it replaced letters of the alphabet with names of body parts. For a while I had spent all my pocket money on medical magazines in search of new vocabulary. Once we were able to converse, life became fun, until our large-scale cheating in tests proved our downfall, for which I was blamed, by teachers, pupils and their parents alike.

In the summer I had failed to get the school to display one of my sculptures, a hair-cutting machine in corrugated iron, bunches of twigs and old razorblades, in the dining hall. I made a fatal fuss that culminated in a petition, which only my four best friends were willing to sign. With ferocious cowardice they dropped out when the hopelessness of the situation became clear. Indefatigably, I signed the pad of paper four thousand times, in as many different hands as I could manage. This cut no ice whatsoever, particularly when I suggested I could use it as a bank account for when I was next punished with lines.

Rivals poured scorn on my schemes and I had been branded *juvenile*. It appeared not to matter that not one of the name-callers could recite *pi* beyond two decimal places, or explain the difference between *apogee* and *aphelion*.

'Where', a typical parent, an honest burgher, once said loudly at a parents' evening, 'is the merit in party tricks like that?'

My swearing had also been noted, particularly by my teachers. Mum swore very little, her oaths being confined to 'sugar', and occasionally a very quick 'blumps!' followed by a hand rushing to her mouth and a coy roll of the eyes, so she was concerned when my housemistress phoned her to complain. She had never heard of some of the books I had been reading.

Bored by the spellings, I twisted in my seat and looked out of the window at the workmen below. The Police implored me loudly, tinnily, from a small radio, almost concealing the sound of flagstones being flipped up and dropped. The exposed earthworms writhed in the sunlight.

The light from Arcturus takes thirty-five years to reach us. Therefore we are seeing Arcturus as it was thirty-five years ago. It may have gone supernova by now. The concept possessed me as I sat. We see the moon as it was a couple of seconds ago, therefore those worms, or the school chapel, or the cottages that raced by on the way to school, appeared as they were in the past, the infinitesimal past perhaps, but still back there, behind. So when I saw myself in the mirror, I saw myself as I was then, not as I was now; the sum of nearly everything that had happened to me, but not everything. I sent the essence (simplified) of these thoughts to Dido in a note. The reply came fairly fast.

So you mean we're seeing chapel as it was
0.00000000000000000000000000000000000000000000000000000001
of a second ago? Wow ace doss hot cheesy! So what?

We'd gone to see *Breaking Glass* for Dido's birthday. I was jealous of her forthcoming bondage trousers, to be bought with money given by her rich granny.

After lunch we all went back to our new study, where, in time-honoured tradition, the four of us drove out the dead wood of unwelcome hangers-on and potential putters-up of Hollie Hobbie posters with a lecture.

Someone's got a wart! All covered in spunk!
Out it popped big and red PLOP!
And the nun said
Mind my twat!

The door slammed shut. I picked up a hockey stick and began strumming it. The other three banged locker doors and mugs.

'The antichrist's a wanker!' we screamed for several minutes.

The housemistress came in and asked us to start as we meant to go on. I had hardly drawn breath and white spots boiled before my eyes.

'Let's start a band!'

We came up with a half-size guitar and a very old Stylophone between us, and planned for the weekend.

On the way to games we caught up with Toinette, who was *popular*. Her face was a deep holiday caramel, and her hair a whitish straw, giving her the appearance of a negative. The other girls walking with her were shaped like your first horse in pottery aged five, or little cocktail sticks, but this girl had a *figure*. Her companions had just started to experiment with make-up, and their eyes were ringed either with lumpy pearlescent blue or, worse, heavy black which vibrated horribly against their north-European Caucasian pallor. Toinette wore little make-up, and her hair stayed together in natural waves and didn't descend into brushwood.

A chorus of wolf-whistles broke the surface of our chattering. A gang of townies was arranged like crows around the buttercross. We girls bunched and rippled, looking down or letting out disproportionately loud giggles. I tagged behind for a moment, rudely adjusting my shorts. I had not yet begun to use tampons, and the thick pad had already begun to slip to the side. One edge was stuffed against me, compressed and soaking, while the other was tucked, uselessly and uncomfortably, under the elastic of my gusset.

'Shame about the boat race!' came the shout.

'Shame about your cox!' I shot back. They imitated me for a second before getting it. Then Toinette caught their eye and I was lost to them. Toinette was not beautiful, with her gerbilous teeth and lips that peeled back several inches to reveal jutting scarlet gums, but at that age garrulity and hair-flicking seemed to be the keys to attractiveness.

I didn't have an awful lot to say to Toinette. Her father was an electronics magnate, which meant that she was in possession of every new gimmick before it even reached the advertising stage, hence her early calculator, and later, more fashionably, her Walkman, which she would ostentatiously share with whichever boy she was favouring at the time. She always had larger watches than anyone else. She was also as thick as pigshit.

None of the above precluded a friendship between the two of us but, as at all schools where there are day pupils and boarders, a complicated rigid hierarchy existed that discouraged it. Expressed as an equation it could be said that the attention paid to a given child increased in direct proportion to the amount of money paid to the school by its parents.

For housemasters and mistresses, there was something agonizingly *brilliant* in having the charge of a scion of wealth, even from farming. The pasty roughness of the day pupils, who bore the taint of their local origins, was not conducive to ingratiation. Most pitiful of all, however, were those boarders who were in by the skin of their teeth, by scholarship or triple-mortgaging, who had no obvious charisma, and whose parents drove reconditioned brown Triumph Toledos in which they insisted on collecting their offspring at the end of every term. These unfortunates were imprisoned at the school for weeks at a time, like donkeys fenced in with gazelles. The stupidity of some of the richer children was overlooked with a mystical forthrightness. Hands that could barely hold their gold Parker 25s would be lovingly corrected. I, on the other hand, was frequently told off for singing, even songs entirely of my own invention.

I walked ahead of the group, tired of their shuffling and the timewasting Brownian motion of their minds as they reacted to their shabby audience. I thought about the chart I was constructing back home of Venus's orbit around the sun and its peculiar retrograde. I tried to imagine what it would be like to live on Venus. On that planet, one day is as long as two hundred and forty-three Earth days, longer, in fact, than its own year.

How could you tell when your birthday was? And what about seasons? Would you hibernate? And how would salaries be paid?

I was struck when I read that the atmosphere on Venus contained vast clouds of sulphuric acid. Sulphuric acid had a special resonance in my imagination, perhaps because I had seen so many horror films in which people dissolved parts of themselves in it. I imagined descending on to Venus in my spaceship amid the white and ochre swirling and the ship melting and disappearing around me and then, in a billionth of a second's excruciating agony, I would vanish too.

I was obsessed with space travel, and knew that I alone of millions was capable of leaving Earth for an endless journey, a quest, going somewhere that no one could possibly guess at. For me, the death of small animals on the screen was as nothing, on an emotional scale, to the departure of spacemen. I would spend hours in the loft digging out and reading my father's old sci-fi magazines. Lester Del Rey and Isaac Asimov knew there must be more to life than this world!

There was a strangled screech as four girls limped past me towards the hockey pitch, one foot supported by their sticks. I took off in pursuit. We hobbled violently through the teachers' car-park and arrived hysterical with laughter. As we stood waiting for roll-call, a coach entered the car-park and proceeded to plough its way through the milling children. Soon the small crowd was divided in two, one half trapped in the corner between the perimeter fence and the enormous green and red bus.

'Sedgebourne cunts,' someone mumbled. Large boys began pouring out of the bus. They were playing Whaley in the first match of term. Every one of them seemed to have prominent cheekbones and a similar angled, gelled hairstyle. They were much taller than their Whaley counterparts, and their lips seemed more chiselled, but perhaps that was merely a trick of the light that radiated from their constantly polished and gigantic transporter. This bus had caused shudders of aesthetic old-world horror among the Sedgebourne staff, but since it had been the gift of a particularly wealthy Middle Eastern parent, no one complained. And the toilet facility on board had more than made up for any garishness. The visitors were ushered away.

Whistles were blown and children herded. There is a particular cruelty in the method certain sports teachers use to divide a group of children into two for the purpose of a game. What is wrong with pointing to the middle of the crowd and making a chopping motion? Or balancing out the teams in terms of body size and skill? Or using hair colour, or astrological sign? No. There are teachers who, with the envy-by-default that comes with the job, particularly at a private school, try their hardest to spread social discord. So they appoint two captains and let the kids fight it out among themselves.

I was sufficiently unpopular not to be chosen by my fellow pupils, and sufficiently bad at sport not to be chosen by even my very best friends. So when the teams were nearly done I would be left standing proud in the familiar, diminishing little group of drongos and spastics, the human mushrooms that time would never heal. I had become used to this by now, and used it as an excuse to throw my stick at people and sulk.

After games I tried to persuade my housemistress to let me off one of the weekly 'activity' periods, which involved either badminton, bridge or community service, so that I could work on my astronomy.

Mrs Hotchkiss (MSc) had a chip on her shoulder, a social attribute which, if discovered early, can be whisked away with a brush of the hand. In Mrs Hotchkiss's case, however, it had long been subsumed in the suppurating wen of self-hatred that it had engendered. It was amazing that she could find off-the-peg outfits to fit her at all, let alone a husband who could tolerate the smell of her hump.

'Sarah! Quite the little intellectual, aren't we! No, is the answer.'

three

KANGAROO COURT, middle-range in smartness as Sedgebourne's Houses went, was an addition from the late-nineteenth century, founded by a hulk-baron eager to make his mark on the education system. Its façade was grey pebbledash, its windows were unattractively proportioned and its garden had a tendency to flood due to the extreme flatness of the area.

James Radger was Kangaroo Court's pastoral tutor. He smelt of pipe smoke that had inexorably built up over time, and was master of a suspiciously sporting physique overlaid with down-at-heelness. He had a slight *bouffe* of curly black hair, and blunt, rugged, sensual dark looks that made his obvious dislike of women all the more insulting to them; his sardonic glare when anything *titted* hove into view was enough to spoil any aesthetic appreciation of him by the female sex. His accent might have been engendered at a private establishment such as this. Closer examination, however, revealed lax blares and twangs which years of private drill had failed to eradicate.

Radger liked to think he understood his Boys. He dreamt still of senior common rooms he had never entered, which made all the more dangerous his wants on behalf of his young charges.

He knew very well how to smile in the glare of the chrome grilles and buffed nails that faced him at the beginning and end of every term.

Above Radger were a deputy-housemaster and a housemaster, beaming unexceptional married men whose amiable superiority threw his rebarbative tendencies into sharp relief. He had cultivated a Terrible Temper of which Stanislavsky would have been proud. Never had child buckled shoe and scurried faster to its piano lesson than his Boys in the wake of his stern shout; never had children moved more noiselessly past a Schoolmaster's study than the inmates of Kangaroo Court.

The less fortunate of society he singled out for particular hatred. His habit of talking as if responding to a left-wing newspaper article which no one else had read was well known among the small, Tweed-scented village circles in which he moved. He drank, of course.

As a little child, I had intimately encountered a man who though not Radger, so resembled him that, when the memory flickered alight, I feared him.

Radger, for his part, did not particularly seem to like me, for reasons I could not fathom. It was probably my parents and their pitiful succession of company Vauxhalls. Not like his parents, all three hundred or so of them. They had all adopted him, particularly the richer foreigners with their exceptional cigars and handpicked ports.

My friends appeared after Saturday lunch with their instruments. Dad noted Lorna's CND badge with disapproval. Her brother had been down to the big rally in London.

'She's too young to get all political with things like that,' he humphed to Mum, feeling cross on behalf of the citizens of the nation's capital who'd been put off their day's work by the lefties. He suspected it was a conspiracy by the increasing numbers of unemployed. My bedroom door banged shut.

'Anarchy!' we screamed, taking it in turns to pogo to the Sex Pistols on the bed. Dido spilt tea on her pink sweatshirt.

'Mum'll kill me! She only washed it yesterday.'

Lorna produced a small silver safety pin. Her parents had not allowed her to get her ears pierced, so I sat down to devise a way of balancing it in place. After failing for half an hour we attached it to the clip-on part of an old pair of chipped gilt hoops. We had all raided our mothers' jewellery boxes for similar attachments in case of failure. Dido sat quietly in a corner making a necklace of safety pins like a daisy chain. MT attempted to spike her hair. I backcombed mine so that for a couple of moments it stood up and made me look, I was told, just like Siouxsie Sioux.

'OK. We need some lyrics.'

Yes I go to a public school!
I'm not a fool,
I'm not a yob,
So I guess that means I'll get a better job!

Then, more in the spirit of the exercise,

Away in a manger, no crib for a bed,
The little Lord Jesus laid down 'is shaved 'ead,
The cunts in the bright sky looked down where they fucked,
The little Lord Jesus 'ad 'is pubes plucked!

Dido extolled the virtues of the shoddy bondage trousers she was about to buy. It was a strange thing, but her parents, although posher than mine, had no objection to Dido wearing second-hand clothes, while mine shuddered at them. Perhaps they feared the street more than the Smith-Browns because they were nearer to it.

'Hey, look!'

There was a thunder of footsteps on the path and two Boys in sports kit galloped past the bottom of our garden.

'I didn't realize you lived so near! Wooooaaargghhhhh! God, you must get screwed the whole time!'

We fought with pillows while Lorna bounced on the bed, safety pins swinging. The door burst open and Billy rushed in and hurled himself among us.

'Death breath. Death breath!'

The curry-brown carpet became a mass of swirling colour and shouts, Billy's tail curled and quivering above it. He issued mewling little barks as we pushed him around.

'This is meant to be a rehearsal, you wankers!' I shouted. We needed drums. We all had the same thought at once.

'What about your mum's copper pots?'

My heart sank. Mum was partial to anything shiny and polishable that had merely the appearance of age. Thus she had become a regular at Jake's Junk in the High Street, a coy little nest of holey Victorian lace cuffs, broken breast pumps and floral pot-pourri sackettes. The proprietor had painted the interior midnight blue and had hung up swathes of faded net curtaining, to give the effect of a pea-souper. Mum was the proud owner of seventeen pots and kettles of various sizes, which she hung around our lum-o-grate and constantly rearranged. Drumming was out of the question, so we opted for a photo-session instead.

It took an hour for the band to prepare. None of us had actually touched our instruments yet, but we named ourselves the Dildos after consulting a dictionary. The photographs were marred slightly by the foreground presence of plates of half-eaten peanut-butter sandwiches and tall glasses filthy with chocolate froth. Perhaps it was just incorrect exposure, but there was some gold in the air that afternoon, the gold of a sunny September teatime in England, the midges crowding against the sky, the pigeons crying in the poplars.

Somewhere out there was an economic slump. Its tentacles had reached into our household in the form of faded bits, worn areas and commodities not renewed, but since the taste-excesses of the seventies had almost entirely passed my parents by – their own excesses being, in catalogue-speak, *timeless* – they were not to be worried by fashion. Fewer people were buying what my father made, or rather assisted someone else who had meetings with another person who officiated over making, but he still had his Cavalier, and the bills, particularly for his commemorative plates and Mum's curio kittens, were up to date.

In a couple of the pictures, the band is lounging on the Cavalier, its doors open, inviting; hedonism and unspeakable decadence against the gunmetal grey polyurethane interior. Lorna is wearing a black T-shirt which she has knotted at the waist. She has drawn a skull on her neck. The CND badge, the size of her thumbnail, is displayed at her chest. MT has a side pony-tail, long purple shirt and a pair of old black wellingtons, around which she has tied a couple of Billy's old collars. Dido has dug out five sets of clip-on braces, the elastic puckered and frail, which she has attached to her jeans. Her neck is festooned with skeins of fat nappy pins. I, feeling a little bored now and thinking about Mrs Thatcher, have put on blue lipstick, a mini-skirt and sunglasses. Ten poses later we were fidgeting.

'Let's go into town.'

We made it to the village square where we stood, not sure what to do next. I folded my arms boldly. Lorna was dispatched for Creme Eggs. There was a snigger behind us. I thanked God for the make-up I'd put on, which covered my blushes. The snigger came again. I turned with offensive nonchalance.

It was Dawn. Dawn Skyles, my one-time playmate. We had messed around for several years until class awareness had finally ripped in two the pantomime-horse outfit that was our friendship.

Dawn's family lived in the council flats up the road. Her dad was a retired leather-cutter with a shoulder injury. Dawn had a mass of curly blonde hair, which might have remained glorious, if it had not been for the inevitable consequences of her upbringing. It would be subjected to relentless streaking, as if sick birds continuously shat on it in delicate arcs of mustard, brass and institution green. Then it would enter a platinum phase, by which stage a short lifetime of successive bleachings would have left Dawn with three or four desiccated skeins of hair the colour of a stained sheet rustling down her back. But that was the future.

My friendship with Dawn peaked when I was eleven, just before our schooling divided. We went on long bike-rides with foil-wrapped apples (donated by Mum) and chicken crisps (by Mrs Skyles). On our last ride together, a mile's pedalling brought us to our favourite field, with its rotten gate.

'Look! White shit!' I screeched as we scrambled over. A dog turd lay curled in the interim grass on the other side. Uninterrupted summer sun and the unused gate had allowed it to lie bleaching, for several weeks, in the same spot. It was pure white and chalky, pristine, absurd. Our laughter shuddered through the grass and sunlight.

I pulled out a magazine and read from the problem page. Someone was complaining of a discharge, the agony aunt replying that there was nothing to worry about.

'White discharge! White discharge! How horrible! I bet you've got it!'

I leapt on Dawn and bit her, accusing her at the same time of having pubic hair, which she did, being slightly older than I was. I pretended to lie back and then pushed my foot between her legs, sandal still on and damp with dew. We scuffled, Dawn only half resisting, perhaps, who knows, out of boredom. I flipped the end of my sandal under her gusset and peeled it back. The hair was sparse but dark, a brutal encroachment like a doodle on her big buttery frame.

I hadn't been sure what to do after my yelp of triumph at the sight, and lay back with my fist in a bag of crisps. Later on we performed a couple of minor acts of vandalism around the post-box.

We barely saw each other after that. Once ensconced at the local comprehensive, Dawn had taken to sitting on the wall in the village square, eating. I was not allowed to sit there. I used to pass her in the car.

Today Dawn was wearing a grey raincoat enviably creased and vile, with boots which were very nearly Doc Martens. Her hair had been spiked and bleached. Her lips and nails were black. Her nose and ears were pierced. She'd grown a lot. She hung out with a crowd who left every place they sat decorated with mis-spelt graffiti inscribed in marker pen, or spray if they were feeling especially daring. *Sult! Carp! Cnut!*

There was nothing to say. After hanging around awkwardly for a while, the group of us went home. It began to get dark and several parents came and took their daughters away from me. I sat in my room, the Habitat Anglepoise spreading its pool of light over my desk.

There can be no months if a planet has more than one moon. At least there could, but imagine the tension. If there were even only two moons, each would have a different orbit. Double the madness, double the tides, and what would happen to menstruation? Perhaps inhabitants would develop two uteruses, or have two sets of periods that occasionally coincided in one gigantic horrible gush. Imagine Saturn, with more than twenty. Life would be a delicious ripple of confusion, little balls of light squealing up and down above as the population knocked its heads against the wall and bled incessantly. Perhaps there would simply be a sea of blood in which females would stand during certain hours of the day. Perhaps each moon would have its own sector, or sect, of the population who followed it faithfully. There would be wars, perversions, hierarchies, histories based on the size of the moons, or their particular attributes.

I liked Pluto best and his massive orbit out there in the dark, the cold dank end of the solar system, Charon whirling patiently behind.

four

EARLY MORNING. ON MY table was propped a geology book, revealing a foetal map of the world pre almost everything. Laurasia and Gondwanaland, the two huge landmasses were called, the mass of water around them the vast Tethys Sea. How could you name a land where no one had ever lived?

The idea that these creaking hulls of igneous rock that inched back and forth, supporting only the most basic life-forms, could somehow be *named* held a fascination for me. I imagined standing stock still as my room collapsed, the house tumbled, the foundations shuddered and vanished, and all around me cells contracting and retracting, genes backing up and fusing as the vitamins were sucked out of them by the spinning sun. Had my parents owned a video, I would have taped *The Time Machine* and watched it over and over.

The land froze and boiled and froze and there I stood alone. The air seeping fog or singing with ozone. The first person ever. But something bothered me. The night before, I had dreamed of seedlings in a field, planted in thousands of neat rows, fuse-green, tiny, two-handed. Then, as always happens in dreams, the proportions shifted and I was thrown downwards and the seedlings grew and began to push at me, and the little leaves became flat rubbery palms patting, punching at me from below.

I pulled on a pair of brown corduroy trousers anciently matted with dog hairs and picked up my telescope. I was going out to look for Venus. My socks were bright in the early light as I crept out of the house, the sky a gentle choir of blue high above the behemoth of shadows at the end of the garden. I walked quickly down to our tree and burst up into its branches. I climbed until I could see over the wall. A thick yellow light seeped suddenly into the gloom of Kangaroo Court, and for a moment the adjacent Quad became a pool of liquid black. Radger was up. It must have been his turn to wake the Boys. He, the housemaster and the deputy performed this disagreeable task in rotation, the early start spoiling the necessary recovery from a large dinner. It was easy to follow Radger's movements through the windows of the house as he prepared to wake the Boys.

Although it was a full hour before he was first due to ring it, Radger picked up the huge bell and walked out into the corridor. Nine times each day it sounded. It was a moment he seemed to relish, although the bell was so massive that it taxed even his busky frame. The bell spent most of its time on a table in front of the window in the housemaster's study, and I had observed it many times. It was engraved with convolvulus, its handle thick and mellow with age. The ringer would open the study door, raise his chest and the great gurgling clang would ring out to the Boys: get up, go and eat, stop eating, get to class. Each burst of rings would send a flurry of sound through the house, the sweet creature-noise of a warm Boy waking, the hopping-scrape of trousers caught on one foot, the bemused canter into breakfast.

This morning Mr Radger toured the freezing beige corridors, halting briefly by each bank of ancient light-switches. He had, I had heard said, a particular love of old switches, with their round protuberant backs and pert little knobs, and would not have them updated. This had apparently caused consternation among the parents, eager that their offspring not be electrocuted before their time.

He vanished momentarily from my sight, then reappeared at the refectory door and held out a wad of short, tapering, curiously slender fingers. The hanging lamps let fall their bleak ochre.

He was quite far from me now, standing still, contemplating the tables. Mr Radger seemed very proud of his tables. They had been there for years and years. They, and the little benches that ran eagerly alongside them, bulged with the laid-down strata of privileged young lives, hopes, dreams. Seventy years perhaps they had been there, or a hundred. The oak rippled in the early light, worn and grooved by the agitation of burgeoning humanity. There was nothing dead about this substance, which had once stood tall in some meadow or forest and now vibrated with history.

Mr Radger walked to the end of one long table, its triple planks undulating gently down a clean perspective. Now he was even further away from me. He laid the bell down. I was not sure what I saw. It seemed a crude juxtaposition, this morsel of human flesh pitted against the great creature of wood that lay before him. His fingers pushed at the table's edge as he pressed his body against it. The wars and their silences, the cheers of victory, the accents – at this table's birth perhaps the rolled spewed 'r' was still used – coronations and special turkey meals, mulled wine, boaters, a million little shocks of semen, all surged brightly at him out of the great gobbet of sentiment that he held so dear.

My attention was briefly distracted by the matron, uniformed, who was moving soundlessly down the corridor, as if with great purpose. I saw her disappear, then reappear in the refectory just behind Radger. She edged up to him with a gentle movement, her body hopeful. Radger spun around and hit her so hard that she fell back and down between the benches, arms and legs caught in the struts that supported them. He turned calmly back to face the table. She got up and stumbled away out of sight. Radger continued to stand until the morning cold seemed to encroach and he left the room.

The acrid smell of bacon came at me from the kitchens. In the gigantic frying pans the cheap, gas-permeated strips of porkflesh were giving up a glutinous white fluid that bubbled thinly. Kate Bush sang 'Army Dreamers' inside the cook's radio. I struggled down from the tree, the leaves wiping themselves rudely across my face. As I walked over the wet grass I found myself nesting and unnesting the smooth casing of my telescope in agitated rhythm. I went to get ready for school.

It was twenty miles to Whaley, a town near the sea although not quite near enough to be fun. Sometimes we were bussed to the coast for an outing, and the icy wind would tear at our hair as we waited to enjoy ourselves. Every morning I was picked up by a vast estate car with rows of seats like a cinema, packed with other Whaley pupils. The windows always steamed up disgustingly. Somehow one person's breath was all right, but several created a curdled amalgam of other people's carbon dioxide rivalled only by dog-sniff in its offensiveness. It was two weeks into term.

'What can you tell us about those polygons as opposed to those?'

Another hoop-jumping exercise in maths. I was so bored I began to rub my ankles together and stick out my bottom lip. The class was silent, frowning.

'They tessellate, sir.'

'Oooooh, you've lost me there, Sarah, what does that mean?'

'It means they fit together without any spaces between them.'

'Sarah, my dear, as I may have said before, you must have swallowed a dictionary.'

I barely heard him. As he spoke a football clanged outside and brought back to me the brief but solid memory of a small incident that had threaded gently, insistently, into my thoughts.

In the summer, my parents had taken a semi near Bath, with Formica kitchen side and inglenook. The boy next door kicked a football into the garden and it hit me on the head. I went red and he smiled at me. Both sets of parents went out for the day and he came round and we had some wine in the garden. He dropped on to me like a stone, so that my breath was squashed inside me. His erection hurt me, pressed into me without the relief of movement. My hands remained clasped across his back, uncertain. He twisted my nipple for an hour and a half. Seeds from the bird table fell sporadically on my face, and my head crunched against the dried clumps of earth at the edge of the lawn. When I undressed that night and pulled down my small greying bra there was a yellow stain inside the left cup. All I could think of was his saliva and how his mouth seemed to engulf mine like a slippery red oxygen mask, pungent from his third ever cigarette.

The incident had left its bead on the pale, pristine agar of my consciousness. For the rest of the summer, as I had lain down to sleep, strange sights had loomed behind my closed eyelids. I was on a camping trip with this boy. We pitched our tent, then he came inside and lay on top of me but kept quite still. Suddenly, silently, the whole tent was awash with white fluid.

I recrossed my legs. There was a rasp as my skirt tore away from the chewing gum stuck under the table. I thought suddenly of the man who, when I was little, had sorted through me as if I were no more than a bag of dirty laundry. And yet that man had spoken romantic words to me, of a sort. The boy had given me none.

The lesson ended, the day ended, and I got back to my grebo which was growing steadily in the garage. He was modelled on any number of wall-sitters and passers-by who caused me and my friends to shriek with disgust. The long greasy hair, the spots, the flared jeans, the duffed-up leather jacket, the filthy T-shirt, the plimsolls. For the spots I was using small bits of knotted balloon with custard in them; for the hair the combed-out stuffing from an old, damp mattress I had found in some bushes near the local tip. That evening, as I teased out the rough hair, something convinced me that I had dropped my scissors down by the tree, where I had been retying the by now disintegrating peacock.

I walked outside, cursing not the darkness but the blinding security light that flashed on as I stepped into the garden and burnt out my eyes so that I saw nothing. It was suppertime, and Kangaroo Court's study windows emitted only brief rays. There were no lights down by the path. I waited for my sight to return and crossed the damp grass. As I neared the tree I had to blink. A tiny orange blob hovered for a second in the blackness before rising quickly, hesitating and then falling again. It seemed to beckon and yet confuse, like a moving peephole in a vast door to another world. It rose again. I walked towards it.

Air was expelled from lungs, after which came a confident enquiry.

'Hello?'

'Hello. What are you doing in my garden?'

It might have been a fairy tale, I in a little yellow dress led by a receiving party of dancing beetles, coming upon a talking molehill that granted wishes. I got nearer, and a rush of hot tobacco engulfed my face.

'You live in that house there, don't you?'

'Yes.'

'I thought so. I've seen you around. I'm Alexander Pulver. You go to Whaley, don't you?'

We talked. Sixteen, Alex sang with Adenoidal Whitenoise, a school punk band. He suggested we meet the next afternoon after school so that he could see me properly.

School dragged the next day. Perhaps it was no more than a coincidence, but I was getting sick of the groans and insults that accompanied my every move in class or out of it. I was reaching a state of mystification where I absolutely could not see the attraction of certain of my classmates, and yet it was these very people, sitting together in corners laughing, who seemed to be having the best time of anyone. And I was getting tired of being so much taller than most people. Those that were my size, boys of course, ignored me completely. *God, it's the Professor,* they would sneer. It had been easy to ignore all that up to now, but the world had taken on a new cast, as if I had blinked and there were no shadows any more, or that all writing had turned into Cyrillic.

Alex was sitting in the folds of the tree, *my tree,* smoking. He had dark, spiked hair and beady brown eyes with a bit of eyeliner, and definitely passed for good-looking. He also had a skiing tan.

'What the fuck's all this rubbish doing down here?'

The peacock had slumped beyond all recognition, its head bent back, looking almost *bashed,* and my most recent, the tall grabber, had lost much of its grace but retained the blue, lurid and cheap now in the early autumn. All three I had repeatedly found bent over as if pushed, and nearly every morning I had righted them, the blood rushing to my eyes as I swooped quickly to restore my pride.

'They're not rubbish they're my sculptures!'

Sculptures! The word seemed to divide and disintegrate as I said it, shot through the heart by the amused sneer that Alex was directing at me. The word took on an effete, pretentious air, as if it only truly belonged to something crafted of white porcelain under a polished glass bell-jar turning on a silver doily on a cake-stand in some pastel salon. I had never actually used the word out loud to anyone before. I sounded like a little child, caught in the act of proudly describing its own excrement.

'Ever heard of a bloke called Henry Moore? There was also this guy called Michelangelo as well. *They* were sculptors, I reckon. I'd give up now if I were you.'

A great axe-head of tension ducked out of the sky and hung

above my skull, waiting on my reaction. It was the way this sixteen-year-old boy was looking at me – not with the patronizing admonishment of a teacher, or the piss-taking caprice of a schoolmate, but with something else I had never seen. It glowed, his look of assumption. It expressed total confidence in his own opinions. It was not an expression I had ever seen on either of my parents, or anyone else for that matter, except on television.

'They've got a bit wet now but I like them.'

It was the best I could manage. I wanted to tell him to *fuck right off, tosser!* but something stopped me. No one, in truth, had ever really complimented my work. The grebo might prove to be a turning point, but he was only half done. At school I was tolerated, but swatted irritably whenever my demands became, in the teachers' eyes, excessive. Mum and Dad indulged me amid a dark drizzle of remarks about the taxpayer, and how I couldn't hope to support myself out there in the big world on the hard-earned cash of people like them. I once asked my mother how washing up, Hoovering and collecting copper-effect kettles differed from art, if both apparently relied on a taxpayer, in this case Dad. My question was not appreciated.

Alex offered me a cigarette. I refused.

'Are you angry with me?' he teased. No one had ever asked me if I was angry before. The world either took it as read in a thirteen-year-old, or didn't need to know anyway. And anger has never been cool in a social context. So I said no. There was a rattling noise. Up by the house Dad was tussling with his lawn-mower. It was always 'his' lawn-mower, just as it was always my mum's washing-machine.

'That your dad? Why doesn't he get a man in to do that?'

It is a peculiarity of some people that they must always ask why, not in terms of the abstract or the mechanical, but the personal, viz., why are you so poor? Why is your bum that funny shape? It is a pointless and cruel form of put-down. However, two years at Whaley had taught me that you only admitted that your parents weren't rich among your very closest and most trusted friends.

'Because . . . because he likes to do it himself.'

'Weird bloke.'

I was getting ready for bed that night when a small stone flew up and hit my window. I pulled back the curtain. Below, illuminated but barely visible through the bald reflection of my messy room on the black glass, was Alex in his school uniform. I opened the window.

'Hello. Do you want to go out with me?'

'Yeah . . . Yeah, OK.'

There was no other possible answer. He beckoned sharply to me, his face again glossy with confidence, all tempered with a smile. I leaned further out through the window. There was a small thud and then a dripping sound. I had knocked a whole glass of water over my desk. The ink drawing I had made of the grebo was bubbling up in great clear flat blisters, the black ink dividing into its constituent green, blue, rust and yellow and spreading, quietly, into chromatographic lichen before soaking into the thick white cartridge paper.

I left it, went downstairs and we kissed, a coffee- and smoke-flavoured kiss. The bell sounded. When Alex had gone I went back and sponged at the water. The paper was puckered. The image barely remained.

five

In class we were introduced for the first time to the great dictators of the twentieth century. Such personalities were completely alien to me, and I was fascinated. How could one person make so many million follow him (always *him*)? I tried aligning the necessary traits with those I knew: my parents, the Batesons, my friend. None seemed to fit. And all the *death* necessary to keep the person in their position; it all seemed so nebulous, so far away.

I had never seen death, but mass movement I thought I knew about, ever since one day ages ago when, retreating slowly in the sunlight, I put my foot on one corner of a broken patio stone and rested my full weight on it. Within seconds, hundreds of gleaming red-brown ants were pouring out around my feet. I tried to tread on them, but with horror I realized that they were merely taking cover in the deep tread of my shoes and were now streaming up and around the stitching and on to my ankles. I shook my foot in horror. I was not wearing socks, and the tiny bites came thick and fast.

Hitler, Stalin, Mussolini. I found Mussolini rather attractive, with his entourage endlessly digging trenches for themselves, photographers stretched out along the ground.

The next time Alex came round he brought a couple of friends with him. They smiled and nodded in what appeared to me to be a very adult way. They both wore long navy blue overcoats with their uniform. They smiled politely at my jokes, asking me if I minded if they smoked. They were introduced as Kev and Keef (the latter known as Cobra) although I gathered that their real names were Jonathan and Harry, who must, I assumed, have in turn been christened Harold or Henry some time in the long past. Both had good skins.

I made some coffee and they joked about the rugby match against Whaley and about someone or other who had been caught wanking and then suddenly—

'So where did you go on holiday this year, Sarah?' asked Kev.

'Oh, we went to Bath.'

'Do your parents have a place there?'

'No.'

'So was this a *rented* cottage?'

'Yes.'

'What does your dad drive?'

'A Cavalier.'

'Is it a company car?'

'Yes.'

'Ah, right, I thought so.'

'Is there a mortgage on this house?'

Alex began thumping Kev. They were both shaking with laughter.

'Shut up, shut up!' he gasped. Keef joined in.

I watched them flailing on the carpet, all this well-groomed young flesh. Alex suddenly broke away from the others, ran a hand through his hair and sat down next to me and put his arm around me. I felt a little fizz of excitement.

'Some people in here are green and hairy.'

There was a brief spate of rib-digging and punching before Kev and Keef stood up to go, their coffee barely drunk. As they walked out of the door they noticed a lingerie advert I had stuck on the wall. There was an explosion of enthusiasm not previously seen that evening.

'Fucking fit!'

'Yeah. *Fucking* fit!'

'God, I love the breasts of a mature woman!'

'Seeya, Alex! Oh, 'bye Sarah, see you around.'

The room seemed disproportionately silent without them. Alex reached over and put on a tape. The Dead Kennedys exhorted us to kill the poor. Alex turned the chubby button to its maximum. The noise became a burning, boiling rush, but was still not very loud, and appeared to be putting the tape recorder in danger. He turned it down.

His kiss was quick and pointy. He shoved me on to my back and clamped his hand over my breast. He pushed one knee between my thighs and kept it there, in an arrested state of ramming, for the next ten minutes. The sensation reminded me of riding a bicycle over concrete. He kissed my neck and put his hand into my knickers. I felt my chest rise as automatically as if it were being led by the moon.

Suddenly I was warm.

We rolled over. There was a crump as Alex's foot became stuck in a cardboard box. I pulled it off him, laughing as I unbooted my cavalier. There was a picture of a hideous china kitten on the side of the box.

'What the hell was in here?'

'Oh, my dad got my mother a pair of candlesticks for their anniversary. Actually they weren't kittens they were swans.' One pink and one blue.

'Oh, really, that's funny. My dad gave my mother two black swans for our lake on *their* anniversary.'

I went to the loo, and came back to find Alex standing on my bed, flicking the animal mobile I'd made out of tinfoil the previous year. It was dull with dust. With each rapid motion, my monkey, lion and giraffe were slowly deformed, reduced to flailing lumps. I rushed up behind him to shout. We rocked back and forth as I tried to stop him reaching up and flicking again. Finally he pushed me roughly away from him, jumped up and patted the mobile out of the air and across the room where it crashed, destroyed.

'Look what you've done to me!'

He turned to me, opened his flies and pulled down his trousers to reveal baggy blue Y-fronts, tented by a vaguely cylindrical bolt of flesh. I put my hand to my mouth and giggled.

'Touch him, go on!'

He stood over me. There was a knock at the door. It was Mum with a tray of biscuits.

Alex swiftly restored his appearance. Mum had obviously been planning this meeting, since there were three mugs of tea on the tray. Alex's face instantly took on another unfamiliar expression, that of ingratiation tempered with a tiny bit of piss-take. They introduced themselves, but there was to be little small-talk, as my mother was soon off on a tangent all her own.

'You should have seen the cake the Batesons had delivered the other day. Honestly you could have bought a ticket and sat on it! Oh God, and Herself was wearing a *saffron* coat with a *fur collar*! Already! I mean, it's hardly winter, is it? She looked like something out of *The Wizard of Oz*. Anyone would think she was . . . well, you know what I mean!'

'Don't you like Mrs Bateson?' I asked.

'It's not a question of *like*, Sarah. They're just not our sort of people. You'll understand when you're older.'

I pressed my fingers together, willing her to go away.

'Of course, Alex knows what I mean, don't you, Alex? Going to that posh school of yours!'

The cringing cramps in my stomach began to radiate, but I was saved by Radger, ringing the bell for supper. Alex excused himself. I went downstairs to watch *Morecambe and Wise* with my parents. I sat cross-legged on the floor.

Eric 'n' Ernie bounced and flirted in their curious ill-fitting suits. As I watched, I found myself dividing my attention between the screen and the thick, bulbous Habitat pottery lamp on the coffee table beside it.

This is a rarely discussed condition, in which a motionless object near the television reveals as much to the observer's imagination as the fictional plots and characters appearing on the screen. Its sister condition often occurs at the cinema, theatre or concert-hall, when the viewer relates some aspect of what he or she is watching to events in his or her own life, and goes off at a silent tangent for fifteen minutes before returning to the drama in hand, having missed a vital part of the plot.

The lamp sat and pointed upwards. The harder I stared at it the more I wanted it inside me. It was a peculiar sensation. As my eyes passed back and forth from screen to lamp, I could not prevent tiny serpents of helpless lust gathering before my eyes, entering me and descending *en masse*. I imagined myself squatting over the popular ceramic and somehow managing to absorb its entire girth.

But after that what? My mind spun for a minute with the onset of possibility. My underdeveloped inner thigh muscles went into spasm. I rose and went downstairs to the bathroom where I locked the door, lay down on the itchy nylon olive green carpet and raised my legs.

There are so many ways to masturbate. Some are art forms, some have a sneaky grace, and some are no more than a *frig*. This being my first time, the latter raw unrefined action was what I now performed, a gush of barely understood images racing through my mind.

It took less than a minute for me to learn, tentatively, at first, with one finger, the middle one, like Alex had used on me. But not going right for the clitoris as he, agonizingly, had but just to the side. The feeling scared me for a minute, but then it became a beckoning. I followed.

The nervous fractals that tide and multiply with orgasm pulled me six times from my Allied bed and upwards, from where I descended like a paper plane, wobbling and diving deliciously to earth. My chest was patched like a map of northern Canada.

'Hello, little Ern!'

The sixth orgasm required some effort, but desire still whirled out of me from somewhere like a genie. All that free pleasure to be got in the street, bollards, police cones, almost any cylindrical form of relatively possible proportions.

Laugher from the television.

When the body encounters an atmosphere or object of its own temperature, the mind plays curious tricks. In spring, when warm gusts overlay the residual chill of the middle northern hemisphere, you may walk in the park and suddenly feel nothing at all on your skin. It is only the movement of hair and clothes that reminds you that you are solid. Similarly, when I pushed my finger into the liquid core of my brimming vagina, it seemed to vanish, the sensation of it elided with the heat coming from inside me. I put my finger in my mouth and again, I had to wait a couple of seconds before my tongue could acknowledge the gel melting on it. From then on the scent of myself would become the quickest way to arouse my desire.

I lay back exhausted and turned my head sideways. Near my eyes was an unmistakable *grolet,* a tiny sausage of used pink toilet paper nestling below the toilet's hull. I leapt to my feet in disgust and returned to the living room. *Morecambe and Wise* had given way to the news.

I went to my workroom. The grebo posed, half-made, against an old chair. I was about to start on his flares. I had taken apart an old pair of jeans and was constructing the widest pair I could possibly imagine, extending the despised flaps until they sailed well out of order. Usually I would giggle just looking at them. I picked up a bradawl and picked idly at some stitching. Music blared from Kangaroo Court, and the inevitable laughter which always puts the seal on loneliness. My body felt hollow. In three weeks, the Dildos had gone absolutely nowhere. The band had shown a marked reluctance to take up their instruments and actually play anything. I had written some songs, but when I read them out I realized that the tone of callow aggression, imitated from a thousand punk bands religiously taped from John Peel, did not sit well with our chirpy hysteria.

The following Sunday afternoon, Alex invited me to his band's rehearsal, in a freezing, echoing hall in the town. I sat awkwardly while the band members swore at each other in immaculate accents and then sang about death and drugs, neither of which I had any experience of, and therefore was not to know that neither did they. Alex did not once acknowledge me, and I became quite agitated waiting for the final conversation about women to end before he walked towards the door. He grabbed my arm without a word and manoeuvred me under the concrete stairway where I allowed him to cop a feel. The familiar hand clasped my crotch like a codpiece.

six

Fat is naughty!
Fat is ugly!
Fat is bad for your health!
Fat will leave you . . .
ON THE SHELF!

Four small girls were dancing around three shoes in a circle. On the word *shelf*, they dived for the shoes, and the slowest person was out. The October air was knife-sharp in my lungs as I wandered through the Whaley campus. Two girls whirled a big rope while another leapt over it, chanting breathlessly:

Kill this bitch
Stab this cow
Prick her with a pin
She's so thin!

Chips are hips
Fries are thighs
Honey is tummy
I hate my size!

Fried egg a hundred
Ice-cream two
Pot of cream five
But I'm thinner than you!

Waiting for after-lunch class, I saw four of my classmates with their noses deep in small yellow booklets. They squatted in a line against a wall, skirts fanned out over their legs and feet, giving them an ornamental appearance.

Occasionally one would raise her head, read something out loud and the others would nod portentously or shake their heads in disgust. I had seen these same yellow books in lunch, consulted and as a result the contents of plates pushed around and discussed.

Bemused, I joined my class to wait for the chemistry lesson. But even here I could not find an unpuzzling haven in which to contemplate. At the edge of the waiting crowd, four girls, including Toinette and MT, were standing face to face with a group of boys. None of them could keep still. Whenever a boy said anything, one of the girls roared through her hair, another rocked back and forth so violently I thought she was about to fall over or at the very least drop her bag, and Toinette kept dancing forward and whispering in a boy's ear, after which she would screech violently, revealing every shining facet of her over-exposed gums and surgically whitened teeth. I attempted to join in. One boy cracked a weak joke about a stone-age bra. I tried to fall about laughing but all I could hear was my own voice. At the next piece of humour I forced the laugh out even harder. Somehow this gin-soaked bray was wrong coming from clean faces, undyed hair and school uniform, but no one seemed to care.

And MT, my lifelong anti-smoking friend, with whom I had once spent hours wandering around Sedgebourne Blu-Tacking up pictures of tar being poured from test-tube to Petri dish bearing the legend *Smoke Now, Die Later*, was puffing coyly with the rest of them.

The teacher appeared. I dropped my textbooks as the jostling began. The little crowd shuffled routinely over them.

At tea I sat near the girls with the yellow booklets, curious to see what they were doing. They talked quietly until suddenly the skinniest one impounded the others' booklets with sonorous strictness and then, picking pages at random, pointed to each of them in turn.

'Lucy! Rump steak, grilled!'

'Two hundred and twenty per hundred grammes, three hundred per serving!'

'It's one hundred and sixty-eight and two hundred and eighteen, actually. Clare! Apples!'

'Forty-six, forty-six. Same weight!'

'Katie! Mashed potato!'

'Eighty, one hundred and sixty. Add fifty-one per individual pat of butter.'

These were girls who, in maths, sucked their hair and giggled and, after much picking of their nails, ventured the wrong answer.

seven

ONE NIGHT, with Patrick Moore's assurance, I took my telescope and left the house with the intention of going into the middle of the playing fields and watching for shooting stars. However, I could not resist climbing up my tree just once to see what was happening in Kangaroo Court. Tonight Radger's study was filled with young Boys, all staring up at him with the look of small animals in expectation of food. There was a softness to the light, as if the room were about to be photographed for the school brochure, and a little Vaseline smeared hastily on the lens. It was, in fact, caused by smoke from Radger's pipe, whose belly gulched forth mustardy veils that hung heavily in the densely furnished room. Radger appeared to notice this and flicked open the window.

'Boys. You probably know why I've got you all in here this evening. Since there are only twelve of you I thought my study was more congenial than the rather clinical common room, and I hope you all agree with me. Are you sitting comfortably, ha ha? Then I'll begin.

'I give this talk every year, and every year I think to myself, why do this? Can't they just sort everything out for themselves?

And then I remember the darkness of my early teenage years, and how I desperately searched for answers to the questions I had begun to ask myself. I even riffled through my mother's diary for answers! You can imagine how far that got me! Especially the thrashing I got when I was caught!

'But first of all I want to tell you not to worry. Women aren't all out to get you – just the ones over three foot eight! But seriously. When you are privileged enough to be able to attend a school like Sedgebourne, it must occur to you more than once in a day just how much luckier you are than the rest of the population. Expressed as a percentage, you're probably in the top ten per cent for intelligence, personal appearance and, of course, family wealth. In fact, it would be safe to say that you can justifiably take a look in the mirror before you go to bed tonight and say to yourself, "Johnny, I'm posher than the next man and proud of it!"

'But you must never be arrogant. And awareness of just how lucky you are will not make a man of you in certain arenas, namely that of the birds and bees, otherwise known as dealing with the unfairer sex.

'Girls probably frighten you a bit, don't they, with their hair and garish make-up, and that mysterious way their skirts blow about? How nice, you must think, to be able to walk around with the wind playing around your legs!

'But that's not the whole story, unfortunately. In my day there were a lot of nice girls that one could date, hold hands with a bit and marry if one wanted to. Nowadays girls like that are pretty thin on the ground, and anyway, all too often you can't tell the difference between them and the disgusting little whores who go round doing it with anyone who asks. But then that's just my opinion. Would anyone like to ask me anything? I am, after all, here to help.'

With these words Radger slammed the window shut. I watched for amusing hand gestures but was disappointed. At the end of the session Radger picked up the bell and the Boys scattered out into the echoing corridors. I searched for shooting stars. None appeared.

I went home to read but was thwarted even in that. My favourite book about the moon was missing. It was an early seventies publication, shiny paper, full of intelligent early seventies speculation, with an old *Save It* sticker peeling on the front. Perhaps it was rotting in the garden, its pages matt and bloated from successive rainstorms. I searched through the collection of outdated geology books that had finally been laid to rest along the bottom shelf in the hallway.

For some reason, such books were particularly effective when read on the toilet. Perhaps it was all the data, all the relationships of scale and proportion and time all knocked into one, whose magnitudes and dimensions fluctated with the evacuations of the body, and needed equal concentration.

Screams echoed sporadically from the living room as I searched. Dad was watching *Doctor Who* with his peanut-butter sandwich.

My first conscious act of feminism was probably to criticize the number of squeals emitted by the Doctor's female assistants, and scoff rudely at the panicking sheen-haired long-booted creature surprised by yet another set of wobbling latex tentacles.

I picked on and on at the shelves, pulling out any biggish book with an unidentifiable spine. But it wasn't there. With a child's crossness I rammed my final mistaken choice back in its place and it fell straight back and into the hollow between the books and the wall. Others followed. Eight heavy books slipped gently on to their back corners and rested before their combined weight lurched them sideways and into the cavity behind. I cursed, hoping there was no spider there. It was the season for them too, when they came in from the cold. I yanked the heavy volumes out. As I did so I caught sight of piles of paperbacks stacked carefully in the dark little space. What a waste! They should be out on a shelf where people could get at them. By the handful I forced them out of the darkness.

Deep Throat, Riding Lessons, The New Panties-offcracy, Supervixens Cast Off!. Their covers depicted young, slim women in various states of undress, sometimes accompanied by men. I took a handful and hastily put everything back. Forgetting the moon's origins, I walked quietly back to my room and shut the door.

For the next few nights I became involved with a cast of characters as new and therefore worthy of attention as anyone else I had met. One woman appeared to orgasm every few seconds, even as she was writing, and thought nothing of going to the supermarket with a live vibrator inside her, buzzing away to the envious chagrin of the checkout girl. Another announced joyously that the best fellatio was to be found in Bologna, due to the particular profusion of sausages there. There was the invented, I presumed, world in which the women were only allowed to dress as far down as the waist, and could be summoned for all variety of intercourse with a simple phrase, 'Bend over, chattel!' Then there were the identical platinum blonde twins who were there to indulge man's every whim. Every hard-on, of which there were many, was an invitation for typing, cooking, driving or knitting to be downed and hands, lips or feet to be applied until ejaculation was achieved.

All these women were *ready for it*, twenty-four hours a day. I, of course, had never read anything like this, and somehow it all gave justification to Alex's urgings which, during our twice-weekly meetings, were increasing in intensity.

'Come on, come on, get him out, can't you? Just lie down, oh go on, go on. Other girls do it, why don't you? Go on! Shall we? Shall we?'

'What?'

'You know, make love, like they say in magazines?'

I had never been sure what to do at these points. The outer shell of my body felt nothing. His cold finger wriggled and dived into my knickers and jabbed at me abrasively. My latest reading matter seemed to imply that a certain reaction was required of me, a certain falling in with whatever was on offer. When I was alone, however, nothing could inhibit the scalding veneration I had for my own sexual organs.

My friends and many others by extension knew that I was seeing a Boy from Sedgebourne. Which transformed the fact of knowing me from a straight negative to a positive that could be compared to an early crocus bud.

October billowed wetly into November. I had entered into hello relationships with several Boys from Kangaroo Court, whose smiles had become so knowing that all I could do in return was imitate them, leaving me with a face like a Greek theatre mask.

One Saturday my parents were out shopping. Alex appeared at two o'clock and we spent the next three hours posed in the various tableaux that come with an approaching sexual crossroads: Alex with one hand clamped on the back of my head trying to force my mouth on to his penis; Alex with his hand firmly pushing mine on to his penis (declaring that it was seven inches long); me with my bra still done up, rucked up under my chin; the top of my head rammed into a pillow, giving me the appearance of a mob-capped kitten on a Christmas card.

It was inevitable that, after a couple of hours, I would be able to squeeze some desire out of this mess of callow physiological ballast. If I closed my eyes, the lampstand from beside the television appeared, to kickstart me. By teatime I was warm and enthusiastic.

'I like you, Sarah. Maybe, ha! I love you. Let's do it tonight!'

The sky was deep blue, the bed a haven, an albumenic niche where everything could commingle in safety. *Timelessness* reared its ugly head. Alex arranged to come back at eight, when my parents were going out to a local townspeople's committee. I preened in front of the mirror. I bathed, I flicked, I applied creams. The radio played Adam and the Ants. Suddenly it began to get colder. Perhaps there was something wrong with the radiators. I shivered. Alex appeared, looking keen and nervous. We went to my room. He switched on the main light and sat on the edge of the bed. The plastic chandelier clung to the middle of the ceiling, as if in retreat. Its facets, bruised from many falls, swung dully as the door closed.

'OK. So it's clothes-off time, then.'

I had hitherto assumed Alex was experienced, full as he was of tales of the wild little numbers he'd *been with*, since he was ten. Something froze me.

'Let's put the light out.'

He did so and we stripped. Unfortunately he then could not see to put on the condom, and I was left sitting there, spread, while he hopped to the switch and back.

'OK, then.'

He pushed and pushed against the dry channel I was offering him. Unaccountably, I found myself thinking of the coelacanth, and how it must carry the most ancient collective memory of any living creature.

'Come on, come on, are you there yet? Are you there yet?'

The harsh stuffing sensation gave way to discomfort. I tried to make a joke.

'"Come on, boy,"' I recited, '"feed me your girth!"'

I hoped I'd got it right, and giggled sweetly. But my face and legs were chilled, and Alex did not laugh. Suddenly his cock slipped into me with a shiny scrape. He moved about a bit for a couple of minutes, and then pulled out.

'Got any porn mags?'

I could not reply. He took off the unfilled condom, wrapped it up and left. I remained on the crumby candlewick. I looked down at my vestigial tail of a body, so unlike its to-be-adult self that I could not possibly, even through narrowed eyes swimming in film, replace one of those models in those magazines with it. Pale, tapelike, with some shape in the middle to be sure, some breasts there, of course, but as if the whole, in a few thousand years, would simply drop away through obsolescence.

I had been too young for this, I knew. I thought about what I had read only that morning. Oh, to be cheap and carefree, to think of nothing but the moment, to ride astride, stained nylon pushed back, small bruises scattered, hair stiff and tangled, as if with seaspray from a ride in a small but powerful boat, make-up lining like African rivers on a map, the orgasm slipping through quickly and effectively, and to stand up afterwards and peck and adieu!

'Enola Gay', at full volume, anaesthetized me against the great drumming cheer that rose up out of Kangaroo Court a few minutes after Alex left.

I did not see him for three weeks. I began to be puzzled by the curious mixture of ignoring and attention I received in the street. Otherwise life remained, on the surface, the same.

My first awareness of myself post-virginity can be reflected perfectly in the first appearance of animals on land. Something, a high wind, a tide, a predator, mutated fins, caused a creature to bump up to the shore and scrape along for a few inches before returning. There was, during this first foray, no predator up there to eat it. Perhaps it would itself assume that role. It could do nothing but evolve.

eight

'SO. DJER FUCKIM THEN?' whispered MT, as we dipped small pieces of fabric in different-coloured dyes.

My hands seeped brown and green as I plunged them in and out of the stained washing-up bowls. There were no gloves left when I had come to get mine. The teacher, Miss Float, did not appear to regret this state of affairs and announced loftily that I would just have to be careful then, wouldn't I?

We hung out our work to dry. Seven little batik anarchy flags in autumn shades dripping messily over the sink.

'Well, girls,' said Miss Float, 'these are truly fabulous. What would your parents say?'

She turned away. There was a 'Kick Me' sticker on her back. We giggled.

'Did he have a big one?' MT demanded.

'He told me it was seven inches,' I replied.

'Golly!' She picked a transparent ruler off the floor and held it up to the light, her finger covering the seven mark.

'Just think! You had all that inside you!'

Through the window I watched as Toinette passed, her lemon-blonde hair almost green in places.

'She says that's 'cos of the swimming pools in Barbados,' I said suddenly.

'What is? Sarah's going red, Sarah's going red!' MT sang in my ear. Going red was something I had never learned not to do. I had therefore developed a defence mechanism to divert attention.

'Get the parachutes! I'm falling!' I shrieked. One foot still on the ground, I raised my arms and other leg, one hand clutching my hair, and opened my mouth wide, howling. Even now it worked, and MT burst into hysterical cackling. Sooner or later I would have to evolve a more sophisticated technique.

That night we went to the pub. To celebrate, in MT's words. Dido came too, sworn to secrecy. They tucked themselves in at the back while I went to the bar. No one ever questioned me about my age. I returned and placed three snowballs on the table.

'Spunk! Hooray!'

As always, my nose got stuck in the small-mouthed glass. My body felt awkward, tucked in the small wooden chair, with its curving, pointless arms.

The following evening I began to itch. I was lying on my bed in a long skirt of such thick material sewn so tightly that I could not possibly have remedied the agony beneath it from outside. Normally this would not have been a problem. I could have reached for the zip, undone it and pushed my hand into my knickers. But tonight I had guests.

I squirmed and tried not to. An admiring glance, like a great greasy bubble, passed between the Boys on my bed. My fringe flopped and swayed with each polite contortion. I twisted and sat up, hoping to crush the itch into submission. There was something called young gentlemanhood which prevented these Boys from acting on their impulses, plus less nebulous factors such as rules and laws and parents in the vicinity.

I tried to nod sagely and flirt while clenching and unclenching my buttocks. Thirty seconds' respite and there was another ecstatic onslaught. I pressed my feet together and prayed. One of my visitors, whose name I did not know, spoke.

'McLeod's sister's fucking fit. You're very tall, aren't you? What the fuck's this?'

'It's Venus's orbit around the sun.'

'Bit of a boffin, then? There's been a survey out, my dad was saying, that proves men are better than women at maths and sciences.'

The itching spread forward into my pubic hair. Between my legs was a delicate inferno of bright pink sparks, as if a wind-up toy car was held against me and the wheels whizzed round by hand.

The other visitor walked up and down my room. His foot caught something sticking out from under my bed. He pulled at it, dislodging several years' worth of paper, and an old shoebox full of toy cars. It was a snake I had made two summers ago, a modest piece of anthropomorphism, created from the embodiment of a child's first brand awareness, the Coke can.

'You make that?' He shook his head and laughed. 'What a load of crap.' His eyes fell on the bra advert on my wall. 'God, fit breasts.'

Over the last few weeks I had gradually begun to cover my walls and ceiling with pages torn from magazines. The poster of R2D2 and C3PO had almost vanished. Whether by accident or design, I had stuck the closest of the close-ups of models' faces around my mirror, so that when I looked in it I was always faintly surprised by my own straight unfurnished features after the shaded glittering holes, button noses and split, shimmering mouths that framed them.

Joy Division came to an end with a click.

'McLeod's got a new Technics four-speaker. Radger's already threatened to gate him.'

'White Riot, yeah!'

'Hold on a minute.'

In precise small agony, I got up and went to the loo. I went to the bathroom and locked the door. Gazing upwards at the peach vinyl wallpaper and balding electric blue handtowel which seemed always to have been there, I yanked down my skirt and knickers.

Threadworms are not sophisticated in any way, unless you count their eggs' ability to survive chyme and other carriers of enzymes. Threadworms do not sit easily with perfumes, rings, unchewed nails, brushed hair, successful dinners and other signs of a manicured character. Threadworms do not care if the door is opened for their host or whether it isn't.

This was a particularly populous attack. There is a peculiar horror in knowing that a living creature, a tiny white spasmodic curlicue of matter, however simple-minded, is living on *you*. I tore and gouged at myself to put out the tiny pale flames and counted seventeen of the gentle parasites.

Back in my room, the audience was getting restive. The pacing one had torn the snake's head off and thrown the pieces on the floor. I was about to shout at him but somehow I wanted to dissociate myself from such childish reactions.

'Whoops, sorry! So do you like men, then?'

'Well . . . they're OK . . .'

'Have you been out with a lot of the ones at Whaley, then?'

My visitors were sixteen, maybe they knew more than me. But I could take a radio apart better than they could. They began talking about a party they'd been to in London, and what they had supposedly drunk and smoked there.

'Did you hear John Peel last night?'

'You listen to John Peel?'

'Yeah. I really like the Gang of Four.'

'I didn't think girls liked that sort of thing. What do you think of the Piss Dogs, then?'

'Well . . . they're OK . . .'

'HA, HA! I just invented them. Girls don't know anything.'

The bell rang and they left. As their footsteps crunched away into the dark, I undressed and lay on my back, leaning my legs against the wall. Taking a small kodak-yellow mirror in the shape of a flower I swung the Anglepoise into position. I peered hurriedly at my pulsing anus, and was rewarded by a tiny white face emerging whose expression I could not discern.

I went to bed and turned on the radio. Ronald Reagan had got Carter out. It meant almost nothing to me, except that Amy Carter had had the Police play at her tenth birthday party. I switched off and put on a Joy Divison tape I'd made. Being taped from FM radio, it had a certain loudness, but was spoiled by a swish of interference at the start, the distortion billowing.

No one has ever really considered how to tap this capacity of even the thickest, most jaded child to love and respond to music. I rewound and played, and rewound and played, my fantasies gradually taking on more colours each time as if on an infinite printer's block.

There was a thumping on the door. Dad had had enough of the bloody noise, the same song over and over again. Why is it that adulthood brings with it an embarrassment about repetition? There is no better way to concentrate the mind than by saying the same thing, or looking at the same colour. Reluctantly I turned down the music.

In the last weeks of term, I began to discover friends I never knew I had. Potentially exciting strangers began turning up at the house demanding to be let in. I tolerated the stream of well-wishers, many of whom had consumed several pints of beer and who sat, slumped in my chair, expectantly. I had no idea why these Boys came, except that occasionally I was informed that one of them fancied me, and the other who always accompanied was acting as a sort of rotating chaperone. A Boy who arrived on, for example, Tuesday night, pissed out of his head, might by Friday have turned into the sidekick. One particularly persistent one, braving the scene alone, managed to get me on the bed, but I turned away in disgust, from his breath, from the coldness of his nose and the stiffness of his huge overcoat, whose rough wool teased my neck. An icy hand was thrust between my legs, which I dragged away.

On seeing the little orange points in the darkness I would walk down to our hedge by the path and ask for Alex. Giggles spurted forth, before being stifled by the polite silence that would extend into these Boys' adulthoods and smother all spontaneity. Exchanged glances cannot be seen in the dark, but they can be felt. I would feel my voice echoing and I turned away, laughing it off.

My thirty-seventh visitor alleged that one of his teachers had been talking about me and had called me a *desperate little floozy*.

'Dad,' I said later, 'This boy I met told me his teacher said I'm a desperate little floozy!'

Dad hit the roof with such immediacy that I had to retract, claiming it was a joke. Perhaps it had been. But the expression that clouded his face during that burst of outrage was more complex than mere fury, and it would be several years before I could perform a sufficiently scientific separation of it into its constituent parts. However, I knew I saw fear there; fear, perhaps, that he would have to act, but could not. Not something a child wishes to see in its father. To see fear in a parent is to see the abyss.

'Whore!' Someone shouted as I walked to meet my lift to school.

'Slag, slut, no-friction, open-all-hours, spreadlegged whore!'

The excessive violence of this outburst was sensed even by the shouter's peers, who shushed him, amid giggles, as they barrelled up the hill to the square. I stooped to hide myself. Waiting for the car, I doodled holly leaves on my college pad. Christmas was coming.

And Christmas went. And term started again, and Alex came back and I was more pleased to see him than I could possibly have imagined.

nine

It was a laugh, but a cruel one, to watch the barnacles ejaculate. Iodine in the water made the male think a female was in the vicinity. These hapless little life-forms never even got to do it properly although, for all we knew, the male's quick clouding of a square inch or two of sea gave him the most exquisite pleasure.

'So, Melons! Do you know the answer?'

I stared up at a bottled baby, mindful of its holy old face and greenish grey pallor, insulting really for it to be in a bottle, wherein it had become a system, a chip of scientific pride, its umbilical cord holding it trivially as if it were a trapped helium balloon.

'Melons? Are you with us? Or are you far away, preening in your boudoir?'

There was a waft of giggles. Meaty Mrs Bottington appeared at the end of our bench. Dido was doing the experiment while I pushed things to and fro. She passed by me and for a moment laid four meaty fingers on my shoulder, in one of those fake balancing postures so beloved of the large. My nausea at her attention was accompanied by unaccountable lust, as if the imprints of her fingers had produced boils. I always sensed her creepy knowingness, but could not help reacting to her.

Later, on the way to games, I passed her getting into her car. She eyed me as she shoved her car-key in the toothy little hole.

'Hi, Sarah!' she called. Every feature in her huge face was tiny, apart from her eyes, which bulged behind her lenses. She beckoned me and offered a mint in the flat of her hand, as if she could, at any time, clamp her fingers over my entire face, the way some people do to cats for a moment of cheap domination.

'Got to keep up your stamina, then!'

'Yes. We're doing cross-country today.'

'Ha, Melons! I didn't mean *that*!'

No one heard her except me. When I arrived at the sports hall she was, to my surprise, standing by her car. I was informed by a friend that cross-country was off, and we were doing PE indoors.

The teacher made us do sit-ups. I was left, as usual, without a partner. Suddenly Mrs Bottington, who had been loitering in the doorway, came into the hall, headed straight for me and held my legs down without a word. The sweet cupboard smell of new Greenflash and heavy nylon gymshorts rose up around me as I stretched out on the floor. I struggled, blushing beyond unfitness, my greasy plod of hair with its mild dandruff, my hips enlarging out of control, the rest of me developing reluctantly. Everything I had come to hate about myself was there, under her. At the end of the little session, she lifted my ankles high up in one slabby hand and dropped them. The shock crumped through my heels and I gasped in pain.

That night was Alex's concert, to which I had invited my friends. I wasn't sure if Alex wanted me to go or not. We had tried to have sex a few more times, but he seemed more interested in taking the piss out of me. Today, however, he appeared two hours before the concert, slurring his words slightly.

'Do you know what Keef said about you the other day? He said your thighs look as if they're about to give birth on both sides! Don't you think that's funny?'

'No, actually.' I turned away from him.

'Oh, for Christ's sake, look, I'm supposed to be at the Hall in an hour, am I going to get a fuck or not? I mean, it's a simple question, I mean, it's not like you're the fittest girl in the world or anything. I could have anyone, but it's easier with you living here. Oh, come on, you frigid whore!'

I acquiesced out of mysterious need.

That evening, I combed my fringe from even further back than usual, so that the thick ends of newly washed hair bounced up in the light like fibreoptics. The colour black had not really reached this class and age-group in this part of England. We thought pink and purple were cool. Dido produced the bondage trousers, and I some CCF combats taken in so violently at the calf that my legs looked like rotten chicken drumsticks. It was a toss-up between those and some fluorescent orange cagoule trousers similarly resewn. I had worn them to see Stiff Little Fingers at the Exchange and had sweated so much that the dye in my socks stained my feet for a week.

'Mummy doesn't really like me wearing make-up, sighed Dido, applying purple lipstick.

Dangling with safety pins and smelly dog collars, wrapped in green bin-liners which we sheepishly discarded half-way there, we walked down to the Hall. The band were tuning up. I knew that the proper behaviour of a girlfriend at this point was to walk up to the stage, simper, roar at appropriate moments and stare around the room with arrogant complacency, but I could not. And, anyway, Alex had barely given me a look. The girls huddled and smirked. Kev and Keef appeared and said hello, but soon dropped me for my friends. I felt tall, and looked at the ground.

Radger and another master appeared, and stood chatting to the band, who had made a real effort. They had all spiked and dyed their hair. Alex had pierced his nose. Groups of Boys came, mostly in the mufti of dark sweaters and jeans, one or two in full get-up. There was a slight smell of smoke. We went to the loo and drank. When we got back, the crowd had grown, and there was a lot of loud laughter. I felt particularly on show, and found myself shuffling behind my friends at every possible opportunity.

Alex ran up on stage with little white marks on his cheeks. His fringe was collapsing slightly, the tips clogged. Adenoidal Whitenoise began with 'Happy Death', a mawkish, violent love song which had the dressed-up members of the audience pogo-ing at the front and the masters peering for signs of intoxication.

Oh Happy Death!
Happy Death!
I'm waiting for you-ou-ou
Gun in my head!

As the evening progressed, the songs became more daring

and Alex, who, in rotation with the rest of the band, kept disappearing briefly, became more lurchingly insistent.

Stupid cow, she'd do it with anyone,
Stupid cow, I want to hit her,
Stupid cow get out of my picnic,
I'm trying to eat my rucking lunch!

They hurried into a number about the IRA (*NO nothing, nothing there, let's drop a bomb!*), and the arrest of Peter Sutcliffe (*God save the pigs, they did something right!*). They ended with some Sex Pistols covers, which I and my friends danced to right at the front. We hung around determinedly while the audience left. Finally Alex deigned to notice us.

'We're going to the playing field after lights-out. We're meeting at the gate. See you there.'

I felt a frisson, a feeling which seemed to dissociate me from the other girls. This was justified in the following half-hour, when Lorna, MT and Dido all started talking about ringing parents. What was it about *girls* that they always wanted to go home just when things were starting getting good?

'Come to the playing field, oh, go on!'

My friends' faces and outfits were drained in the harsh sodium light as we walked back to my parents'. There was a general whine of *No, can't, can't stay the night, got to get up early and help my brother go shopping for some trainers, I'm tired, can't be bothered*. I despised their cowardice and bravely sat it out until eleven-thirty, by which time they'd all gone, and my parents had finished watching *London Night Out* and were in bed. It was a warm night for late winter and I thrust my hands deep in the pockets of my school duffel coat. I had half a bottle of rum. No one else liked it.

As soon as I was out of the house I opened the bottle. I walked for ten minutes, along the road and out of town, to the playing fields. The streetlamps ended. My way was lit by the occasional car and the sodium glow of the village. There was a loud laugh. A little group of Boys stood there in the darkness, the familiar points of light waving as they talked.

ten

WHAT ANYONE MIGHT have seen approaching was a large, rather uncomfortable-looking teenager in too-tight trousers wearing a bit too much green around the eyes. I arrived at the gate and peered. Someone struck a match and I had time to see that Alex was not there yet.

'Hello, Sarah.'

Had it been daytime, I would have realized I was looking into the palest eyes I had ever seen. It was Tom, drummer and heart-throb. I had met him once before, in someone's room.

'Did you enjoy the gig, Sarah?'

I should have been suspicious of his charm, too easy even for a rich seventeen-year-old. I gave gauche assent and was so busy being amazed that he was actually talking to me that I did not notice how quickly his attention left me and returned to the group.

'Look, we've got a girl!' he said, not bothering to introduce me, since they all knew who I was and I them. There was a murmur amid the clinks in hidden plastic bags. I did not really feel like a girl. I felt big and greasy. My trousers cut into me if I bent my leg more than twenty degrees.

Alex appeared and ignored me. At an invisible signal, we went into the sports field, where I had walked Billy so many times as a child, and had, more recently, paraded archly with different girlfriends, pretending not to hear the wolf-whistles and clip-vowelled obscenities we attracted.

'What about here?'

'Nahh – too near where Radger walks his dog. Let's go in the spinney . . .'

We continued in silence.

'Look! That's where Cobra screwed Treena. She had her period but he didn't realize until afterwards.'

'God, that's disgusting! Isn't she a bit of a dog, anyway?'

'Fit breasts.'

'Dark, isn't it?' I said, trying to sound flirtatious. I walked next to Alex, who was smoking manically. There was a silence, a silence with a seriousness about it, a concentration. Someone resumed a story which had obviously been interrupted by my arrival.

'Braithwaite swears they'd done something to the ball, but the old bastard in charge of the other lot wouldn't even talk to him and just kept on walking back to their bus, and so finally Jocko calls out—'

'Here we are,' said Tom.

We sat down. The grass was damp.

'So how's Whaley, then?' said Tom as he opened a bottle of whisky, suddenly turning his attention to me as if it had never been away. 'Lots of men there you like?'

'Oooh, hundreds,' I said, my hand in my hair. Alex snig-gered. I looked up to see the bottle, waiting in mid-air for me to take it. I attacked it greedily, trying to kill the unease in my stomach. More swigs brought on a familiar warm feeling. A few more and I was making plans in my head as they talked. Suddenly I began to feel accepted. Tim, the bass player, was talking about a party.

'All these fucking women were just sitting there. He said they were pretty prolistic, but shit, who cares? You can't see the white shoes when they're round the back of your neck! – '

The speaker paused for a response and was rewarded by a rousing guffaw.

' – And one of them started coming on to him! She was absolutely desperate for it, and she kept saying things like, "Oooh! What's it like wearing that posh uniform all day?" and "Do your teachers cane you and stuff?" And he told her to shut up. Anyway, he takes her outside and she's getting a bit pissed off for some reason so he gives her all this stuff about his dad's place in Antibes and how he'd like to take her there in the summer and all that romantic crap—'

' I think we're talking RADA here.'

'Yeah! So that warmed her up a bit, so she pulled up her skirt and said, "Ooooh! Give it to me, darling," and he's not really ready and – does she mind?' The speaker jerked his finger back in my direction.

'I don't think there are any ladies present. Carry on.'

Tom interjected. 'Excuse me, would you apologize to Sarah, I don't think that was very nice, was it?'

'What! You're mad! OK. Sorry, Sarah.'

Now my eyes were accustomed to the dark, I could see Tom was giving me a very secretive, practised glance which spoke of warmth and privacy, of arms encircling and hands entwined. I suddenly felt very safe, liked even. Alex barely looked at me.

'God! Selina's breaking my heart, you know,' someone suddenly piped up.

'Oi! I haven't finished the story.'

'Well, come on, then, did he fuck 'er or not?'

'That's the whole point. He'd drunk so much he couldn't get it up, and suddenly he felt a bit funny, and she was pushing him and everything and he said, "Look, dearie, I can't, how about tomorrow?" and he puked all over her!'

Their laughter pealed back and forth. I even found myself joining in.

'I promise you, he could see everything he'd had for dinner, some sort of veal in wine thing with peas and chips and it was all over her tits and dripping down her boob tube—'

He broke off with great swabs of laughter. Alex and Tom performed a duet of echoing shrieks.

'And she started going on about her dry-cleaning, and what would her husband say, and he told her to fuck off and then Ben found a taxi and they pissed off before she knew what was happening!'

'Brilliant!'

'Fuck! He'd do it with a packet of Angel Delight if it cleared off before sunrise.'

'Or a girl from Whaley.'

'Thanks a lot!' I shouted, drunk, my voice high.

'Thanks a lot,' one of them imitated.

'Has she had enough to drink, do you think?' continued Tim. 'God, look how much she's had. I'm quite impressed, actually, though have you noticed the way girls who think they can drink suddenly sort of pass out?'

Tim had it in for me. Perhaps he had been one of my rejected visitors.

Tom interjected again. 'Now, boys, I've told you before, Sarah isn't like the other girls, are you Sarah? What are you two talking about so quietly?'

'He's smitten for Selina. We may have to call a doctor.'

'Tell us about it, Johnny lad.'

'His bed was shaking so much last night I don't think we need to know much more. I nearly called Radger.'

'I don't know what to do. She's just so fucking, fucking . . . fit! She's a real *lady* too. God, did you see her parents at the start of term? They came separately, her dad in a Bentley and her mother in an E-type Jag. That's just so fucking cool! Selina's beautiful, there's something pure about her, I dunno, I want her cherry. I bet she's hot in the sack. I could teach her everything I know.'

'That wouldn't take long, then.'

'Fuck off! I've had more women than you cunts put together.'

'Yeah, yeah! Dream on! I've seen you tossing off.'

They leapt on each other. I sensed their attention falling away from me, but I felt I could do little about it. I leant back on my hands and stared at the sky. The cloud cover was thick, any light diffuse and soft. There were no stars. Alex had not even looked at me. He sat and smoked. A foot seemed to fly out of the air from the pile of thumping, pushing bodies and hit my face hard.

'Ow!' It hurt enough for tears to come to my eyes. There was a small silence. Tom, who had distanced himself from the scuffle, came over and sat next to me, putting his arm around me and encouraging me to lean against him.

'I think you're well rid of Alex, Sarah, he wasn't good for you,' he whispered, confidentially.

Had I been sober, I would have wondered at just what point I had actually become rid of Alex, but the thought soon evaporated from my confused brain.

Although no taller than me when sitting, Tom contrived somehow to look down into my face. 'You're very attractive,' he whispered. 'Do you know that? Everyone talks about you, they all say how beautiful you are and how they'd all like to go out with you. You're so pretty, you know that, don't you? Let's try this.'

And he pulled out a plastic bag and a bottle of Tippex, which he shook and poured into it. He put it over his face and inhaled. The record-shop bag jumped up and stood to attention as he sucked in his breath. He put down the bag, breathed out, poured more Tippex in and offered it to me. 1,1,1 trichlorethane was something I had never tried. Although I had come across many solvents in the course of my hobbies, it had never occurred to me to inhale them. I felt buzzy and strange. I shivered. Tom's hand began to move against my waist, stroking gently. I was too involved in my own gratitude to feel his body shake, as bodies generally do when one arm is gesticulating rhythmically, as his certainly was.

'Tosser!'

Thumps and the sound of kicking. I felt Tom's hand moving slowly back and forth and gradually upwards towards my breast. I felt the whisky bottle pushed against my lips. As if to encourage me, he took some as well. The rim clashed against my teeth. There was a light frothing noise as Tom brought the bottle down too fast and it thumped against my leg. His hand made contact and began to squeeze.

'You know, Sarah, I've always thought how mature you were, so different from the others. God, I wish you went to Sedgebourne – maybe in a few years, hey?'

'But you'd be gone by then,' I might have said if I hadn't been so pissed.

Soon my eyes began to close and I lowered my head, an atavistic gesture, interpreted by beasts of prey as supplication and surrender. He squeezed my breast harder. 'God, I wish those lot would piss off. We could really have a good time, just you and me.'

He leant against me as we sat and I found myself losing my balance. I tensed my stomach muscles to prevent myself slipping further, but this only made me quiver with the effort.

'Hey, relax – why don't you just lie down?'

He prepared me another bag of Tippex. The scuffle had lost much of its momentum, and attention was turning, like a gigantic vulture slowly scenting carrion, to us.

I could prop myself up no longer, and flopped back on to the cold grass. Tom half lay on me, his hand pushing into my trousers. It was very dark, the low light touching only the strongest facial bones.

'Come on, then, no one's watching.'

There was the familiar sound of fingers against seamed fabric, and a descending zip, and then a slight sweaty smell. There was the familiar reaching for my hand and pulling it over and pressing it against the small hardish stick of flesh. But my hand flopped as soon as he let go of it. He spat out an expletive.

'Too fucking pissed!'

He took my hand and again wrapped it around his penis and rubbed it up and down hopefully. My hand fell back once more. Why did I not struggle, protest? So much of me was warm in my amniotic nest, however false. Reality was a distant TV screen seen through curtains from a speeding train.

'Fucking cow! Did you give her some white stuff?'

'Did you get up there? When's our turn?'

'Do what the fuck you like, she's out of it.'

They crowded round me.

'God, they're always desperate for it, aren't they?'

Alex prodded me with his foot.

'She's shit in bed but at least she's got a cunt.' There were sniggers. I moved a little, rose and fell like a discarded detergent bottle in a half-hearted estuary.

'No you fucking don't, not after leading us on like this, no way.'

I could hear them, but could not distinguish who was saying what in this misty kaleidoscope of sound.

'God! Did you know that doctors take students round hospitals to examine women who are having abortions? When they're knocked out, a whole group of them come round and stick different-sized vibrators up them to see how big their cunts are and how wet they get. It's true.'

'Fuck, I'd kill any woman who poured my baby down the sink,' said Alex. 'That's what my father always says. When we were skiing last year—'

'Well, I don't know about you boys but I'm taking it where it's going free.' Tim knelt down and took out his limp penis. He tore open my combats and tried to pull them down. Then he tried to rip off my Kickers but they were so heavily laced that he was obliged to put one of my feet between his legs to undo it, rather as a loving mother might do for her tired child after a long day's playing.

There was a harsh streaming sound as Alex pissed nearby.

'Why don't you do it in her mouth?' someone suggested.

'If you get any of your piss near this little fucklet I'll beat the shit out of you and I mean it.'

Laughter. He undid the other shoe and threw it down hard so that it bounced away into the darkness. He pulled down my knickers.

'Stop it,' I might have murmured. The grass's coldness against my neck and cheek was bringing me back.

'Stay where you are, bitch! Oh, fuck this bitch I haven't had a fuck since the Christmas holidays and I'm fucking desperate for it. Christ, it's all the bitch's fault with her fucking pussy. God, you could fit a fucking fire engine in there.'

Tim took a deep sniff. 'Bet she stinks. No wonder my dick won't do it.' He stood up, kicked me in the leg, and then sat apart.

Tom came over and tried. 'She was getting wet a minute ago, I'm sure.'

He peered at me and began trying to stimulate my clitoris. His hands were cold and muddy from the fight. I moaned. The virgins of the group looked at their nails. Tom got inside me but could not come. Alex was the same.

'The worst I ever had!'

'What's the point of women, anyway?'

There was a silence.

The gate opened and closed.

'Shit!'

They rushed to assemble my clothing.

'Find her fucking shoe!'

The last sound that came from the little scene was the high-pitched whizz of corduroy trousers rubbing together as the Boys fled away across the grass. A torch bobbed as the newcomer approached. I opened my eyes at the light that suddenly burned in my face.

'What the hell's going on here, then? Wait a minute. It's you, isn't it, Sarah, you naughty little thing, the local girl made bad.'

I murmured thickly.

'You, my girl, are drunk. I think we'd better get you back to your parents, hadn't we?'

Tears appeared on my cheeks. Radger stuck out a hand to pull me up.

'Now, I don't know what's been going on here but we'd better keep quiet about it, don't you think?'

He looked at me, threatening through sympathy in that *adult* way.

'We can't have your reputation getting any worse, can we? You can't even walk. Hang on. Don't you know the difference between left and right? Too pissed, I suppose, you silly little girl.'

My shoes had been put back on the wrong feet. Roughly he sat me down and pulled my shoes off, relacing them violently and far too tight. He put his arm around me and started to walk me back towards the light. I leant into him heavily so that my nose became squashed against his rough tweed jacket.

My memories stirred, enticed out of the darkness by the

metallic, urinous smell of pipe smoke that I helplessly inhaled. I snorted with the exertion of movement and constriction, while snot and tears exchanged places with the odour and soaked into the cloth. As we shuffled down the road I remembered being scooped up, my head in a similar place, my legs folded. I was carried, I was small enough then, curled and raw like a shrimp, my heart beating. Once upon a time, huge, hard, leathery hands like these had taken me and adjusted me for life.

Radger returned me home unseen. Luckily the door was on the latch or I'd have been in real trouble.

eleven

A DARK EARLY EVENING in late February. I got out of the school car in the town square and steeled myself for the walk home. I hurried along the street, walking on the grass by the pavement as if to hide the sound of myself. Cutlery rattled in the kitchen as I passed by. The dew gave a mad shine to my shoes, and as I skidded I remembered the pain of grazes and the grey dust and blood and singing skin. I scuttled towards the warmth of hearth and home, the yellow of the light-bulb, the dairy cream of the lampshade and Mum letting the blind down with a whoosh and a crack as the plastic base hit the sill. But I was not home yet.

I experienced this terror earlier and earlier each day at school. The waiting, the getting in to the car, the ride of forty-five minutes or so, the constant looking at my watch, the constant assessment of the likelihood that the Boys would be returning from lessons and I would have to walk home among them. What did I look like? Was I carrying too much? Would the handles of the carrier bag break? The agony of crawling around on the ground picking up pens and plimsolls and bits of paper and in the end grabbing everything in a lump, scrunched in a panic-grip as fierce as any on a clifftop railing, while they called out obscenities to me and laughed.

This evening there had been a major roadworks and the journey from school took nearly twice as long. Safe! I stood in the garden and looked at the stars while I waited for supper. There was music in the Quad over the mindless glockenspiel of a ball kicked with young men's fused forces. Quick as a monkey my hand responded to the itch at my back. Without thinking I tugged up my white nylon school shirt, already untucked, letting the harsh wool of my waistband grate at me. I scratched for the eighth time that day. The skin there was a patch of broken blood vessels.

My character seemed to dissolve with the days as I worried and worried about who might see me under the sodium lights on the way home. I masturbated more than ever, and when I was not masturbating I was spending my pocket money on something other than sweets and nail varnish. I had discovered the personality quizzes in women's magazines, from whose conclusions I could choose from domineering, flamboyant, the mouse or the home-loving type, whose a, b, c or d responses I would cheat and manipulate in order to give the desired answer: an interesting, magnetic, flamboyant, individual woman, not a thirteen-year-old child.

And then I discovered horoscopes, which took even less effort than quizzes, and I was away. Venus in the sign of Aquarius meant that I was going to enjoy the weekend. Leo rising meant I was a really strong person, and really artistic. My own sign endowed me with qualities that I did not particularly respect, but being able to find out what would happen to me the following day, week or month gave me something to cling to, a strip of driftwood on a tide of opprobrium.

Mum and Dad noticed some sort of change in me, but since I was spending just as much time as before in my room with the door shut, but ceasing to litter their home with Fablon, there was little for them to complain about. Especially when I decided to clean the house, every day.

You can only be told something about yourself so many times before you start to believe it, and my parents' home had been derided so much that I thought that by scrubbing every sill and polishing every doorknob (except that we did not have doorknobs but aluminium push-downs), it would become respectable.

My mind became a patchwork of character summary and obscenity. At school, I sat at a table, in the lab, scratching the filthy black surface of years of people and experiments and wanted to shriek and shriek and shriek at the person who was presuming to teach me physics.

I went for a haircut, clutching a photograph from a magazine of a model with a massive jaw and a wart-sized nose. I emerged with the style that adolescent girls get from female hairdressers who scent their urgent need to appear grown-up, but are damned if they're going to let them.

I screamed. I screamed because I looked even less like what I was supposed to look like. The following morning, before school, I woke up, reached for a mirror and looked, thirteen, young and big, and I hurled the small mirror away from me. My hair, layered in that useful easy-to-care-for way, had bounced up, resembling a light-bulb. It did not suit me.

Mum and Dad, although confident that this was no more

than a *phase*, sensed their daughter's misery and decided to take me to the theatre. I climbed obediently into the Cavalier. It did not occur to me that my evening would be anything more than a quick bit of culture and back home to watch a repeat of *The Goodies*.

The forecourt was dense with Boys.

'I'll just pop the car over here, then!' jollied Dad. I was rigid with terror. I slipped out, my chin firmly fixed to my chest.

'Look up, Sarah, dear!'

I glued myself to my parents as we entered the crowd. I heard the now familiar sniggers. Boys stared. I felt too tall, too fat, my clothes too cheap.

'Sarah!' called Mum, brightly. I had been staring so hard at the ground that I had momentarily lost them. I wanted to vomit.

The comedian performed his usual stunts. Like all good comedians, his talent lay in sensing the main political thrust of his audience, and pushing particular jokes in their direction.

What a gay day! he parodied.

The laughter burst forth from a thousand young lungs, forced almost to asphyxiation. The room was, for a few moments, terrifying. On and on they guffawed. Great buckets of laughter hurled against the walls and dribbled down. The comedian began to get cross. They were interrupting his flow. He mumbled something to himself. As one section of audience quietened down, another chorus of rippling shrieks would ring out somewhere else. The comedian stood with his hand on his hip, waiting. He opened his mouth to speak, mistaken in the idea that his very presence would cause them all to shut up and take notice. The seats around me shook and shook with each new haemorrhage.

'THAT'S ENOUGH, BOYS!'

Radger, in the front row, stood up and faced them all down. There was a shaky silence.

In the interval, I ran into Kev and Keef, who seemed oddly interested in my parents.

'Anyone for a wine?' asked Dad.

That weekend I decided to redecorate my room.

I wanted it to be sophisticated. Magnolia emulsion, therefore, was purchased. I took a dustbin liner and tore at my walls. All the adverts and the residue of ancient posters beneath them came tumbling down as I pulled. I jerked back the bed. Mobiles, monsters, poems, jammed in together, were suddenly exposed, powdered by months of dust. My rainbow-coloured shelves were taken to my workroom, stripped and painted *crème*. My charts of the solar system I held on to for a day, before remembering how I had accidentally got all the answers right in a quiz at school and had not been allowed to forget about it. My old sketch-pad stuck out from under the bed. I got up as if radio-controlled and tried to pull it out. But it would not move. I knelt down and heaved at it. There was so much else piled on top of it, so many graphs and Saturn's rings and instruction manuals and radio bits, that it had become completely stuck. I jerked at it and raw sobs burst forth from my lungs. The sharp end of the metal spiral tore down the length of my finger.

The work took a week. Last to go was the grebo. I had been so proud of him. However, my studio was ripe for conversion into a *snug*, as Mum quietly pointed out to Dad.

Paint dry, my walls were adorned carefully with a poster of

Adam Ant and another of my star sign and its attributes. The third available wall held up a large, full-length mirror.

'Look, dear, did you see? Ruth Lawrence got her O-level maths and she's only nine!'

My room was lit by three small Habitat spotlights. My Kleenex box was covered by a shiny white plastic cover. Only the cleanest of my books were allowed to remain in the shelves. Anything paint-stained or torn had been placed in a box and thrown in the dustbin.

My desk was clean and varnished. All that lay on it was my new Secret Folder. I decided to set up a club. It is a great insult when people tell you they know everything about you and what they do know is not very interesting. Mystery is what attracts people to people, isn't it? I wrote out a list of rules, a list of membership fees and a list of activities available to members who could, with permission, invite non-members to participate. It described the place and time of the weekly meeting and suggested clothes that the members might want to wear. 'The Club' it was called, and the documents remained in the folder on my desk, proudly asserting themselves. All it needed was a member.

The following Monday at school, the atmosphere in chemistry was different. There were whispers, giggles, looks on teachers' faces. I assumed that I was the cause, but then I saw the empty seats in the row behind me. Four of my classmates and two others had been caught snogging. Suggestions of what might actually have gone on abounded, but it seemed to amount to little more than a quick hand on a breast, a sweaty cling. Whatever the truth, their futures were now in the balance. For a bit of kissing! I shuddered. The mere *thought* of my being expelled from school would have sent my mother scurrying to the kitchen for an aspirin. *What would people think?* she would ask herself, almost every day, about almost every subject that involved a spontaneous act of personality, something she had long since given up.

'Sarah, tell us the word that describes the properties of this element.' The chemistry teacher interrupted my thoughts. He held up a strip of magnesium, the soft grey-white metal that burns with tiny furious incandescence, and twisted it around. I stared down at my book. All I could think of was people's backs, backs of heads, everyone turning away from me. Silence. *Malleable,* my brain explained. *Malleable,* my mind screamed, repeating from what the teacher had told the class only ten minutes before. I was drowning in the silence that throbbed around me. Someone dropped their pencil case with a rattle. Giggles passed around the class.

'Come on, Sarah! What's got into you?'

Malleable, my brain explained. *Malleable, malleable, malleable,* but I was sick of attention, sick of the spotlight, *malleable.*

Murmurs popped up around the class.

'It's malleable, sir!' chimed out a voice.

'Thank you, David. Sarah, why don't you listen instead of staring at your nails?'

His nails were filthy, I hoped with shit.

In break, a crowd surrounded another girl, bursting with yet more news.

'Oh! Jackie's gone to hospital!'

'Who's she?' said someone cruelly. There was a general snigger.

'That's so mean. Didn't you know she's got anorexia?'

Tall, lanky Jackie, with her grey-blonde greasy curls and pink-rimmed NHS specs held together by a plaster, her squeaky voice and unexceptional marks. She simply did not eat. And now she was gone, leaving behind her a trail of lectures and leaflets about eating properly. I had never even seen her with one of the little yellow books either.

And so several months passed in a patchwork of apparent activity. I stopped speaking in class. My room contained almost nothing. On my desk was a row of felt-tips and a small furry dog that I had found buried inside a cardboard theatre I was about to throw away. In my spare time, of which there was quite a lot, I stared and stared, waiting for phones that did not ring and visitors who had stopped coming. The only reliable was the television. I stared and stared, at my reflection, my nails, my shoes, my walls.

My emotions were silting up, the bright hues slipping down and mixing to a uniform grey that was building up slowly, irreversibly. And yet I could still crawl on all fours across my bed and put my hand into myself from behind, and find myself wet.

If several months sounds a long time, I'm talking about teenage time, in which aeons can pass under the influence of what must, to all intents and purposes, be called misery.

twelve

A SATURDAY IN MAY. Exams loomed. The evening, like so many others, spread out in front of me like a pool of fat. I sat at my desk and held a blue Ball Pentel vertically and rotated it until a dense dark spot appeared on the blank sheet of paper, into which all my emotions poured. I stopped moving the pen and examined the tiny dent it had made. That was all I was, flattened, gone nowhere. Something was boiling somewhere, but it seemed several feet away, not inside me at all. The light bounced coldly back at me from the magnolia walls.

Outside insulted me, with its warm sounds and fresh smells, with flowers, leaves and birds. Escape. Where to? I wasn't a runner-away. I didn't know how. Footballs rang in the Quad and Grace Jones sang out. I could not imagine myself in a nightclub.

Another night in. I felt incapable of movement. A group of Boys ran down the path. Automatically I jumped up and started doing my hair. I walked up and down the room. There was nothing, no one, anywhere in my life, no one I could *go to*. Only in other people's families are there those mysterious selections of interesting older friends who enter the children's lives as mentors, fucks, initiators into drink or drugs, or simply to show the young that not all older people are parents or teachers or repositories of bitterness and envy.

I strained to imagine such a situation. What would this person be like? Inevitably my mind made the whole thing into a story, about how I would be visiting some cousins and their friend, thirty-two-year-old 'Joe', would look at me significantly in the kitchen and be heard to say 'heartbreaking legs' while I fought with the dog in the garden and later that night would sit up late talking to me and gently pull my *panties* to the side with his finger.

I had watched a TV play the night before in which a poltergeist invaded a house where there were two adolescent girls and it smashed glasses and picked up scissors and stabbed people in the leg, and then I started to wonder why there wasn't a poltergeist in this house too, and it would serve everyone right and justify everything and then I could go away somewhere else. I strained and strained to make something move, to push a jug off the shelf or start the washing-machine, but nothing happened.

I walked slowly into the living room but could not sit down. Every time I moved towards a chair it was as if on the seat were tiny drips of something disgusting, undefinable, which might edge into my clothing and seep into indelible patches. I looked around to see if any calendars needed changing.

I fought a familiar urge to wipe the pinkish dust from the shelves, to run a duster, damp, along the smooth wobbly row of books. Some stuck out more than the rest and there was an inevitable build-up of dust, a moraine that would gather behind a particularly prominent one. I tried the usually satisfying flutter of a pencil along the spines but it gave me nothing. I leant over the table to stare at *The Times*. My upper body remained at an angle of forty-five degrees for several minutes. I was far away.

'Sarah, dear, what are you doing?'

'Nothing, Mum.'

How untrue that is! Always a lie: even if the body is motionless, the breathing silent, the mind is still a rat in the maze of its everchanging. Today, more than usual, only the surface of my mind was blank, a dangerous blank. Nothing!

I picked at the chewed flat top of my nail and hoped my mother would go away. She moved towards me.

'No no no, everything's fine.'

I looked at her with the exhausted fierceness that transcends humiliation.

What had I been in a past life? Axle? Vegetable barrow? I went back to my room. God, there was a spider there, near my chair. I became rigid. I threw something. It sat. I picked up a can of Elnett Firm Hold, once used to fix my drawings, and fired a thick spurt at the creature. I sprayed until the can was empty, my finger in a hysterical grip. The spider vectored a few paces and got as far as a small crack in the skirting before scrunching up in agony. One leg raised and quivering it died, pathetically. I hated even their dead bodies and felt hunted by this one.

I picked up the pencils that lay on the floor and began trying to stuff them into a plastic cup. Their chewed, gaudy variety irritated me. I picked them up one by one and jammed them in. They became more and more tightly packed until it would have been impossible to pull one out without the rest coming with it. The last pencil, a 3B, one of my old drawing ones maybe, was thicker than the rest and would not go in. I forced and forced, and finally threw it in the dustbin.

For the next twenty minutes I counted pigeons' coos in the poplars, and then rewrote the titles on my five tape boxes.

Then I left the house and walked down the road to the fields. It would have been quicker to take the path, but I could not face anyone in such a narrow space.

I went through the gate and down the field, conscious always of any shouts that would indicate the presence of another. The evening sun. On the way through the little copse by the big wheatfield I found a set of handlebars. All my life I had been imbued with a sense of others' *property*. Even when the School had dumped a huge broken-down minibus in front of our house, preventing Dad from getting to work, my mother had physically restrained me from writing junior obscenities on the windscreen.

'It's not yours, there must be a reason for it being there.'

Eventually this terror of others' belongings sank in. But now there was no one around. I bent down into the little fountains of grass at the edge of the copse and picked up the mechanical limb. It was not from a racer but spread, like antlers, with a rigid, rusty gear lever attached.

A tractor hummed in the valley. The sounds of Kangaroo Court were finally deadened. I did not care about my exams. The tractor's hum was replaced by a deep buzz. A fat oval object dived out of the air, a disgusting June bug. It sailed stupidly into me and clung to my sweatshirt. I wanted to retch with horror at the huge, sticky-legged creature. I bashed at it with the handlebars, barely noticing the pain in my breast. The insect squashed in an ooze of pinkish grey, like ice-cream. I rubbed the stain madly with a wad of couch grass.

I had just recovered when out of the soft golds, came a bright red and green object. A Boy was coming towards me, smaller than me but confident-looking. He stomped through the grass, apparently oblivious. I glued my chin to my chest and walked on.

'Hi, whore!' he mumbled, jauntily. Somehow if he had shouted it would have been better. I would have snapped out of myself and shouted back. I felt my first post-insult breath squeeze out through my nose. I stopped. He strode on.

I turned, leapt up and knocked him to the ground. He was a lot lighter than he looked. I had never had a fight with anyone in my life. I had never pushed anyone over but, rather, spent the time avoiding having it done to me. So I had to learn quickly.

I twisted him onto his back. My knees on his chest, I raised the handlebars and brought them down hard on his face, four times in quick succession. I must have stunned him slightly because he did not move when I jumped up to kick him. Everywhere, not a piece of flesh spared. Then I went for his eyes, then his lips until they bled. His floppy hair fell back and for a minute his face looked like one of the models in my old adverts, swollen, pouting lips, eyelids down, face darkened and glistening. I pointed one end of the handlebars at his shoulder and thrust my whole weight onto it.

He began moving around. I shrieked, that kind of shock-scream which is so instant that all you hear is the echo and wonder why people are looking at you. I rained blows on him, the metal grasped in both fists. He began to cry. I had never felt more enormous. He rolled onto his side. I pulled back my foot, with its cheap plastic pointed toe, and stung it between his legs. He whimpered and his hands flew down, curling in torture like the spider. I jumped on him, pricking him with my little metal heels, grinding and grinding at his flesh, his tracksuit tearing. I yanked down his greying underpants to reveal his genitalia, sitting like small creatures, the proportions unrelated to any other body part. I brought the metal down one more time and stood up. He contorted with agony.

I threw my weapon into the air. A great arching throw. The handlebars spun majestically and for a second flashed silver in the sun before crashing into the bushes. I turned and walked home.

Back in my room, I sat on my bed and kicked off my stained shoes: instantly the room was filled with a strange odour, as the smell of my foot-sweat mingled with the cheap, lurid perfume I had sprayed into them. I went upstairs to my parents.

'You're not a very happy little girl, are you?'

The counsellor, whom I towered over, was a woman in a pilled burgundy jumper. She recalled the reading ladies and piano teachers of my earlier years, who always spoke in the same strangled monotone and always had unnecessary perms done on their short curly hair.

'They said my home and family were shit and then a group of them fucked me and Sedgebourne is just a whole load of cunts—'

'Now that's not very nice, is it? The School looks after the town very well, doesn't it? I think you'll have to do better than that, Sarah. That little boy's had his life completely ruined and you'll have to live with that for the rest of your days, won't you?'

I stared blankly at the woman as she went on to explain that every time I did something *I must think of others first.* I had felt quite powerful after the incident, but now everybody seemed to be trying to shame me. I had tried to explain but somehow could not describe what had happened to me.

My parents were speechless, and regarded me with fear. I had not come back and sobbed, which might have made it easier, even in England. In fact, their greater terror was of the School, whose first line of attack was a visit from Radger.

'It must be said, Mr and Mrs Clevtoe, that we have been aware of Sarah for a very long time. Let's just say she gets around and leave it at that. We're aware of her drinking.'

'Excuse me, er, sir, but our daughter—'

'Mr Clevtoe, one of our boys had been blinded in one eye, and that's barely the beginning of it. The doctors have not yet discovered the full extent of his terrible injuries. Of course, the School's prominence means inevitably that the press will be here *within hours,* but for God's sake don't say a word until I've sorted out the statement. Oh, yes, and Ben's parents'll be here soon. I'll be sending them straight up.'

And with that, he strode out of the door. The boy's parents! My father would have felt a cold rinse in his bowels at the thought of the huge shining car halting outside our house, and the camel-coated two getting out and slamming the doors and marching up, every plank, every breezeblock in the little house shaking with shame, the long, suited arms of lawyers reaching out from behind them like the fingers of a great hand, and he having to justify what he didn't understand anyway, and why should he have to, it was Sarah with her pretensions and her bloody cleaning and he and her mother preferred her when she'd been littering up the house and no wonder those bloody boys didn't come round to see her any more and now what was going to happen to her bloody exams and all the money they'd spent on her school fees and what was all this about her drinking and her mother had gone without new clothes for God knows how long—

His tirade, directed throughout the house, was interrupted by a ring of the doorbell. Dad left me in the lounge, and went to open the front door.

Through the window, I could see a small nervous grey couple standing there, she in a faded flowery dress and white cardigan, he in a shirt and ill-fitting trousers. They sweated in the fresh May sun. Their Dolomite, a dull ochre, was parked, rusting, behind them.

He let them in. They were still waiting to hear whether Ben would lose his cricket scholarship, or whether the School would look kindly on them, as Mrs Brees put it.

''E 'ad a talent, 'e 'ad, 'e really did. What did 'e do to your daughter, Mr Clevtoe, tell us, please, so we can understand what she did?'

As the conversation continued, my father must have realized that he had the upper hand, and cashed in as hard as he could.

'Well, it was easy for the boys to take advantage of her, her being so young, and all that. Your boy's sixteen. They've got around quite a bit by then, haven't they?'

'But 'e says 'e just walked past 'er up at the field and she went for 'im with a metal object.'

'I know that much, Mrs Brees, but Sarah is finding it very painful to talk about all this, and she may not be ready to tell the whole story.'

The notion of someone being 'ready' to discuss a painful incident would have been a recent one to Dad, who had devoured the recent trial and imprisonment of the Yorkshire Ripper with fervour. He'd come upon it during the bit about counselling for the girls Peter Sutcliffe hadn't quite managed to kill.

Mrs Brees began to cry quietly, while her husband pursed his small mouth, one of those mouths that at the beginning of its life might have had the potential to expand into grins of joy, but was now so overwhelmed by the surrounding skin leaning heavily in on it that it had admitted defeat. This small skinny man began to rock back and forth, constantly half swallowing and tucking in his lower lip.

'I – I don't think you realize 'ow badly injured Ben is. We worked all our lives to send 'im to a school like this, so that 'e could 'ave the same chances as the rest. And now it looks like 'e'll be in and out of 'ospital for ages – 'e's got to miss 'is O levels and everything.'

'We want to talk to your daughter, Mr Clevtoe, that's all,' said Mrs Brees through her tears, looking back and forth from my face to his. Saying nothing, I ran away, out of the back door and straight into a reporter, who began asking me about the discipline problem at Sedgebourne and whether there was any truth in the story about the theft of children's gravestones from the local cemetery by drug-crazed heavy-metal-loving pupils, even before asking if I was Sarah Clevtoe who'd had all the underage sex and tried to castrate the poor working-class scholarship boy whose grandparents had spent their last pennies to help his parents—

I fought free of him and ran.

paresis

thirteen

AFTER MY EXPULSION from Whaley, I remained in an education system of sorts until the age of nineteen, when I went to university. Having done little but study and collect fossils in the interim period, the academic institution I was able to attend was a prominent one, a highly traditional establishment whose very name attracted applicants as the rich scent of game-gravy leads bony strays to the kitchen door. The stench of history in this place was so strong and thick that many mistook it for clothing. Its alumni posted frequent cheques to keep it viable, while most of those currently attending were so anxious and miserable that had they been able to donate their agitation to the national grid, there would have been no further need for nuclear power.

I pushed my brand-new trunk over the pavement and dragged it along the corridor. My room in St Drew's college was small, green-tinged. I sat for a moment on the narrow bed feeling that a small part of history was indeed being made. People milled outside. I went to meet them.

I realized very quickly that my love for Mrs Thatcher was not shared by any of my peers, apart from a small set of loudmouthed, unembarrassed and unfashionable young men. The more fashionable treated me with curiosity, allowing me to join their ranks largely because of my clothes: leather trousers, obscurely cut away shirts and tiny, holey, knitted mini-skirts. My hair was now fourteen inches long from crown to ends. Examination in the mirror revealed that my face had more obvious character than previously, but I could not tell what kind.

I discovered a certain talent for getting on with people, gravitating towards those who seemed the friendliest. I did not think that my new companions remotely resembled anyone from my earlier years. Their faces seemed so fresh, their demeanour so relaxing, that I felt far more at ease with them than the less confident, poorer students who did not have the benefit of a vast network of old schoolfriends to socialize with. I had no fear of running into ex-classmates here, so I felt I could begin again with a self reconditioned and retuned. I was, in reality, merely *clocked*, but refused to admit it to myself.

I learned quickly not to admit to any hobbies. Expensive leisure interests involving complex equipment and aeroplane tickets were acceptable; small-scale activities needing postage and bus-rides were most certainly not. I rushed quietly to join the Astronomy Society. I was the only female at the first meeting; the twitching creatures who ran it excluded me with ranked, sweatered backs and refuge in tedious theories. My numeracy had weakened in recent years, and I could not compete with their equations.

Two days after arriving, I joined some of the other students and went to meet the first of my three teachers. This was the first and only time I would encounter these men in the safety of a group. It was an odd teaching system, in which young people were sent alone to the room of a middle-aged man to recite a redigested hash of someone else's opinions. The whole effect was of standing between two huge mirrors and seeing the same image racing back and forward, utterly unchanging. It would remain unclear to me for quite some time whether I had any opinions of my own.

Dr Rhyll worked in a vast, white-painted room, lined with convincingly large numbers of books and Impressionist reproductions. We arranged ourselves on the fat sofa and cosy chairs. Some of the little group found it impossibly luxurious, some had not known what to expect, and some scratched their ankles and wished they'd stayed in London.

A thin, nervous-looking man with a sparse fluff of mousy hair appeared in a sweater. He had a half-buried history of attendance at right-wing rallies, and membership of the Monday Club, whose student-cell dinners he reputedly attended in rented black tie, proudly and swiftly streaked with vomit. He spoke, nasally, from the side of his mouth.

'You're all here because we chose you. You're the best of a very strong competition, so you should congratulate yourselves. I hope you all believe in the great Men of Literature, because if not we're going to waste an awful lot of time!'

His laugh, so desperate to boom, sounded as if it came from the end of a hosepipe. I guessed he was referring to Shakespeare and Dickens, and probably Jane Austen by default.

'Do we need to read the critics?' someone asked.

'Of course! But for God's sake read the modern stuff. Try to keep everything after nineteen hundred or so, it makes things much easier. And for Christ's sake stay away from anything to do with Marxism. This is literature we're studying here, remember, not politics! Ha ha!'

I had had no idea that politics had any relevance to the study of anything. It was not something I had ever been taught at school.

Everyone seemed to be looking around for someone to fancy, so I copied them. A stocky, cubular Canadian soon offered himself to me. I had spied him from afar, dark, indelicate, brutal-looking, striding around in sports kit. I made myself known to him, both personally and, before that, through the strange indefinable network of sidelong glance and simultaneous ignoring by which hard, attractive people mated. We had a couple of walks around the college garden. The second time I momentarily forgot myself and plunged into a mound of leaves, shrieking. I loved dead leaves, the burning life in the colours and the springiness of them! The Canadian waited patiently while I bounced, the white breath puffing quietly out of him, his hands dug deep in the pockets of his ski anorak.

He knew a lot about the Finnish cheese industry, and talked about it incessantly, having just cornered the export market. I was impressed by his sophistication until I happened to mention that it might be fun to go on the college trip to Istanbul.

'Don't do it, Sarah! It's dangerous in the Middle East. They're real primitive out there!"

We had a disastrous dinner, during which he asked me what my parents did – I had almost no idea by then – and the names of the family pets from the time of my birth onwards. I did not want to discuss my circumstances or my past, and therefore short-circuited quickly. I stared at my plate in misery and fury.

'Sarah,' he asked, concerned, 'do you like art?'

Back at his room, he lay on me like a penitential slab of granite. I had no desire to shout, 'More weight!' despite my obvious martyrdom. After a while I fellated him, but the taste of his semen so ill-matched the sweet and sour sauce that had come before it that I spat it out onto his chest.

'Now a fool would have swallowed that!' I mused. He did not laugh but wiped my head from his vicinity with a hand the size of a breadboard.

The next morning he called out to me as I went to meet Dr Shabbie, my second tutor. I was so amazed not to be ignored that I tripped and fell up the steps. The heel of my hand oozed red through the grey dusty stain. This pleasantness was to prove a temporary aberration. The Canadian faded quickly when I became irritated at his lack of finesse. Brutality seduces and then we feel cheated when it won't peel back to reveal a soft, automated trellis of multi-limbed, multi-tongued brilliance.

Dr Shabbie had Old Master reproductions on the walls. Built like a prop forward, he bounced into the room and grabbed a hardback book from the table. He held it out in his hand. He was pale and freckled, with orange curly hair running to silver, and soft wet lips. He was rumoured to have made at least two of his students pregnant, and then to have threatened them with failed exams when they attempted to make the situation public. He waved the book in someone's face. 'You! What's that?' he shouted, his hair bouncing with the percussive demand. The student he had addressed looked terrified for a second, then decided to fall back on what was expected of him.

'Well, it used to be a tree, dinnit?' he replied, smirking.

Dr Shabbie sighed before speaking. His voice was even more powerful than his swashbuckling body implied.

'This is whatever you want it to be! Ignore the name on the cover, the author's irrelevant.'

'How can you say that? Of course he's not,' said a girl with a growing-out perm who would have shaved the whole lot off within the week.

'You see, you don't understand because you're all so bloody bourgeois. God! Another intake of establishment *ingénues*.'

'I'm not bourgeois,' said the same girl, sounding genuinely hurt, 'I'm working class, I always have been.'

'Then you can have a gold star!' he shouted, sounding like Albert Finney at the end of *Scrooge!*. He threw her a small wooden star, painted yellow, one of several lying around the room.

'I give these to my working-class students, and occasionally to women if they're very very good!"

His bacchic shout echoed around the room. His eye alighted on me and he smiled. For a moment I saw before me a blend of Mother Teresa and Marlon Brando, there for me and me alone, ready to take me away from all this yet also wanting the best for me as a free and equal human being! My needs, my desires became the most important things in the entire world, *ever*. My face burned. To bear a child by this man seemed for a moment the most wonderful, logical thing I could ever do *in my whole life*!

There was a knock at the door and the divine beam flicked off. I shook my head, as if to dislodge trapped water from my ear. We shuffled out, ignored, as Dr Shabbie turned his attention to his next visitor.

Like Bornean cave swifts with their nests of hardened saliva, people began to form social cells around them. Personalities bloomed and faded. One afternoon I went to a tea party, given by a pleasant young man who treated me more politely than anyone I had ever known. I assumed he must have fallen in love with me, and I responded with gratitude. He kissed me on both cheeks, which I found romantic. I followed him into his room, trying not to trip over the guns and golf clubs which were stacked everywhere like tepees. Proudly I produced a boxed set of profiteroles. He thanked me, expressing amazement that I had spent so much money at the town's best *pâtisserie*. On the table was a Tesco's Battenberg cake and some custard creams.

Three other, strangely familiar, young men lounged about the room. One of them farted loudly as I stretched out my hand in greeting.

'Do I know you?' he said.

'Well, you do now!' I responded, brightly.

'Wasn't your brother at School?' said another. Not understanding this shorthand for the country's most famous educational establishment, I replied that had I a brother he most certainly would have been. He gave me a strange look. Just as I was about to speak again, my host put on a tape of *Carmina Burana*, turning it up almost to full volume. No one in the room seemed to mind at all.

A Monopoly board was produced and one of the guests began setting it up. My host rose to go to the loo. He returned five minutes later, whereupon I got up to go. He halted me with an ominous wag of the finger.

'Phwoooh! I'd stay out of there for a bit if I were you,' he shouted over the singing. I was not sure how to respond. To accede and hang around with cramps for five minutes would imply that I couldn't possibly *go* in the presence of the smell of someone else's shit. However, to ignore my host and head straight in would denote a suspicious ignorance of etiquette. I pretended to look at his hunting prints until a suitable time had elasped.

The game began. I wanted the top hat but somehow got the dog. Within twenty minutes each of my co-players had formed a consortium with one of the others, and were buying hotels and borrowing more money than they could possibly ever pay back. I became puzzled. Not having forged any under-the-table alliance, I ground to a halt.

'Sarah,' sneered one, on a winning streak, who I could have sworn had been at Sedgebourne, 'are you so weak-willed that you can't even play a board-game?'

I left soon after.

After several weeks' unaccountable delay, we were invited to meet the third and last of our tutors. This time there was just a winking screen in the corner, over which someone had stretched a home-knitted bobble-hat. We waited for a while but nobody came. Then a bustling woman appeared, dowdy, efficient, with the universal tight bright Shetland sweater pulled down over a pleated skirt, an outfit that declares dogged acceptance of English middle age and utter renunciation of youth. She tutted on catching sight of the hat and ripped it away with a deft flick of her wrist, then turned to us and smiled professionally. 'Welcome all! This is Professor Davidson, who's taking part in our new university scheme. He's a brilliant man, but he finds it difficult and time-consuming trying to communicate with other people so what we do is wire him up to a simulator and let him twitch his ideas out on that! His thoughts are turned first into radio waves and then translated into spasmodics on a special screen which converts them into text for you to copy at appointed times. I know he loves the set-up, and I hope you will too.'

During this my first year as a student, I was buoyed up by little other than my own naïvety. I redrew my personality in sand every single day. My memories lived with me but they had been housetrained, and could be commanded to lie down, even if they would not go away. I was vaguely aware that there might be something wrong with me, that I needed an outlet for my thoughts not provided by my peers, but the idea of seeking outside help filled me with misery.

The division between myself and others seemed so enormous as to be invisible, as if I were an insect among sequoias. Sometimes a fury would rear up in me that made me sweat and twitch and *react* to what seemed to others as nothing. My companions would reassure me with slight puzzlement as I fulminated, my body arching involuntarily. I barely registered their discreet leers.

My tutorial relationships remained a blank as I tried to fulfil my teachers' varying ideological demands. In desperation I read the critics, copying and repeating until all I had to offer was an obscure chutney of other people's ideas. '. . . in a sense a complete metatext-as-metaphor, since every character through his or her suffering has an obviously socio-economic role and speaks directly to the reader. By the same token, the signified—'

I was cut short by Rhyll's emaciated howl.

'You'll never get anywhere with me, or the markers, if you bring in that sort of half-baked political flatulence,' he shrieked in a monotone.

'Dickens is a creator of plot and character – those are his fortes, that is what he is here for, and therefore he is a fundamental building block of the British literary tradition. Dickens worked his imagination bloody hard to get his serials out, and you're reducing his hard-wrought words to representational cardboard, puffs of flabby political commentary, the politics of envy! Get lost, girlie! And don't darken my door until you've understood the *themes*, my girl, the *themes*!'

The truth was, he hated my clothes. I had begun to wear more leather. Inside, however, I felt there was nothing more substantial than cheese, and if someone leant hard enough on me I would deflate rudely, the pale ochre aggregate inside me frothing out and dribbling messily down. No one, least of all Dr Rhyll, cared about my theories on evolution, or about the great age of the series of fossils (all genuine and authenticated) that I had collected with Chivers Jelly tokens when I was eight and had treasured ever since. Naïvely, I had thought that fossils were the epitome of history, that these nubbly relics in their garish display box represented true heritage, next to which this merely medieval institution should have been suitably humbled. But no. My trilobites and sharks' teeth implied a *pastime*, which could not, of course, be tolerated.

I spent my first summer vacation making sandwiches and staring into space. Earth and planets moved, and my second year burst upon me. I made a new friend, Pyrrhus, who tolerated my femininity, and I his fish jokes. He and I took to indulging in *frottage* in the Duke of Barry, an expensive cocktail bar crammed with hairdressers and creators of designer stationery. The profusion of soft caramel Italian leather and batwing sleeves drove us both to distraction as we competed to pass through the room and back, one saving the seats while the other glided up and down in expensive *frisson.*

His friends became grateful for my presence. Having neither the inclination nor the courage to attempt a genuine relationship with the opposite sex, they used me as a dummy for their speculations about the female intellect and anatomy. To them, I was a palimpsest of theories and hypotheses to be tested and thrown out, or proved with knowing laughter. Although they considered me reasonably intelligent, I was to know that I, as other women, had no idea of *concepts.*

One day, driven to paranoia by other people's careerism, I panicked and wrote seventy-two, individually typed letters to newspapers, banks and advertising agencies, asking if there were jobs available. I forgot to include the bit about working for nothing, and received seventy-one polite nos on sheets of paper so thick and creamy I tore them up and dissolved them in my coffee.

Gamely, I decided to try student journalism. I approached the editors of *If,* the university magazine, and managed a very respectable four articles in the first issue of term, to the chagrin of many. Total strangers began coming up to me at parties, saying, 'I think you're very pretentious,' and walking away.

None the wiser, I attended the next editorial meeting at the beginning of the following term. The room was full of short haircuts wearing high-necked black sweaters and leather jackets, saying, 'Fuck, yeah!' and 'Fascist!' My studies of militaristic periods in history indicated that there were few styles more

Fascist than close-cropped hair and identical dark-coloured uniforms, but I sensed this was not the time to point it out.

I stared round the room. *Fast for Namibia!,* a poster proclaimed. I thought it was suggesting a race. On closer inspection, I was bewildered to discover that a lot of rich children were about to sit down and starve themselves for half a day on behalf of people living on the other side of the world. These dietary games would then be proudly inscribed on CVs as evidence of compassion. At the time it did not occur to me that these students were having simple fun, playing with their developing feelings of caring as I myself had played years ago with my swingball, testing the elastic as far as it would go. I felt a rage at them which I could neither explain nor justify. I filter-fed on the conversations around me.

'Fuck, so we got to the house, stopped the car and gave 'im the cash. Well, of course 'e didn't come back, did 'e? Seventy quid! 'E ran out the back while we were sat there for a fuckin' hour! I'm never scorin' off 'im again.'

A girl touched me on the arm and said, 'That means "buy drugs", Sarah.' I flushed. I could drink and drink until my face and mind had melted and re-formed enough to face the askers in the outside world but I could not go beyond that. I could accept alien flesh and sperm inside me, pinioning me, running me up against walls, but to take drugs I would have to join a clique, *be* something. I did not have the confidence, even when drunk. Self-hatred had gripped my head for too long between its ratcheted thighs.

I looked up and caught sight of someone from my college who, I had heard, had recently been offered a scholarship. I rushed up and congratulated him with gusto, not realizing that he had previously declared to his friends that he would never, ever, accept such a trapping of imperialist flunkeyhood. His companions turned on him instantly. These were people who constantly urged each other to get off the fence, but when they tired of the height would stagger quietly off to their parents' second homes to recover. (It had taken me many years to understand why anyone would bother to have two houses.)

I blushed at the scholar's hostility and walked away. This crowd were so utterly devoid of vitality, of sap, that I imagined them to be like the *Graeae* of legend, with half a bollock between them, which they were obliged to pass around in order to act independently.

The editors wanted someone to do a piece on Greenham Common. I grabbed it, trying to salvage something from the dismal meeting. The following Saturday I spent a drizzly afternoon in the open, sitting with five women on a huge, splitting sofa. Sometimes, apparently, a sweater would never, ever dry. I did not know it then, but that was the first afternoon of my whole life I had spent with true believers in anything. I arrived expecting to scorn them, and came away puzzled by my excitement.

My friendship with Pyrrhus developed as far as it could. In public, he tolerated my desperate cuddles with no more than a rigid politeness. Back at his room, however, he would clamp his hand on my crotch with a spaniel-like helplessness in his eyes. Every Saturday afternoon I watched his mawkish, drunken attacks on me as if from a distance. Once he went for me with a coat-hanger, another time he masturbated into a glass of beer. I offered to drink it for a dare, but as I raised it to my lips I caught sight of the proteinous swirl suspended in mid-flight; it so resembled a raw egg that I found myself nauseated and unable to continue.

We decided to see how quickly we could reach orgasm in public places, the loser buying dinner for the other. After a heavy lunch, I elected to lean on one corner of the college washing-machine and he on the other. Passers-by did their drying and left. We both found it impossible to come, and decided to try the new art gallery. Neither of us would have admitted it, but this was something approaching a relationship.

All my efforts at social integration seemed futile, however, once I crossed the corbelled shadow of the Haight family. A dynastic phenomenon, there were seven of them, four siblings and three cousins, at the university. Their provenance was frequently disputed. Cutely, they referred to themselves as *Etruscan*. The sisters were professional virgins, and respected for it, particularly by the type of Englishman who is terrified of real sex, but revels in waving his finger under the noses of his peers afterwards.

When I encountered the Haights I tried to converse with them but it was an unrewarding exercise: their faces remained fixed in a delicate sneer, as if arrested by a passing gas leak. I tried particularly hard with Mirabelle Haight, first because everyone else did and second because for a time, my efforts seemed to have paid off. There was a talent inherent in girls like her for making you think they had something special, something *important* to talk to you about. They never did actually take you aside and impart this special communication but the secret little smile was enough to keep you in thrall, for a while.

The Haights' paintings could be seen hanging discreetly in

various colleges. They were indifferently talented, and it puzzled me that Charlie Haight's *Tuscan Scene* should have been chosen for display in preference to an extraordinary statue by a fine-art scholar who had already won several national prizes. Gabriel's piece had a hundred arms like a Tibetan deity, and in every hand he clutched a bust of a great person of culture. No one could tell whether the god was throwing them or protecting them. It shone in the light like a jewel and glowed peacefully in the dark. I, among others, campaigned to have it displayed in the junior common room, but Charlie's bland pastel of the *Chapel of the Sacred Girdle, Prato,* won the day. There were dark hopes expressed that it was beer-proof. In the end, someone simply drew a moustache on one of the *putti* and left it at that.

For seven years I had lifted neither pen nor brush. I had simply read. I felt a twinge when I saw the sculpture, not, I hoped, the I-could-have-done-that-if-only twinge, but a memory of sitting in my cold bedroom surrounded by dustbin bags.

I remained in the town during my second summer, waitressing a little, working in a shop and learning a certain patience, a fatalism perhaps, a restructuring of the Hope Hormone. Then I met a man called Michael.

I first caught sight of him in my last winter. His hair and clothes were indistinguishable from the darkness made deeper by the bright lamp on the wall above him. Part of a hand in a pocket, a slit of cheek, were all I really saw of him, but as he moved to face me the light bit back from his pupils.

I didn't know which college he attended but he hung around St Drew's a lot with a pair of cheery, roaring men who seemed like boys in comparison. They hunted together at weekends, their early-morning shouts and thumping car boots the cause of frequent complaints among the other students.

The first time I approached him he was standing at the college gate, tossing his hard hat from hand to hand. As I spoke to him the tossing slowed, the hat's dark blue felt reflecting no light. The crop that hung from his wrist swung lazily with every movement.

After that, we always seemed to speak in the dark. Even in the middle of the shining lawn in front of St Drew's, a great Monty Python thump of a building that looked as if it were about to chug away into the distance, even here, the sun went behind a cloud whenever we met. Michael rarely smiled, but viewed me from his jacketed height with unblinking agate eyes, as if millennia of looking down on others had rendered human interaction obsolete, and my submission to him was guaranteed.

What we talked about I can never remember, but there always seemed to be the preamble of an arrangement, a loom of possibility, a slow, headcocked reckoning. Michael would never have been so vulgar as to gaze openly at my breasts or my legs, but all the time I stood before him I felt the points of daggers dragging softly up and down my body.

I did my best to shine for him at the start, and for a moment felt a flicker from an almost forgotten time, when I would thrown a book to the floor and run and shout my childish enthusiasms to the nearest person, Billy capering behind. I thought that this would endear me to him, that my attempted brilliance would somehow meld with his.

Eventually one night we brushed against each other. We left a party together, without a word. I followed him back to his college. The porter nodded and smiled as we strode silently past him. Michael did not speak until his door was firmly shut.

'Get down on that table.'

I simpered. I wanted lips and arms, sweet entanglement and giggles before surrendering.

'Get down on that table or I'll fucking rape you.'

He pushed me, not truly violently. I sat back on the rickety desk and waited, gradually submerged under the cold, damp exhalation of the modern annexe he inhabited. The badly designed steel structure bled damp into the plaster. Black stains crept out from each corner of the ceiling, pointing inwards, downwards at me. A Porsche poster hung on the wall, rippling in the yellow light of a small, stained, part-melted lampshade. The fox-tail that hung next to it seemed incongruous in the ugly room, like something won at a fair. Metal shelving lined one wall, marked by years of stickers ripped off as teenage allegiances changed. Those were the before-condom days, when minor infections ran riot, and the sperm ran itchily out of you like dead breakers from a minor inlet.

'Wait.' He put out the light. 'I always screw in the dark.'

I realized why when I put my arms around him. His back was covered in enormous spots, scattered cleanly like fenland oast-houses.

A little after his orgasm, I screamed as he pulled sharply out of me. An old, mildewed chill replaced him. My soft inner walls collapsed.

The anonymous nature of our relationship worked for a while. It provided a sensate focus for my desires without the tiresome nodes and arcs of a developing intimacy. What we were doing, of course, had nothing to do with intimacy. The passing of my vaginal fluid to his penis, from his penis to my mouth and back to his and then back to my vagina, had nothing to do with intimacy whatsoever. I loved the secret glamour of taking off my underwear at a quarter to twelve, and walking through the night to his room wearing only boots and a battered full-length Barbour I had found bunched smellily at the bottom of my cupboard the previous year.

Nature plays cruel tricks on the vulnerable, and after a while I found myself wanting to go for coffee with Michael, and talk about life and stuff and the universe and philosophy and say all the things I had never said to anyone in all my two and a half years at university. Once I even tried, playfully, to introduce the idea of our having a conversation, but to no avail. Besides, over the past months, something had taken me over, along with many of the other females around me. I had become dedicated to *results*, not proud achievements but mere panic-driven entries on lists. In the shadow of my finals – the long, pointing shadow that tickles the timid, flayed skin of the middle-class aspirer that I was gradually becoming – Dr Shabbie reduced me to tears.

I arrived after a sex session with Michael, which had split the upper layers of skin at the entrance to my vagina and left me with fifty-nine tiny bruises on my neck and chest.

'So. What have you learned this year, Sarah?' Shabbie was rocking back and forth with exaggerated boredom. He had not tried to sleep with me. He had seen early on that the intensity of my loneliness would not interest him for long.

'I'll be honest with you, Sarah, your insistence on the existence of plot and character in literature will not endear you to at least one of the examiners I know—'

I could not, it seemed, please anybody. I screamed as my coffee flew through the air. I was summoned to see Professor Davidson on a piece of continuous paper.

The seventy-second reply to my frenzied job applications arrived. I had been offered a placement on the *Skip*, a recently established national newspaper. I found it odd that they had not wished to interview me formally first. Obviously they believed in the value of a good *tranche* of further education at a reputable establishment. I began to read newspapers. One day they were full of something called the Poll Tax. My fingers blackened with print, I started to think.

I began to have hideous dreams. Four-thirty one hot afternoon I lay down on my bed, the light a lurid teal through thin slubbed curtains that barely joined. I found myself standing in a garden, listening to the plants. I looked down at my breasts and saw penises growing out of them, some perfectly formed, some vestigial, fingerlike, all sprouting up and up like hands from a grave. Suddenly the image vanished and all around me was seafood: lobsters, crayfish, crabs, running, running, past me and across the grass and disappearing.

My fears rose up higher as the exams approached. Like Gerard Manley Hopkins with his half- and quarter-point marking system, I steamed myself up until I was frantic with diarrhoea. With hitherto unseen precision I wrote and rewrote my revision notes, fluorescenting and refluorescenting carefully scripted boxes, and learning quotations I barely understood. Like every *girl* I worked too hard, in the superstitious fear that some Grand Designer would see everything if I did not read and digest every single line and chapter of every single book, however trite and pointless.

Afterwards I collapsed. Answering my body's Pavlovian call, I went to Michael's room. The door was opened by a pair of ruffled Americans who had taken it over for the summer. He had gone.

I went and lay on the college lawn. I closed my eyes and was still as other students came and went, celebrating. I felt a tickling against my ear as an insect passed by, feeling its way with tiny horns. Suddenly everything went dark. I opened my eyes to see a halo of white-blond hair surrounding a face that temporarily eclipsed the sun. Gabriel. The artist for whose work I had campaigned in vain. I exhaled violently in surprise, having been holding my breath without realizing it.

'I thought you'd gone,' he said, turning a little so that the sun caught his face. He was almost albino, but his pink mouse-face had a marble dignity. He looked as if he had risen out of the crawling slab of human viscera and emerged, pale and clear, unsullied. He was astonishingly beautiful, avoiding entirely the appearance that some pale-haired men have of having been printed with one colour missing from the block.

'You look tired, Sarah.'

His voice was soft after all the shouting and the echo of the examination halls. I tried to shield my eyes against the glare but could not.

'I'm sorry. I can't see you.' I covered my face with my hand and opened and closed my fingers, translucent scarlet slats. Gabriel laughed gently and sat with me, without saying a word. I was lulled, not to sleep but to a calm. When I looked again, I caught a vision of him dressed in rough white cotton pyjamas. His hair rippled in the breeze. He was sitting with his knees drawn up looking outwards, upwards. I asked him about his recent trip to India, wanting vicarious excitement. He talked about the streets, the noises, the people, and I imagined him stepping with magnificent gentleness from rickshaw to bus to café seat, above the petty frustrations of the ordinary traveller bent on the penny's difference between satisfactory fare and diabolical rip-off.

Today he had his sketch-book with him.

'What's that?' I asked, as I tried to interpret the cyan squiggle and fit it to a woman, a tree, a building. I wondered if I was simply too bourgeois to appreciate these wispy epiphanies.

'Why try to define it?' he replied and smiled with the golden certainty of an evening sun reflected in a vast shop window.

We talked for the next two hours, about his sculpture, his exams, my exams. I had, in truth, nothing else to talk about. I had no interests, I realized, save sex and occasional searches for new clothing. I had a job, but no other connection with the life of the mind, for want of a better way of putting it. Gabriel was so full of stories, of his travels, his thoughts, that I felt as if someone had turned on a vast ionizer that gave out great gulps of mountain air.

'But what about you, Sarah?'

He looked at me.

'What about me? Sorry, I don't understand.'

'Sarah, I hope you don't mind me saying this but you look so sad.'

'I—'

And the tears came, not the first by any means, though tears in such a situation were rare for me. I did all my crying alone in bed, my makeup turning to two charcoal blocks under my eyes.

'Sarah, Sarah, what happened to you?'

He put his hand on my head but did not stroke. So often people try to stroke your hair and all their sweaty palms do is tug, and the irritation destroys everything. He simply moved his fingers, pressing the palm gently but firmly. I could not stop crying.

'Sarah, I'm here. I'm not going to go away.'

For a minute I cared if people saw, then I felt ashamed. Who cared? I rested my head in his lap and he squeezed my neck softly. The fabric of his trousers smelt sweet, not of hot human but of sugared almonds, or coconut or frangipane. I soon stopped crying. I stretched out my legs. Barely having seen the sun they were a greyish beige, the scars dull white grooves. I had not shaved them since the beginning of my exams, and they were furred with tiny vertical sticks of growth that gleamed in the light.

'Let's get some food.'

We split apart briefly to stand up. As I got slowly to my feet I saw I had left a brown-black stain on his trouser-leg, which was only just covered by his tunic. He did not seem to notice it. I now expected a cool, English promenade to the delicatessen, the flow of air between us negating irrevocably what had gone before. Instead he put his arms around me as soon as we were on our feet.

'Look, you've got—' and he pulled out a Kleenex, wrapped it around his finger, licked the tip and, staring intently at his work, wiped the fallen makeup from my face. No one had done thar for me since Mum, so long ago I could have invented it.

We ate carrot cake and salami and candied chestnuts, and drank elderflower cordial. In the evening we sat on St Drew's steps until it became too cold, then went, without speaking, back to his room, his huge-ceilinged room hung with canvases, full of half-finished creations. We lay down. I touched his head. The bone-white hair was shockingly soft, like chick fur. He put his hand on my stomach and looked into my face. He did not touch me anywhere else. Something kicked inside me and the old fear danced up like a big spider in a sink.

'Sarah, we don't have to.' He took his hand away.

'It's just that—'

'Sarah. We don't ever have to if you don't want to.'

Relief washed over me before my fear had time to metamorphose into desire, the spider quieten and sprout into the silky darkness of pubic hair.

We talked and fell quiet. We crawled under the duvet, which was covered by a dark red bedspread appliquéd with bulging, shining elephants. We curled up together, I with my back to him. All I could hear was his breathing. We were both still dressed. In the night we awoke hot and stripped to our underwear. With our skin touching I expected the usual edging up, the catches in the breath, the pointy shove below. But nothing. We returned to the same positions and fell asleep. In the morning we embraced, but in such a way that I could not tell if he was even hard. I was grateful.

The hundred-armed statue sat in the corner, dusty. Beethoven was the nearest face I could see peeking from between the burnished black fingers.

Two more days of this and he told me about his uncle's flat in London. Moving in with Gabriel was the first spontaneous act I had committed in years.

fourteen

LIFE BEGAN. I did not as yet know enough of London flats to find this one irritating. It was a basement in a part of town known as smart, with a transient population of young Europeans all dressed in navy blue which set off their tans perfectly. Old women, their time-gone clothes immaculate, walked small dogs up and down. Large metallic-effect cars basked in the gutters, occasionally heaved into action by people of all ages, colours and nationalities, linked only, but strongly, by their wealth. Detached houses were white, with intense little gardens paved and preened by visiting people in housecoats. Our flat was in a tall building, one of thirty or so in a cramped little lozenge with a green space in the middle. The building was populated by both rich foreigners and the upper-middle-class British who hated them but could do nothing about it. Thus it seemed apt, and somehow safer, that I lived underground.

The flat was so low set, and the surrounding buildings so tall that, whatever the weather, it was always pitch dark when I opened the front door. As I felt my way down the pointless corridor, I was assailed by a rainbow of smells, first of damp, then shoes, then indefinable old dust, then unlaundered clothes, and finally occasional puffs of sewage from the drains outside the kitchen window. All overlaid by the narcotic tang of Gabriel's paints, glues and polishes.

We painted it and the gloom took on a pearly shine. The smells, however, did not go away and we battled sweetly over air-fresheners. I had a month before my job started, to which I gave barely a thought.

At night we lay together on the big, damp futon. Gabriel had long ectomorphic fingers with which he stroked my body. I simply lay, thinking of nothing but safety. He never pressed me, and I let him rest his eyes against my breasts, closed, who knew with what patterns burning themselves there. Desire was absent, that familiar crawl at my back, the steel shaft of terror that descended through me and walked me towards darkness like a puppet.

I spent my days exploring London, an *A–Z* discreetly covered with a page of Sunday supplement. Sometimes I would despair, in Soho, standing over the book on a street corner, my chin glued to my chest, my hair curtaining, as I tried to read the map upside down, desperately calculating lefts and rights, not knowing even which direction I faced. I read newspapers. The pointlessness of politicians, the madness of City salaries. And yet I was to have a salary too.

It was the Summer of Love, or one of them. Gabriel took me to a club. He rammed something down my throat calling it Ecstasy. The taste made me gag, and reminded me of the little pink worming tablets we used to give Billy, but I said nothing. The music was single-noted, electronic. Suddenly Gabriel was off, a wraith in the dry ice, spinning his whole body, more active than I had ever seen him. I stalked him frailly round the floor as he whirled, my face bashed to the right and left by driving hands. I gave in and joined them. For a moment or two I felt a twitching in my spine, a cold chemical slither that may or may not have been attributable to the drug I had taken.

Back home, Gabriel stomped round the house, jerking back and forth to some similar music. I lay in the bed, inhaling the dankness as dawn climbed above. He flopped down next to me and instantly fell asleep.

So I had nested. I had real breath next to me, a network of veins and arteries and motor responses that cooked for me, put my things in the washing-machine occasionally, rubbed my bruises, let my orifices rest unforced.

One morning I woke to find him already up, investigating something at the small round table at which we ate. Gabriel was tearing up a rose. He had a palette of oils on the table, with which he was trying to copy the various hues of the huge flower. He must have taken it from one of the local cottagettes. Its colours ran from deep pink to burning orange-yellow. Its heart had not yet opened, and Gabriel was peeling it away petal by petal, leaving a damp, mashed little core of deep magenta. He was engrossed. I watched him for a while.

There was a forced splendour in the air. I knew I would have to play the appearance game at work, and discovered that I loved the thrill of walking home after a day's shopping, my hands turning blue, the circulation cut off by the weight of the bags, handles of rope and plastic, the sharp, annoying nudge of shoebox-corner against my shin, the bump of thick card and the pantomime thunder-rattle of giant paper carriers. And then the relief of dropping it all flamboyantly as the door slammed behind me, and for a few moments my hands, palms upwards, remained fixed, frozen, purple fingers turned up in supplication until the blood returned to them and the deep grooves, the stigmata of commercialism, disappeared.

We fought over who would put up the shelves. I won, and banged in nails while he made risottos and avocado ice-cream. Tired, after four hours' measuring and carrying planks, I leant over him. I rested my breasts against the skinny breadth of his shoulders as he bent over a drawing, my chin on his head. We became like two rocks, the strata leaping and falling in millions of years' descent towards oblivion. We could stay like this for hours, I leaning, supported, while he rubbed at his work. He did not seem to mind me in this position. In fact, I found it quite an effort, but somehow the difficulty, the tension as my lower body shifted to get comfortable, the rippling grip in my back muscles as I strove not to put my whole weight on Gabriel's quiet form, satisfied me in some obscure way. He never knew the delicate mechanism that balanced me on him, so that all he could feel was two cotton-wrapped balls of softness and the warm pad of my stomach down his back. I would emerge from these positions stiff yet strangely purified. Gabriel would remain at the table, working.

And so summer bleached its way through London, and I taught myself to find the perfect spot in Hyde Park from which I could not see anything but trees and the sun flashing through them and then the light sagged, and August ended, and September, like a huge dog waking, brought the revolving barrier of life back to square one. My new job, my first job.

On my first morning I woke very early. Gabriel was not in bed. I got up to make some tea and padded noiselessly into the muggy darkness of the hallway. I peered into the bathroom and was greeted by a ghostly white form. Gabriel, his long shirt rucked up, was masturbating, his head pressed against the doorjamb, his lips jutting forward, the breath hissing through his teeth, restrained, barely cutting the air.

I stood, frozen. His hand was moving so fast it barely registered in the darkness, except for his signet ring, its dull gleam flickering. There was a sound, a strain, and a neat, military shake of his body. It could have been tiny shards of bone he was shooting out of himself, that fell ticking onto the floor and collected in a careful little fan. Slowly he bent and I heard the rustle and smoothing of toilet paper as he cleaned up. I backed into the bedroom and folded up under the duvet. I felt a tiny kick of arousal. We were so completely unsexual together, he was so careful with me, that I had forgotten, almost, that intercourse was necessary. Every night, it was as if we had retired to hibernate, curled in complementary shapes. He came back into bed. I hoped he would not feel the coldness of my hands and feet. He crawled in and laid his arms across me. We slept. The alarm squalled. We fell apart like a dead shell on a beach.

fifteen

I INHALED WITH PRIDE the tube train's nourishing stench, the resulting exhalation joining the hundred or so others around me that helped to form the city's great infective subculture. In the coming months I would become fair to middling sick every five weeks until my constitution had been broken and re-formed.

I emerged above ground and smiled with the sun behind me as I walked along the fast City road, still golden in the morning light. Cars raced by, hooting their horns with jubilee verve. Life was simple. I had cracked it. Failure was a ravening fissure into which others fell.

My new employer, the *Skip*, was the flagship newspaper of Intranews, a large media corporation. The *Skip* claimed a special niche in the reading market. Neither broadsheet nor truly tabloid, it stretched the minds of half its readers while providing a much-needed break for the rest. The less cultured could discard the review section before friends had a chance to mock their pretensions, and those who imagined themselves more mentally elevated could slum it by revelling in its sex scandals and rabble-rousing harangues.

As I had understood from its recruitment literature, the *Skip*'s directors were eager to employ university graduates both for our youth and the superior organizational skills our education had conferred on us. I had joined as the youngest, therefore my snot-stained pinafores and broken vases, fingers in the butter and thefts from mother's purse would be indulged with the greatest pleasure. Gems of miraculous wisdom would be gleaned from my chatter, the whims of the *enfant savant*.

I waited while a big man frisked me at the door with an electric truncheon. His eyes were fixed on a flickering screen just above my head. As I walked towards the lifts a woman in a pillbox hat shrieked at me, 'Coat check!'

She looked at me with the agonized brightness of a society hostess encouraging a female dinner guest to *withdraw*, and patted her thighs as if welcoming a boisterous retriever. I handed her my coat, for which she demanded a pound.

'You can claim it back later!' she told me loftily. Later I discovered she was a harmless performance artist allowed to operate in the lobby so that the *Skip*'s directors could tell people it supported modern English culture.

I passed through a heavy glass door and was offered a choice of directions via inlaid wooden arrows on the parquet. There was a quiet streaming noise, air-conditioning. Two broad, suited men approached me, heading in the opposite direction. I towered over them. One of them looked me up and down. My feet stopped sounding at the appearance of carpet beneath them, dusky pink with a grey stripe. In the lift I peered into the smoked-glass mirror. My hair was copper, my face a milky beige, my one spot already crusting with mismatched blemish-hider, but discreetly.

I stepped out into a vast sea of pot plants and piled papers, monitors, clocks, flashing televisions and heads bowed. One or two faces rose up and examined me before returning to their original position. Suddenly I felt a stinging on my cheek. It was a spitball, fired from a biro. There was a chorus of giggling remonstration as I made my way across the room. Pushing a long green frond out of the way, I knocked on a door. Silence. I waited, staring over an adjacent woman's shoulder at her computer screen. A message flashed up. *Suckmypenispurple!!! love, Ivor*.

She erased it quietly. I waited for a few more seconds then opened the door with a smile of ingratiation. A man looked up at me, puzzled. I explained my business.

'Oh right. Yeah. You're one of the Juniors. Yup. We're putting you all in there for now.'

He indicated another room. I had no idea I was to have rivals. I felt an agony of competition. At school I had never needed to vie with my classmates, who had swirled below me like boiling rice in a saucepan.

The room contained two people. The girl pouted as she talked about the sausage-delivery firm she had set up during her year off, the word repeated and repeated until all I could feel was the hiss of her sibilants and the blast of her smugness against the flapping sliver of meat that was trapped between her front teeth. The boy had run a local radio station, written for several national newspapers here and abroad and developed his own saltwater-powered car. All I could offer my companions were days spent staring out of windows. To distract them I began a discussion of the glass tank filled with murky grey water that sat behind us on a fake ormolu stand. Then the door opened.

'Hello, everyone!'

A voice echoed round the room. Ranged on the other side of the table, we saw nothing. There was a puzzled silence.

'Well! You lot aren't going to be much cop as journos if you can't even find your own boss!'

The voice, which tinkled like a tin lid on concrete, emanated from somewhere below the edge of the table. We craned forward. A tiny woman, no more than three feet tall, was standing there, all pink suit and gold chains and shiny black bob and bolshie superiority. Her shoes had heels like skewers.

Small women had a definite role in my personal mythology. I had always wondered why the combination of idiocy and sublime nastiness that these little beings could embody prompted neither accusation nor disapproval in the general population, particularly men. As a tall female, I had always felt a deep resentment at having to kiss them socially as it involved ugly, ungainly movement on my part, while on theirs no more than a turning upward of the face as if pretending to be a sunflower in a children's pantomime.

'I'm Lyndi Brill,' the creature said. 'I'm the deputy news editor. I've no time for whingers and arty types and a lot of time for hard workers who put in as many hours as I do!' She winked absurdly up at the male Junior, who smiled back, to my irritation.

'Say hello to Archibald, then!' she cajoled. 'You've all been so mean not to introduce yourselves!'

She pointed to the tank and indicated that we tap it. The crusted surface rippled and a small, flaking, once orange fish appeared, slowly, sadly, as if overcome by millennial misery. As it did so, a reporter bounced into the room, flicked cigarette ash into the tank and bounced out again. The fish bumped once against the glass before turning and retreating into the pale gloom. As we shuffled out of the door, Lyndi caught my eye with an expression similar to that of a primary-school teacher who has just caught a small child with its finger in its anus *on its first day*.

'I was watching you earlier. We don't wear leather jackets here, Sarah!'

I had to bend almost double to hear her. I folded myself up like a piece of origami, one leg stretched forward to allow the rest of me to cant over in an attempt to balance.

She flashed a big tiny smile. 'You'll learn!'

I noticed that, beneath the pink polish, the fingernails of her right hand were engrained with a rust-coloured deposit, almost *red*. She saw me staring and spoke suddenly, with strangely unwilling conviviality. 'There's no fucking soap in the loos. It's hell when you're on the rag!'

We were each assigned a reporter with whom we were supposed to work. I sat down as if at a bar. The man looked up briefly but continued to chew. He was a fine example of the Home Counties Aryan, all dull dark-blond hair, matching eyebrows, skin grey pale, dead blue eyes, thin lips, a large physique without being in any way striking, and a slight tendency to hills at the waist, despite weekend rugby. No sense of humour of any kind, except when it came to the latest comedian. Possibly married, in order that the families combine the automatic curtains (double lined) of Gerrards Cross with the inglenooks of Epsom.

'Hi!' I effused. I expected the man's face to light up at the thought of me perching opposite, given the attention that had been paid to my legs as I had crossed the room, but he merely demanded a set of cuttings from the library. I ran eagerly to the lift. When I got back, I was given the list of winners of the week's crossword competition to copy up. The male Junior had got out of it, declaring sweetly that he did not know how to type.

There were many other women in the newsroom, most of whom were either carrying tea trays or stuffing envelopes. Some wore gingham nylon and smelt of sweat and disinfectant. All of them scurried, like terriers in showcoats, as if higher forces had explained politely but firmly that their own and others' lives depended on the speed of their little feet. The men, ill-shaped in good suits, merely *strolled,* pausing occasionally as if to buy souvenirs on some palm-fringed walkway.

As I examined my surroundings, I wondered at the design of the Aryan's computer. It was similar to the rest in size, shape and colour, but its surface was a mass of matt, asymmetrical lumps. Perhaps it was a one-off, a pilot product, offered to him when no others were available. I was about to ask him if it had been photographed for a magazine when I saw him remove his chewing gum from his mouth and stick it carefully on the edge of the keyboard. At lunchtime we three Juniors made our way to the canteen, where we ate tepid Cornish pasties which were entirely hollow save for lumps of iridescent jelly. Mine also contained a false nail.

We shuffled to the deputy editor's office for the news conference. On and around his desk was a vast array of family photographs. Some were indistinct, taken straight at the light, the spice colours of autumn and the welts of red-wellied toddlers greyed out; some were from school, with gunmetal blue or orange Dacron backing, the children's clothes resolutely charcoal, hair shining like the ends of little banisters. Those unframed flapped and shone with the air-conditioning.

I was roused from my peering by a large body shoving past me and spinning my scratchy brown chair without apology. This was Ivor, the chief reporter. His hair was bleached primrose yellow; his tennis-coach arms were orange and rumbaba-sheeny with a permanent light sweat. Rumour had it he injected himself with Ronseal in an attempt to hide his carious complexion, the result of late childhood chickenpox followed rapidly by teenage acne. As compensation he had become a body builder and then a sports writer, helped by the fact that he sounded Australian but was in fact from Hastings. Today, his right arm had bits of straw clinging to it, which someone discreetly pointed out and he wiped away hastily.

I considered him. My sexuality was urging to return and I opened the door for it, helplessly. But I did not really know what to do. For I had never really *needed* to charm anyone. Since my childhood, I had found it easy to obtain sex. I simply had to exist and somehow men came to me. Not that I was so beautiful or so alluring, but they could sense that someone had already taken a coin to me and rubbed out the silvered square that was my innocence, revealing a manageable price beneath.

The news editor appeared and, after a couple of rounds of *stone, paper, scissors,* started the meeting. Reporters offered up their ideas: motorway tolls, reservoir pollution, benefit cuts, feminist Bibles, the weather.

As I sat, my attention was caught by a persistent, small-scale movement to my right. The Aryan, staring into the void, had placed his little finger in his nose and was probing, with an eyesurgeon's delicacy, for a desirable titbit. I tried to look away, but the tiny process gnawed pettishly at the outer reaches of my vision until I was forced to crick my neck roughly in the opposite direction in order not to throw up.

I distracted myself by watching the other female Junior cross her legs without actually resting the upper one on the lower, so that her calf didn't spread. It would have been terrible for her spine and I was about to tell her so when it came to my turn to offer up an idea for the paper.

'I thought it would be really interesting to study politicians' physiognomies.'

'Fizzywhattywhatty?' came a *sotto voce* squeak from Lyndi, swinging her legs.

'Well we could get a couple of phrenologists and I read the other day about someone who relates facial features to personality and they've managed to discover certain traits that keep cropping up and we could see if there's a definitive Tory, Labour face and so on, and we could look at sincerity, aggression—'

'Jesus bloody Christ!' came a gruff voice, 'This isn't some bloody glossy magazine for bloody *rodarse bitches* languishing on the *fourth toilet*! This is a fucking newspaper. News, darling, news! Live and breathe news! Not poncy prancing arty crap!'

Amused nods of assent framed this rant.

'That's interesting!' I piped up. 'Judging by your reaction, it sounds like it had quite an effect on you. Perhaps you're rather impressed by the idea! Or am I being a little *pocket Freud*?'

The air-conditioner thrummed. The plants waved. The waters of interest closed over my head and they moved on. I was to learn that, at work, as when dealing with the police, being clever does not pay.

My attacker, a tired-looking man with a misshapen, thinning cap of greying mousy hair was the political correspondent and resident Jack-of-all-tirades. A man who had well and truly worked his way up through local newspapers, who had done so much 'time' he was rumoured to have the date of his entry into journalism, 1958, tattooed on his upper arm. He fulminated about the old days on the *Chard Express*, and resolutely typed his copy on an old Remington. A tattered paper would then be handed magnanimously to a secretary, and then to me, since I was the nearest Junior, to input into the system. When the *Skip*'s executives staggered by after lunch, he would bark out a greeting in a gloomy, portentous monotone, occasionally adding a quip if the addressee could stand up long enough to turn and face him.

'Didn't like Heseltine's speech one bit! Couldnearim! Might do better if he loosened his *truss*!'

Or, 'Dullards yesterday, the whole lotofem. Couldn't get a word in edgeways, bloody woman! Need a bloody good dose of *cascara*!'

The executives' silver sleekness, the odour of New Car interior spray floating heavenward from their rumps, barely registered his timegone humour, which had long been wound in antimacassars and laid to rest in hard, cream, oval suitcases without wheels.

Someone raised the matter of a new government scheme: schools for creative children, performers and artists, to be set up in the capital.

'I think it's outrageous that they aren't giving scholarships to kids from out of town!' I burst out, remembering the distance I had once felt would never shorten. 'There's just as many talented children out there in the country as there are here! Why don't we go round and find out who'd lose out? We could do it by region . . .'

I looked round at my colleagues. The girl Junior recrossed her legs, again the precarious balance. A cloud of impassivity settled momentarily. Lyndi picked her nails.

'Weren't you born in London, then, Sarah?'

'No, Grimsby, actually.'

The parliamentary reporter grunted, and shot a significant look at the rest of the group.

Afterwards, as we shuffled out of the room, Lyndi, Ivor and several of the other seniors turned sharply towards the lifts and vanished.

sixteen

'SO HOW WAS IT, THEN?'

Gabriel seemed very concerned about my first day at work.

'Well, no Watergates as yet, but they're letting me sort some files on famous people. I phoned Eric Morecambe today!'

'But, Sarah! He's been dead for ages!'

I'd been so excited I'd forgotten, and it was late in the day, and I'd been so eager to please after the disappointing meeting. I laughed as hard as I could.

Gabriel had the look of someone who has been in the house all day. He chewed his little finger and looked up at me from where he sat. 'Look. I made this for you.' He indicated an object on the kitchen table covered by a large white napkin. It was always his way, to reveal something he had just made as if he were the Queen, or some passing dignitary. I turned eagerly, knowing by now to let him have the fun of taking the two corners in his hands and flipping them up to reveal another creation.

It was a life-size bust of me in fruit. Me, carved from melons, plums, bananas, all flayed and scraped moistly into shape, like a Renaissance medical model. The fruit had been underripe, and there was very little scent.

'Hey, wow!' I said, marvelling at the lip-red Victorias and translucent green Galia flesh. It never occurred to Gabriel to doubt his own work, and so it never occurred to me either. Everything was shown and discussed with the same pride as when shrill Ian-from-the-gallery called up to ask how things were going.

I wasn't sure what to say next. It would have been wrong to eat the sculpture then and there, but it needed a degree of protection from the late summer flies that collected at the kitchen door with every new deluge from the drains above. I put it on top of the fridge with a piece of clingwrap tucked around it.

'It's lovely.'

'I thought it had a certain representational value. A certain . . . symbolism.'

'You mean it's an example of nature in its beauty improved by man's ultimate creative hand?'

'Yeah. Something like that.'

He smiled at his food, the kitchen light playing on his oiled-looking eyelashes. We settled down for the evening.

I still did not really know *why* I was working at the *Skip*, or why they had taken me on, except that I felt safe in the thought that my method-acted ambition had not been found wanting. When I told acquaintances where I worked, however, they made dark references to a 'jungle'. Jungles in their eyes were dark, dangerous and unpredictable places. I laughed inwardly at their interpretation. Jungles weren't unpredictable, they were tightly run social systems! Every shrew, every liana, every teak-tree and sticky-legged swamp-nymph willingly shoulders its belief in the continuing survival of the macrocosm! Food chains knot and twist into a great macramé'd skein of nature, a graceful organism utterly dedicated to survival. I had a definite role in such an environment. Nothing *could* be there that should not, where death froths underfoot but viridescent wads of life pump out of the canopy at ten billion germinations a second!

Days became weeks as I waited patiently for recognition.

The *Skip* became keen to promote its surveys section, for which we Juniors were on permanent call. Members of the public were called at random and questioned on newsworthy topics, whether government policy or a new food scare. The memory began to grate of how, on our first day, the three of us had put our heads together and giggled about the poor saps reduced to selling advertising space for a living.

One November morning we were summoned, with smirks. There had been several cases of bodies being robbed while being laid out and a certain slackening off of embalming skills. With Christmas encroaching, bringing with it the inevitable catalogue of health problems and expensive emotional retribution, the *Skip* had decided to expose the country's undertakers for what they were. Telephone directories in hand, we were put to work. I hated the telephone, its heedless helpfulness and whorish availability. Mine was often foetid from late-night use. I gritted my teeth.

'Hello, is that Mr T. Atkinson? Er, sorry, I don't know your first name—'

'That it is, yes.'

'Oh, good! Hello, yes, it's Sarah Clevtoe here from the *Skip* in London. We were just doing a survey on undertakers and we

– I wondered if you had had any bereavements in the family recently?'

'Well. Funny you should ask but yes, yes, my wife died last month . . .'

'Right! Well, I wondered if I could just ask you a few – of course I'm terribly sorry to hear that, Mr Atkinson – a few questions. OK, right. First of all, the undertakers. Were you a) very satisfied, b) quite satisfied, c) reasonably satisfied, d) not particularly satisfied, e) very unsatisfied or f) not satisfied at all?'

The photocopied response sheet was almost illegible.

'Sorry, dear, what was the third one?'

'Um, let me see. Reasonably satisfied.'

'Yes dear, that's the one. Although I wasn't so happy about the way he kept laughing.'

'Er, sorry. Who did, Mr Atkinson?'

'What?'

'Who was it who kept laughing? The undertaker?'

'No. No. The butcher. The family butcher.'

'He came along, did he?'

'For a short time, yes.'

'OK. How well was the body – your wife, of course – how well was it, she that is, sorted out? Very well, quite well, fairly well, average, not very well or bad?'

'She had eyes like stars, my wife, and hands like living ivory. When I moved inside her it was like Apollo thundering back and forth across the skies—'

'So they made quite a good job of it, then.'

'You worker ants in London don't know anything about love, do you?'

He hung up. Afterwards, Lyndi asked me to put the telephone directories back in alphabetical order. I glowered in the direction of the secretary, who was about to leave. Lyndi frowned and beckoned. I collapsed myself like a deckchair to listen.

'You should be better at the job than Susie,' she admonished. 'That's why we picked you, Sarah. Because you're a graduate.'

I noticed her nails again, blackish red filth decorating them as before. The ends of her sleeves were flecked with something like bran. She pulled her hands down quickly as I stood up, until they were impossibly far below me, like children seen from a steep-sided skyscraper.

I felt a vicious frustration. Back at my desk, the Aryan was looking at some very blurred holiday photographs, mostly of irregularly shaped bits of people from behind, or overexposed sea shots with a vast black knob of finger in the middle.

'Oooooh!' I called out at one particularly inconsequential view of part of a flip-flopped foot with a dropped ice-cream next to it. 'That'll be the Via Spodulata – and there's you in anal congress with a muleteer!'

He did not even look at me. Irony had less convertible worth here than milk-bottle tops. At least they could be given to charity.

One morning, after I had sharpened all the pencils and Tippexed everyone's initials on the backs of their chairs, and was preparing to pore over the pile of parish magazines and community notelets left out for me in which to find a *story*, Ivor beckoned me portentously to the newsdesk. He offered no explanation, as he was in mid-performance, standing in full view of the entire newsroom talking on the phone to alleged bank robbers and runaway celebrities no one else could track down. He very rarely took notice of me, my attempts at humour and dour in-the-trade quips falling on fallow ears, but today, however, he took my arm in one huge, padded, marmalade-coloured hand and led me into one of the side rooms.

'This could be your big break, Sarah. It began as a City story, but it's so massive that it's spread over to us.'

He shut the door as he spoke, and pulled down the blinds.

'This is a story about how companies hold back an idea, or a product, until just that perfect moment in the market when they suddenly pick it up and it drops effortlessly into place. It's a huge story, and it'll have massive impact on our most influential readers, the ones we care about most. There's something in it for every section of the paper – the books section'll be covering it, the arts lads – only sport aren't getting a slice of the cake and they're fucking pissed off, I can tell you!'

I craned forward over the scribbled notes on his pad, which he quickly turned back towards himself. The fluorescent light gleamed blue-pink against my skin. I could see every blackhead on his amber-tinted nose, and the shiny stripe of light down the middle like a skier's warpaint. He drew closer to me. I caught the puzzling odour of TCP. The inside of his arm, what I could see of it, was covered in scratches, tiny ploughed trails of crusted blood. He pulled his sleeve down.

'Now this is a lot of responsibility we're giving you here, Sarah, but since the story's got to break this week, we've decided to put the spotlight on you, as a Junior. After all, that's why we took you all on, to find the journalists of the future. It's a big deal we're putting on your shoulders – basically, we're splashing it.'

And so it was that an hour later I found myself in Knightsbridge, my face a mask of ingratiation, asking passers-by how they felt about the impending appearance of a new edition of the *A–Z* with revolutionary spiral binding.

seventeen

'NOT SO GREAT, your little career thing, is it?'

Gabriel was frying some onions.

'What do you mean?' I was crestfallen, surprised.

'I never understood why you wanted to piddle about doing all that stuff.'

I had never questioned my own desperate search for civic identity. Everyone had been dashing for the jobs ferry, and they had just unlooped the last rope when I got my letter and leaped for it, skidding to a halt on the slippery, smelly deck. But at least I was aboard. Yes, *Welcome aboard!*, that was it, that was what the man had said to me on my first day.

'What do you suggest I do, then?'

'God, I don't know, be decorative or something. Go and stand over there with Hoodlum and Saraswati.'

Gabriel always named his sculptures. I could not see the look on his face, but then I did not really recognize his tone either. I sat in silence as he finished frying, the banded white flesh turning transparent against the Teflon. Another new pan, Le Creuset, of course. Where did he get the money?

Something prevented me from bantering back. It was as if

someone had put an invisible bridle and bit over my head, and I could feel the cold burn of metal at my cheek and tongue and the pull of leather at my forehead, crunching the vertebrae in my neck.

That moment, the moment of Gabriel's first ever off-handness to me, laid a whisper of a foundation for a structure without a damp course; without buttresses. I was not really in love with him, but I had taken for granted our emotional unification. Six months ago he had rescued me from my loneliness and taken me on. Now I felt myself *reacted against*, as if I had become an antigen in our previously harmonious cell.

I stood to take off my jacket and skirt. I loved the safety of being at home, where I could shut the door and strip and wander round half dressed, unsuitable for outside viewing. My shirt was absurd with its squared-off hem, the tights shiny, pulling my flesh in like iridescent sausage skins.

'God, you've put on weight,' observed Gabriel.

He barely glanced at me as he said it. He tipped the onion and tuna into a saucepan of pasta bows. There was something trivial in their shape, as if they had fallen from the necks of a hundred deadbeat comedians. I sat down again and my body sagged. I wanted his arms around me, not this. In truth, too, I wanted his face between my legs, which was something he had never offered, or I had ventured to ask. He had got as far as kissing my breasts and resting his head on the bony plateau between them, and up to now I had been grateful, but suddenly it was not enough. His turned back and now his coldness made me yearn for the true dislocation of physical pleasure and the accompanying pain.

We ate in silence, while he scribbled sketches on a pad of cartridge paper. There was a rich new note among the more acrid scents of the kitchen area. Since it improved the overall miasma, I said nothing, nor looked for the source of it. I tore a strip of butter from the hard yellow block and watched as it sagged and slipped between the little steaming shapes.

'You'll get fatter if you do that.'

'Stop it!' I stood up and came round behind him and rubbed my cheek against his T-shirt. He patted my thigh and carried on sketching. I squeezed him and stared at him. Suddenly everything seemed huge. I bent and kissed his cheek, leaving a gleaming patch of butter from my lips.

'What the fuck's that on my face!'

I returned to my plate, fury rising out of nowhere and spreading out, lining me. My face must have looked like an old leaf, because he looked over.

'What's wrong? I'm sorry, Sarah.'

He put his hands out. I did not take them. I stood up and took off my tights, staring him in the eye.

'Oh, God, *must you*?'

'I'm hot,' I said.

Gabriel frowned, his beauty rippling with the aberrant movement. He had a peevish, bullying look that usually only appeared in the presence of bus-drivers. It was always the same with upper-class men, however avuncular, however sensitive. Burst through the shell of politeness and decorum they have built around themselves and they turn on you, brick-red with aggression.

His voice that evening, and increasingly, contained a note of aesthetic exhaustion. He had been working on two dogs fighting, in scrap pieces of wood and metal overlaid with papier-mâché and ceramic strips. Each animal had disproportionately long jaws that wrapped three times around the other's body like snakes. He carved with delicacy, the torn ligaments of the smaller dog shining in a lump of veined wood against the rough mass of hardened paper flesh.

I wondered how he could keep going. To have such respect for his own ideas and creations, to have sufficient light to descend into the mineshaft of his unconscious. My own mind was a tangle of fears and self-doubts, of excuses for inaction in the small cold face of female perfectionism. I could just recall a time when I would rush into my room, arms full of tin cans, yanking string and Sellotape from rollers, throwing paint. I never knew where the ideas came from, they just came. But perhaps that was just childhood.

I turned full round in my chair, like a bored child, and looked at the dogs. My full stomach had not expected this torsion.

'I started a sculpture of a bloke in flares and a bomber jacket once. That was made of scrap too.'

'Sounds profound. Why did you stop?'

'Well, I was only thirteen.'

'Oh, yes, your time of trauma that you won't talk about.'

I lowered at him and belched suddenly.

'Oh, for Christ's sake!'

His long fingers, so elegant when resting that they might even have had an extra joint, rubbed against each other in disgust.

'Sarah, can't you go out tonight or something? I mean, it's getting a bit oppressive with you coming back every night and moaning about your day and then sitting there in front of the television . . .'

'Where do you suggest I go, then?'

'Sarah. It's *my flat.*'

It's my body, I might have shouted once upon a time. I squeezed my thigh absently and looked at him. He shot me a pitying glare but spoke quietly. 'You really want to get *fucked,* don't you?' he sneered. 'I knew it! Desire really does turn women into performing vegetables!'

I sat quietly at the table. Too early in my life I had learned to dislocate my defences. It sometimes took days, weeks, even, for me to react.

I had, of course, nowhere to go. There were people I could phone, college friends with whom I had shared bottles late into the night, but I couldn't impose on them further. I simply wanted to curl up and wait for day.

Gabriel stumped into the bathroom, but I heard no noise. He reappeared five minutes later. As he was passing my chair, I put my arms around his thighs and pressed my lips against his jeans. There was an intoxicating odour of something household, corrosive. I shut my eyes. He did not return my touch.

'You're a masochist, aren't you? I can smell it on you.' And he pushed back my arms as if they were turnstiles.

Time slowly sank its teeth into me. Something was missing from the *Skip,* a spiritual resonance, perhaps. Once, just once, there was a tiny incident which made me feel that *something,* some other force, was trying to make contact. Nearly everyone else was at lunch, and I was alone at the big bank of desks, doodling on a piece of paper. One finger gleaming with ink, I pressed it down, the tiny rifts of skin imprinting intense bushy clouds. It was so long since I had been able to draw a living thing. Everything that was not writing was merely a structure of interconnecting lines and shapes that enclosed a tiny, pinioned core.

I looked out of the sealed window. Below me stood a naked tree, the only one in the street, undulating silently in the wintry gusts. The conditioned air rushed gently at me from above. Suddenly every phone on the table began to ring at once. Twelve of them calling to me simultaneously, a great musical roll of sound that would not cease. I could not answer them. I felt that if I did, I would be dissolved into billions of shimmering electrons and dispersed into the sky. I sat transfixed as it crashed around me, this deep liquid reaping of time.

'Answer those fucking phones, for chrissake!'

The harness fell again. I picked up a handset, but met only silence. The same day I began to itch, and a thin white substance issued from my vagina. Just as at school, when fear of blood coming through on to my skirt made me sweat with fear and therefore think it really *had* seeped out, I kept thinking I had my period but every time I went to look, the same slippery mixture of sweat and nacreous discharge met my eye. I felt a stabbing urge to scratch, a delicate agony that was also part ecstasy, a strange sparkle.

Lyndi reappeared. I approached her desk to offer some ideas, not really believing in them, but responding to the survival mechanism that throbbed weakly inside me. She was already on the phone.

'Give him one, did she? Fuck knows why! So I called Dudley

on the desk and said, "Look, mate, we let you run that story first last week and you fucking know why now get off my fucking case why don't you I've had enough of trying to justify your deals every fucking day of the fucking week."'

The knife-sharp odour of onions leaped up at me from under her arms. An odder smell also came off her, almost of shit. I stood patiently, looking at the ink stains on the dove-grey Dacron panels that enclosed her desk on three sides. On seeing them, on my second day at the *Skip*, I had told a Rorschach joke which fell on deaf ears.

Her monologue continued. I waited, patiently. She could see me perfectly well. I reflected on the different kinds of wait involved in my job, each with its own special vibration and emotional colour.

There was the *Wait To Be Noticed While They Look Busy*. I would stand, toes turned inwards, the photocopy in my hand dampening and stretching. My addressee would be deep in conversation about football with a colleague. There would be the odd brief lull to mull over a goal during which I would advance, bending slightly at the waist while raising my chin a little, and with a quizzical raise of the eyebrows would open my mouth and begin to form the word 'Sorry'. The addressee would look me right in the eye, so I would open my mouth a little to start my speech. This look, however, was no more than a glance, the attention on me no closer than if I were a yellowing reproduction of the *Mona Lisa*. The eyes would return to the colleague, and the gesticulating hand describe another goal.

Another popular wait was *Wait To See Who's Going To Leave First*. At five-thirty all true employees suck the remaining salt and vinegar off their fingers, close their handbags, do up their coats and depart. But not here at the *Skip*. The other Juniors would start to cluster, like evening pigeons, around one or other of the editors, cooing and brushing themselves down. I never understood this activity, since all they seemed to be talking about was sport or royalty. I would sit and turn over and over the pages of a tabloid, wondering if anyone would notice if I left. Many others were wondering the same thing, but there was an embargo on moving for another two hours at least. I would sit it out, watching the clocks turn and turn, the news bulletins flash up and down, the tea trays flying, the mysterious visitors emerging from dark corners of the room, the suits convening, and reflect that all over London people were drowning slowly in these wasted hours. Books remained unread, flowers unwatered and lives unloved; children cried and were lonely because their parents were out fighting this battle no more useful than a video game. This was time tortured, its skin flicked up with scalpels and ripped back so that all it could do was fall forward onto its raw, smashed knees and *wait* for death.

On Fridays we would all, by ritual, dive for the lift at six and go down to the Lifer and Chain, a nasty allegedly pre-Shakespearian hole on the edge of one of the City's bleaker highways, where blind shopfronts and dead façades looked onto narrow pavements and lonely high-speed traffic, the odd dark green and cream *winerie* casting its brassy loom over litter-strewn streets. Here, another game was played. The reporters would eagerly mount the bar, returning with enormous quart glasses, one of the Lifer's selling points. They would clutch these proudly, their immense weight and shape forcing the drinker to down the contents as soon as possible.

My colleagues would stand there, glasses resting on bellies. Those as yet without sufficient stomach forced forward their pelvises in pathetic imitation. And so the men would stand, while the women hung around and attempted to fit in with them. Occasionally I tried to start a conversation. Once, after some regulation goading, I even attempted one of the quarts myself. Barely able to lift it to my lips, I simpered in the correct fashion and gripped it harder, but the slippery vessel rushed down through my hands, and a great splash of beer leapt from its huge lips and splattered all over my shirt, rendering it transparent. It was a good shirt too, the colour of Dutch butter, and baked interestingly into little puckers like a piece of kitchen roll. However, the revealed lace of my bra caught the eyes of my audience for no more than an instant.

'Fucking *ay*! Goal before half time!'

I had barely registered my increased intake of alcohol. Most people I knew discussed theirs so frequently that I vowed never to indulge in such callow grandiosity. However, returning home on a Friday night, the tube train's harsh braking motion would dislodge my hand from its tenuous grip on the greasy grey ball and catapult me headlong along a row of laps. I would murmur some polite justification as crushed newspapers were irritably straightened out.

As it got colder and darker in the evenings I began to slip away from these rituals, ignored, apparently unnoticed. One night, when the winter wind jerked madly at my hair and coat, I returned to the office, drunk, to collect my bag. The burly security guard frisked me desultorily. The coat-check artist was silent, knowing by now not to try it on. I jabbed the lift button and leaned with my face squashing against the mirror. Three paces out of the lift and I realized I had got off at the wrong floor. There was no open-plan newsroom but a silent, white-lit corridor. Amused by this adventure, I walked down it on the sides of my shoes to make the least sound. I was just starting to feel a mixture of nervousness and boredom when a distant high-pitched squeal seeped out of the silence. I followed the sound around the corner and along. Music and laughter rang out at me, and then another reedy, metallic screech. I instantly thought of sex, a good old behind-the-scenes office *screw*, but the screech was too long drawn out, and unpunctuated by gasps or exhortations. I noticed a little puff of straw or something clinging to the carpet. There was a bellow of 'Oh, no, you don't!', more laughter and the drag of table leg. I thought I heard Lyndi's voice say something about needing water, and the tap of her heels coming towards the door. I fled on tiptoe back to the lifts.

The next day a memo appeared on all the desks;

> To all staff from Lyndi: In the light of the Youth Culture that is sweeping the land at this time, we have asked a selection of school-age children to help us edit the next few issues. It's going to be really fun so let's make it happen OK!!!

Five skinny supercilious young people appeared, ranging in age from nine to fourteen, all wearing black and all carrying very expensive leather bags. The size of their shoes increased in inverse proportion to height, so that the nine-year-old's resembled small kegs.

We Juniors were assigned a Young Editor to look after during their stay. This meant sitting next to them and looking encouraging, while noting with interest their every suggestion. The adults quietly took care of the real news while the children fought over whose parents had the largest number of homes. The twelve-year-old shrieked suddenly, 'Mummy says it's wrong to drink Nescafé because they do horrible things to tribes!'

'We've just had our house decorated,' rejoined the fourteen-year-old, not to be outdone, 'and they've used this special paint which is enviro-mental and costs twice as much as the other ones!'

'Daddy always makes Mummy vote Labour,' smirked the youngest girl, who looked, with her vile *retroussé* nose, about forty in a miniature leather jacket and chainy hanging purse. 'He always says, "Well, we can afford to!"'

As luck would have it I was to look after this nine-year-old, whose name was Tabitha. Her face took on a look of ineffable superiority. 'My sister was wearing those two years ago. God, they look so *dated* now.' She did not even deign to point at my shoes as she spoke.

'It's different when you're as ancient as I am,' I tried, boredly mimicking the staggers of an aged crone. 'And where did you learn a filthy stylographic word like *dated*?' I hissed as an afterthought. Her face remained sternly blank. She stared at me fixedly as I worked away next to her, phoning the winners of the crossword to congratulate them and explain the size of their prize. Finally I became unnerved, at which she smirked and asked, 'Why is your nose so big?'

'Because it grew that way,' I snapped.

Instantly she began to scream. 'God you're so horrible! That's really nasty. You're taking it really *personally*. It was just an *observation*!'

Tears of pure acid began to crawl down her little face. The desk's bilious green top almost steamed as the vitriol dripped and pooled.

Lyndi came running over. 'Sarah! Stop bullying the Young Editors!'

Grimly I carried on typing. But as I did so I could not help but visualize winching her up to the ceiling, upside down and trussed carefully in razor wire, and flaying her with the rusty ring-pull of one of her adulterated Tizer cans. And there I would leave her, a dripping scarlet chunk, rolled up dead like a fly in a web, as I performed an honorary *sevillanas* on the floor below.

I was told the next day, to my horror, that she was to accompany me on all my vox-pops. She would stare at me with an expression almost of pity as I clammily approached the public in Oxford Street or Knightsbridge on drab winter afternoons, vomiting ingratiation. When I was rebuffed, my snarls had taught her to snigger only inwardly.

My relationship with the public was not straightforward. When collared by me people were either suspicious to the point of rudeness or boringly excited, the latter by far the sadder. Telephone conversations were even more depressing, Tabitha's presence beside me even more irritating. I would ask to speak to someone, and my heart would go out to his wife at her childish excitement.

'Bob! It's the *Skip* on the phone. Come on, hurry up, the young lady's calling from London!'

I would talk to him and I would write down what he said to me and then I would pluck out the most exciting aspect of his reply, however minutely relevant to the issue in hand, and I would run with it until a Story appeared, a Story that bore so little relation to the truth that he would barely recognize it. A few average lives, with their average love and average endeavour, with their average faults and average dishonesties, would be pinned back on the dissection board, slit open and ruined for ever.

'Don't tell me anything!' I always wanted to shout. 'And I'm not even anyone important!'

As I walked the rainy streets I contemplated my role in the structure of Intranews. My name had not yet appeared in the pages of the *Skip*, and I was starting to wonder if anyone cared about my existence at all. To conceptualize the organization in which I worked, it is necessary to narrow the eyes slightly so that colour and light begin to swim and meld subtly, like fields and skies at sunset, and to imagine a tiny money spider, in its traditional role as lucky little creature, standing on a square of asphalt, or the bitty dark surface of a playground, such agony to fall on. See it sitting, waiting for a hand to crawl and crawl on, pushing past hairs like reeds.

Then focus back, a fractional movement of the ciliary muscle, until you see that over the money spider sits a grey garden spider, one of those that spurt unseeably through the grass. And, back a bit, over that, sits a smallish, brown house spider, and over that a large, greyer one, and over that a medium-sized one of the type you scream at and then feel ashamed, and then a large one, the largest Britain can provide. But this is barely the beginning! Refocus again, and now you will see a great, crouched clamp fifty times the size of the first, each leg immense, anglepoised. And now you are looking up, you are craning your neck, and there is something else, a crouched tower of exoskeleton, a haired black limb the width of a house and the height of a radio mast, and then beyond that! Recant your lenses, for you are now also underneath, and you will see a fur of distant bolts like factory chimneys on their sides. They are rippling hairs from the legs of the biggest arachnid of them all that squats as far as the eye can see, its belly an infinite black cloud.

I suppose it maligns the spider to talk of commerce in such a way. Spiders kill worse creatures than themselves. They do not pollute or spread disease but destroy it – the greasy cockroach and the fly, with its pathetic cargo of shit and sickness. But my disgust at them was automatic, my muscles flexing involuntarily at even the thought of this sightless pubis, this grip of life, its body, obese, a double belly, or pinched, athletic, like the seat of a racing bike.

All the time the itch between my legs more than merely increased, it developed. What had begun as a shy piccolo of feeling, running around my vulva like a penny zig-zagging down through a charity collection box, became a screaming motet of sensation which I could not relieve through my thick coat, skirt, tights and knickers. The doctor, on my third visit, became irritable. He was young and pale-haired, and abseiled at weekends. I wondered how he managed to square bracing icy winds, flapping cagoules and the creak of maddened ropes with poking dispassionately at the forty or so warm, submissive sacs of dysfunctional life he examined each working day.

We were both becoming tired of the sight of me flat on my back with an arc lamp streaming between my spread legs.

'Look, Sarah, I've tested you for everything under the sun. I mean, are you expecting me to *taste* it or something?' He laughed disgustedly. 'You'll just have to live with your discharge. I mean, a lot of women do, and you're not any different from them, are you? And anyway, isn't that why women wear knickers? To catch the drips?'

He must have noticed the sob building up in my face, because he quickly wrote out a repeat prescription for a suppository that had already not worked and, on the way out of the room, called to the nurse to come and sort me out. I had, of course, tasted my discharge. It had an acrid cast, to which I could find no reference in any medical textbook.

Gabriel was out more and more often when I got back to the flat. When he returned he would be swaying slightly, overexcited, bruise-lipped amid his creamy pallor, like a Pears baby in a fruit field.

'Sarah – Christ what's that smell? – why aren't you out there fucking other men? I mean, we don't really *do* anything, do we? Maybe you'd be a bit happier or something.'

He staggered into the bedroom. I wanted arms around me, but I sat for a moment before following him. The door swung closed, bounced off the latch and opened again noiselessly, nearly revealing the bed before being shoved back in my face.

'Just wait a minute, will you!' Gabriel hissed. I turned away and leant against the hall wall. I felt like some crippled creature waiting to be harnessed, some ageing pack-beast expecting to be hit. I often imagined there was a shadow behind me, of a bent, injured being scraping along on two sticks, or dragging a limb on rollers.

Gabriel burst out of the bedroom and flopped down on the sofa. He picked up a paper and feverishly scanned it, as if he were looking for something in particular.

'Now where was I? Mirabelle Haight! Weren't you at college

with her? Look, she's writing a book! What's that ... "sure to become a feminist classic"! Bloody hell, Sarah, you'd better get your skates on. It's time you actually *did* something with your life, isn't it, instead of all this minor clerical work? I mean, you haven't even had your name in the paper yet, have you?'

It was all right for Gabriel, with his mysterious income, I might have said, but all I did was stare into space, absorbing his scornful advice like radiation.

'Oh, Sarah, I'm being unkind aren't I? Really horrible.'

He came over and gave me a brief, brittle, reptilian hug and granny peck on the forehead. He'd stopped touching me in the night.

'OK, darling, you can take Fulham. Sarah, you can choose whatever part of the East End you like.'

Ivor had been put in charge of us for 'Stab the Stripy Shirts!' a weekly slot in which a prominent piece of advertising was put to the test. This week we were testing the assertion that Chariots of Fire Inc could get to a roadside breakdown in less than fifteen minutes. The advertisement showed the requisite immaculate, terrified woman broken down in a windswept alley pulling out her portable and telephoning, shortly after joined by an enormous, lantern-jawed motorcyclist who made her feel much better and sent her on her way.

'So. You lovelies are going to sit there with your portables and wait. Here's a stopwatch each. You might want a sandwich or something ...' He jerked his head towards the canteen. The girl Junior, with an uncanny prescience I had come to suspect, had already set up a Tupperware box with two chicken legs and a Miniroll. I trotted off. One small stale pickle bap remained on the cold shelf. We were given keys to a pair of beige Fiestas and sent on our way. The photographer, Dirk, went with the girl.

In the spirit of the exercise, I picked the roughest, most rotten backstreet I could find. There were no bins here to overflow, just rubbish gently tossing in the night breeze. It was very dark. I could just see the gleam from a tiny pub at the other end of the street, one of those odd-one-out cottagy little places that look as if they were put there by a giant child, their proportions nothing to do with the cubic council blocks and corrugated fencing that lined the street.

I turned the engine off and sat in silence. The sound of singing floated at me through the glass. I dialled the number.

'Hello! I'd like to report a breakdown. I mean, ha ha, mechanical rather than emotional!'

There was a silence.

'I'm in the East End and I'm alone!' I shrilled a little.

'Right, darlin', gis the address.'

I had no idea where I was. I described the locale. He was on his way.

I sat for a while. There was no radio so I made do with the strains of football songs and smashing glasses coming from the other end of the street. A man ran lopsidedly past, stopping only to retch. Closing time. I began to feel hungry, and imagined the other Junior and the photographer, rescued hours ago, musing flirtatiously over a couple of bowls of *linguine* in a Fulham trattoria.

I was just nodding off when the phone rang.

'Hi, Sarah, it's Ivor! How's it going?'

'They're on their way, apparently.'

Silence. I hadn't really reached the flirting stage with him, and he was keen to assert his superiority. Through the electronic fuzz I overheard a high-pitched squeal which I put down to interference until I heard laughter, suddenly cut short.

'So, Sarah! It's Friday night, isn't it? Bet you're sorry you couldn't go to all those . . . Kensington parties tonight.'

'Sorry, what parties?'

The idea of going to a party was alien. The evening would have consisted of a bottle of wine in front of the television and bed by midnight.

'Come on, Sarah, don't come the little choirgirl with me. I bet you could show me a wild time in – what is it? – Imperial Square or wherever it is you live. I bet you've got coke coming out of your fucking ears!'

He gave me no time to reply.

'Why do girls like you bother trying to work on newspapers? I've seen the clothes you wear, I've heard you talking on the phone. We should go out together sometime! Hey, how about it? I could really help you, you know.'

His voice had taken on a tone I presumed he saved for the most pliable interviewees, those who were involved in high-level fraud but had also recently lost a child.

'Well?'

I did not know what to say. I could have slept with him, and indeed had speculatively staked out his large frame several times while filing. But now he was swooping on me from a great height. I felt tiny, helpless.

'Well, how about it, Sarah? Is it yes or no?'

The car's interior smell was artificial, sickening. The wind blew and it shook perceptibly. The doors felt thin, hollow.

'Put it this way, and I've got money on it, you look like you fuck, is that right?'

I wished for someone, anyone, to come down the street.

'I know a girl when she's been fucked and you've been well fucked indeed, Sarah, haven't you?'

His voice continued, slowly, insistently. The phone's LCD dial glowed greenly in the dark. I held it away from me, swallowing. And yet it was just a condensed mass of microchips and filaments. It could do me no harm.

'You know what I'd like to do to you, I'd like to fuck you up the arse and then shove a fucking great slimy *herring* up you. Ever seen a fish die of shame, bitch?'

'Fuck off!' I screamed, and switched off the phone.

There was a rumble of engine and a luridly striped van appeared with a green flashing light on the top.

'Are you all right, dear?'

A small, chubby, balding man with a toolbag jumped out and tapped on my window.

'You look a bit shaken up, love, did someone give you an 'ard time?'

I sat and stared forward, rigid, my screaming mind running round and round and round.

eighteen

MY SUBORDINATE ROLE had seduced me with its simplicity. I felt more and more as if I were walking on glue, rubbery fibres clinging to my feet and inviting me downwards.

I found myself turning, for solace, to women's magazines. These publications featured the same subjects (relationships and fashion) every month, but their creators managed to put a slightly different spin on them each time, and the readers remained entirely faithful. The magazines behaved exactly as a sister should – they made the reader feel good about herself while suggesting, obliquely, that she is really pretty inadequate.

I tended to head for the problem pages for solutions to my discharge, but found myself waylaid by a particularly repetitive editorial exhortation – that every so often it was necessary to have *clear-outs* in one's life, both material and emotional, which would reveal an improved persona and herald the dawn of a brand-new era of self-respect. I was reassured by the pictures of a smiling model determinedly holding aloft a bulging dustbin-liner. Further reading convinced me that there was a confident, superior person nesting inside me – I just had to let her out. I examined my life, attempting dispassion.

Gabriel, once my lifeline, was undermining me slowly, carefully. And he would not fuck me. The physical contact we had, such as it was, was filigree, scientific, small-scale embroidery. I wanted bullfight sex, roaring breath, barbs tearing into my shoulders.

My path to an identity, the *Skip*, was fast turning into a dead end. And so my thoughts turned to Nick, a boy I had known at university who'd had a soft spot for me, an emotional fontanel that allowed him to take me out but never to make a pass as we sat in expensive restaurants, over steaks cooked so tenderly we ate them with spoons, wild mushrooms reduced in brandy and double cream surrounded with flamed twists of firm, rubbery offal and gentle pats of dark, bituminous matter designed to process some alien nutriment that passed out of our food chain long ago. If lighter food had been available, he might have got further with me, but all this, washed down with deep, grainy red wine like liquefied tree-bark, absorbed all desire into the body's overworked defences. He would kiss me goodnight with the most wistful of erections, daring only slightly to pull my hips towards his.

Now, however, Nick was a successful journalist on a paper which, as a publicity gimmick, paid its new recruits more the younger they were. I had seen a picture of him, dark-blond hair smoothed back, black polo-neck delineating a newly jutting chin, a leather jacket moulded as if part of him. Suddenly I imagined forcing him, through repetitive licking, to find me a job.

I tracked him down by phone and he summoned me in a brand-new drawl to Blair's, a drinking club that, conceptually, resembled one of the waist-high green boxes on street corners, which, if opened by a technician, reveal great retches of multicoloured wire.

'At least you're going *out*,' snorted Gabriel.

I entered Blair's. Eyes scanned me like tractor beams. Nick appeared and beckoned me over to a table of what appeared to be genuine grown-ups.

'Hi, everyone, this is Sarah Clevtoe, who's, er, on the way up.'

'Well, she's never going to get anywhere dressed like *that*.'

These words were spoken, in a strangely fluctuating accent, by a rat-faced man whose small yellowish eyes were fixed on me with that bald stare so beloved of the successful and unsympathetic in the presence of the young and wanting. I frowned. I *liked* the red, pink and orange rose-pattern of my cleverly converted full-length ballgown, and I did not realize that any irritation I felt at this potential *contact*'s condescension had, by ritual, to be subsumed in a modest self-deprecating giggle. Nick hurried me on to the son of someone who had written a definitive history of pistol grips. Since this man had once been married to a daughter of the third lord something, columnists still phoned him for quotes about his ex-wife's family's tenancy disagreements. I smiled insanely. He shuddered.

'And this, Sarah, is Amity Rudd of Cherish Productions, Tommy Tompkins, who's a commercial writer – aren't we all? ha ha – and Claudia Smith, who you've probably heard of.'

Amity, glamorous as a cake, picked her nails while Tommy, fat in a tweed jacket, seemed more interested in my legs. I smiled the smile of a Hallowe'en pumpkin.

'So what do you *do* exactly?' Claudia spoke with particularly pitiless astringency. She had a pale, puffy face, in strange contrast to her scrawny chest, which poked bonily out of a half-unbuttoned silk blouse like a ship accidentally bursting through a pair of curtains.

'Well, I'm a Junior on the *Skip*—'

'I know *lots* of people there and I've never heard of you.'

There was a round of sniggers.

'Oh, dear. Let's try again. Have I seen your name anywhere?'

'I don't know, have you?'

'No. No.' Her exasperation was almost fond.

'Look, just relax. You haven't really *arrived* yet, have you?'

Her face imitated kindness as a Dobermann's might when trying to cheer up a bone. A little later, for some reason, the subject of my birthplace was raised.

'Weren't you born in London, then?' came the mongrel accent, striped with heritage like a liquorice allsort. That question again! I could not work out why all these people were so interested.

'No, Grimsby, actually!' I declared proudly.

'How lovely!' came the chorus, every face dappled with superiority. 'How's the Bullring? Or is that Manchester? How are you finding it here?'

Up to now, I had scorned those who declared that, come the revolution, certain social groups would be 'first against the wall'. But now I understood completely. I wished ardently that I had a small bomb, and that I had thrown it at these people, and that they were now rearranged floppily, some dead on the floor, the rest draped over the backs of their chairs, twitching in agony. I imagined the arrival of medical teams, to whom I would bravely and efficiently say, 'I'm a trained nurse, actually,' discreetly pocketing their proffered supplies of morphine for resale at a later date.

'You're very defensive, aren't you?' said Tom, rippling my musings.

'But very beautiful in an interesting sort of way, isn't she?' added Amity. 'You know, Sarah, you look *rather* sweet, and you're *rather* tall, but don't you ever get people trying to – water you?'

I found myself nodding slightly to some faint internal rhythm. I drank on, while, inside me, massive escalators laden with melting, stinking prawns bumped up and down, goading me into a response I could not articulate. I wanted to beg them to like me, but had no words for that either, save the offer of sex, a girlish squirm that could drag a single persecutor to me and silence him in me. To a group like this, however, I could offer nothing save my whitish throat.

Gradually the group dispersed to parties, other bars, and I was left with Nick, who was pressing his thumbs together while pretending not to examine me carefully. He bought me another drink.

'Do you have *anything* in common with those people?' I asked.

'More than you realize,' he replied, smiling. 'Would you like me to get you a job, Sarah?'

With that, he began to rub his nose against my scalp. It was a big nose, and a squashed one, as if some past rejected woman had hurled it at him, crying, 'Take your nose and *go! Just go!*'

He whispered in my ear and we made for the door. He hailed a cab and we sat in silence. I had forgotten to eat. When we arrived at Nick's flat I went quietly to the fridge. There was nothing in it but indeterminate medical supplies and camera film.

'You didn't want *food*, did you? Why the hell didn't you say so? I think there's some dessicated coconut in the back of the cupboard, but it might be a bit old.'

I looked at him, gangling in the doorway with one hand squeezing the upper frame. I was hungry enough to vomit. I turned to the cupboard, and, without shame, reached four fingers far back into the bulging, dust-grey bag. The dull, musty flakes absorbed every bit of liquid in my mouth. I ate on and on. Finally I turned furtively, my tongue still slathering against my palm which tasted of tube rails, newspapers and synthetic ham. Nick was standing in the same position, aghast.

'I've never seen anyone do *that* before.'

He turned and walked away. I remained still in the white kitchen. Was this rejection or an invitation to follow? If the former, should I just go quietly? If the latter, how could I compensate for this terrible gaffe?

I felt as if I had finally been *collected* by the divine taxonomist, and I was already boxed in wood and glass with brown-tinged labels designating phylum, order, genus, my essence analysed so that none need bother with me ever again.

'What the fuck are you doing in there?'

Without another thought I went into the next room. Nick was sitting on a corduroy sofa, one leg hanging over the side, staring at the television.

'Take this and you'll cheer up a bit.' Without looking at me, he held out a small tablet.

'I'll need some water,' I mumbled, returning to the kitchen. I remembered pill-taking from my childhood, agony hanging on the tongue as the bitterness spread in my mouth, my throat closing in panic. Sure enough, the pill made me gag. I tried to stifle my coughing.

'You don't usually take drugs, do you, Sarah?'

I shook my head as I came through the door.

'That's very provincial, if you don't mind me saying so. You'd better forget that attitude if you want to get anywhere.'

He pulled off his shoes and threw them behind him. One of them hit me. I did not think to mention it. His jaw was moving.

'What are you eating?' I asked, resentment surging after my humiliation with the coconut.

'Sarah! Where have you *been*? Cocaine makes you chomp.'

I stood in the light of the television, my dress shining. Nick began to talk, sniffing occasionally. I don't remember what he said, but it was about himself and his career. He did not invite me to sit down. I was not exactly sure what he had given me, although I presumed it was Ecstasy. After a time, the lights began to smear, and everything within my vision became part of a continuous, disproportionate structure, like an abstract, three-dimensional patchwork quilt.

Nick seemed to sense this. 'How are you feeling, Sarah, do you want to sit down?'

I wanted warmth.

'There's a deal in everything, Sarah, and this evening is no exception. You can only sit next to me if you get that fucking awful outfit off *now*!'

'I'm thirsty—'

He stood up quickly and glared down at me. He pushed the heels of his hands into my cheeks, stretching my dry lips back until they split.

'Look what I did! Oh, Sarah, sorry sorry!'

And he began to lick the blood slowly, his big face moving regularly, thoroughly, like a mother dog's. My dehydrated tongue desperately sought out his saliva and I began to suck the flesh of his mouth, gulping at the thick fluid. I leant into him, and felt his heart clapping against his skinny frame. Just as I was about to give up my balance, he let go of my head and ripped down the sleeves of my dress.

'Oh, this horrible horrible thing!'

He tore it off me, scratching at the zip before ripping it from its seam. It lay on the floor, a pool of bright colour. I tried to kiss him, my learned response rattling to be let out. He threw me on the sofa. I did not bounce on the flabby cushions. His hands rushed to his zip. So he was going to rape me. Instead he pulled out his limp penis and urinated on my dress.

'What a woman!' he gasped fervently, addressing the heap of fabric. 'No one's ever actually let me do this before!'

The dress, which had bubbled with the air as it fell to the floor, was gradually deflating as it soaked up the yellow liquid. It seemed to move as if to avoid the relentless stream. Automatically I put out my hand to pet it. I began to feel afraid and very lonely. I closed my eyes. The outside world had finally presented its back.

'Sarah! Are you there?' he shouted, his voice metallic with excitement. 'Sarah! Shit, it must be bad stuff! You're supposed to be all over me! But he's a good dealer! I think it's just you, Sarah. Maybe there's something wrong with you.'

I felt him come nearer, and his hands rip apart my tights before parting my labia. I winced at the sharp tug of my hair which he did not bother to separate properly. His warm tongue fluttered briefly before plunging into me. He recoiled instantly.

'Oh, God! You taste disgusting! Like bath cleaner or something. Get yourself checked out, for fuck's sake!'

I heard his voice high above me, and the dry spitting of his lips, but I registered it as no more than a colour, a part of the rainbow of gentle nausea that was striding across me. My stomach lurched.

'It's true, Sarah. You really are a *loser*!'

His breath came harder. He called out to me again. I drew my knees up.

'Sarah! Look!'

Somehow I opened my eyes into the singing garden of sensation around me. All I could see was his back. He appeared to be squatting. Some vestigial notion of good manners made me squint harder into the delicate confusion of lights and shapes, to please him by praising his actions. But I could see nothing, and so lay back as he left the room. Sleepless, anxious, the night fell cold on my body as the radiators rattled to a halt. I felt worthless, unsuited to this world I had entered. Perhaps my soul was a stone's, quiet, ancient, that had spent the whole of time sleeping off the pain of its brutal, flaming birth. After a while my bladder demanded that I empty it. I could not find the bathroom, so I used the kitchen sink. At dawn I fell asleep. Nick woke me an hour later with a curt shake.

'So are you going to get me a job, then?' I said, my mind locking briefly into the conversation we'd had earlier the previous evening. He looked at me incredulously. I grabbed my hair and stared hard at him through the ends until they appeared huge, like birch twigs.

'Look,' he said, 'I'm not trying to be rude but you really are *naïve.*'

When is anyone ever *trying* to be rude? I wondered. Through my crusted eyes I felt the boredom that comes from fear, my lips like lead.

'Have you any idea how many bloody boring people are trying to get a job in the media at any given moment? Thank God for The List, that's all I say. It gets passed round every few months or so – some names have a red star next to them, some have nothing, and some, I'm afraid, have a black one. It saves *acres* of filing space.'

Amusement entered his voice. 'I mean, Sarah, have you considered taking a catering course? It might help you serve yourself up to the sharks! Ha ha. Although they won't eat you up if you taste the way you did last night!'

I wondered where my dress was. He said he'd put it in the machine. He then quickly went out, ostensibly for a paper, but did not come back.

The television was showing a sitcom about a disabled family circus. The actors' fresh-faced happiness, and their plucky refusal to be defeated by their physical predicament made me sob with self-pity at my own state, which was merely a consequence of bourgeois decadence. I stood shakily and wandered about. I looked in cupboards for something to wear, or read. My nails grated on the tinny wood. In a drawer I found paper, headed with two words, The Club, in a thick, muscular, modern typeface masquerading as a long-established one. Underneath it was a picture, heavy with chiaroscuro, of a fat cosh, its wrist-loop curling suggestively round it, almost like a smile. For a few minutes I studied this, and the matching calling cards. Why had I not read mysteries as a child? I had been too busy with one finger jammed in *Pride and Prejudice* while the other leafed indolently through the dictionary.

I looked up and realized the washing-machine had stopped spinning. The kitchen was very hot, and there was a scorch mark above the plug which had not been there before. Nick had turned the dial to maximum. I opened the door and was nearly scalded by the steam that belched out. My dress was destroyed, the colours killed, every seam split or stretched obscenely. I flapped it out. It was half the length it had been. There was a brown stain on it that I did not remember. There was no dryer. I had no choice but to put it on and go home.

People laughed at me in the street. I tried to imagine that I was in a medieval drama, and was being openly mocked for my brave transgression of stifling moral laws. Fatal, that, the addiction to escape fantasies. The waiting for the phone, the gelled, tousled prince at the wheel of his Alfa Spider, kick the accelerator and fly! Ambition's fat, angular pill, which I had swallowed to give me a golden streak in my hair like everyone else, was rotting me slowly from the inside. I bought a bottle of wine and sat at the bus stop. I began to cry and could not stop myself. I felt bent over, as if something was at my back, a huge larynx waiting to resound. A wave of itching shook my vulva and I scratched, fervently, painfully, forgetting the excitable dames on their meaningless journeys to the shops and back, who looked at me and sniffed.

At home an hour later Gabriel extracted most of the story from me, sighing in exasperation through the fusted gloom. It did not seem to bother him that I had entered a sexual situation, in fact he seemed positively encouraging. He sat down opposite in a parody of sympathy.

'Sarah: I'm going to have to say it. I don't know why you're surprised about all this. There's no *mystery* in you. I mean – how can I put this without sounding cruel? – for God's sake, get yourself some *secrets*, can't you? I mean, you're just *you*, and that's not enough. You give away all your power in the first two minutes and there's nothing left to interest *anybody*. And you're grabbing at me the whole time as if you were a little child. It's repulsive and actually quite boring too. Can't you give me some ideas to play with, something that sparks my interest? You're really not much fun to have around, to be frank.'

Mystery. That burgundy nylon négligé every woman must clutch to herself, occasionally letting it fall part-open to keep the punters interested.

My hands were shaking so much that I put my finger throught my tights as I tried to get out of them. Taupe, the colour's called. Mule, maybe. I saw his eyes glance over my thighs. I pulled my tights right off, stiff and stinking from the night before, and found my toes were laced with tiny, redundant fronds of skin that rolled into tiny worms as I flicked at them.

I pulled down my knickers, already limp and damp. A harsh vinegary scent gusted up. Gabriel looked up at me. His fingers were mercury-shiny from the charcoal he had been rolling between them. Quickly I moved over to him and grabbed his head.

'Here's some mystery for you.'

I leant on him and pushed his face into my pubic hair. For a moment his blue eyes caught mine, wide, horrified. He recoiled and shoved me violently back towards the kitchen table. The scrape of wood on tiles was atonal, hysterical. A cup fell and smashed on the floor. His shouts spilled out, muffled behind his hand as he desperately wiped his mouth.

'You fucking disgusting cow!' His vowels didn't go with the words somehow, too manicured. 'God, you are the most pathetic human being I've ever known—' I shoved my hand between my legs and, trying to retain a sarcastic sneer while the sobs rose, drew a cross, for want of any better symbol, on his forehead. He hissed with horror, and I fled to the bedroom. I heard the kitchen tap turned up hard, the water beating madly into the metal sink, the pipes screaming.

I went to bed. The air was thick. I began to cough. A greenish, metallic-tasting white gum issued from my lungs. I had never smoked. Gabriel came in and sat on the bed. His hair looked different from usual in the low light, but how I couldn't tell.

'OK, let's fuck, then. That's what you seem to want. Look, I'm actually hard, fuck knows how. And you were wet just now, funny that; you secrete but you can't secrete. Interesting!'

I turned and curled into a ball, a streaming sound in my ears. Gabriel prodded me briefly, realized he was getting nowhere and began to masturbate. And so we lay, that Saturday afternoon, I rigid and round like an ammonite, he long and milky, staring at the ceiling.

Snow came and went, late winter cast its pall and moved on. One morning on the way to work I forgot my name. It happened just like that, as I walked the long road. Everything became unfamiliar, the warehouse walls, the smeared mirror-glass that passed me back to myself squinted and grey, hair in my mouth from the frozen winds.

Like a crooked paving stone flipped up by a heavy foot, my mind slipped sideways out of this world and into a redundant space, a shaft of no-light, a blinding void. I broke my step and everything came back with a clarity a hundred times more violent. This was not my world, this seamless organism of people dealing, people creating, pushing, slotting ever more intricate pegs into waiting holes. I was no more than cardboard in that world, a cut-out human pleasantry gone wrong.

My eyes felt abraded. I coughed and coughed. At the office, everything lurched as I put down my bag. I made a vast tumbler of coffee and poured it into myself, then ran as my bowels kicked back. I sat on the loo and waited for the cramped, burning deluge to end, my head singing.

I hid at my desk, hoping to spend the day there, head in my arms, quietly. Suddenly there was a shout. Lyndi came running.

'Sarah! Get your coat on! Lorena Adams is about to throw herself off Raleigh Bridge. Dirk'll drive you down there.'

I staggered to my feet.

Raleigh Bridge was different from the rest. It was suspended and much higher, with great jutting lamp fixtures that could only be reached by clambering over the side of the bridge and leaping onto them. The leap once made, there was only room for one person to sit safely on the convex surface. The police had cleared the bridge of bystanders, so press and public crowded the pavements on the north bank of the river. We joined the mass of cameras and leather jackets jostling for position. Lorena Adams, famous actress beaten down by divorce, drugs, God knows what – the *Skip* would doubtless reveal all – had clearly had enough. She looked frail in a green, fur-collared coat. Her hand kept going to her face. Dirk offered me a telephoto lens to peer through. She was blank, repeatedly touching her auburn hair slowly, distractedly. The wind flapped. She must have been freezing up there. Religious groups appeared and said their pieces. She turned and looked at them and turned away again, staring into the distance. She staggered to her feet.

'She's gonna do it!' hissed Dirk. He positioned himself and programmed his camera to take a picture every second, just in case she jumped.

'Come on, old girl, go out gracefully. Christ, that wind's so strong she'll probably just get blown against the bridge. Oh, fuck, come *on*!'

The camera whirred and clicked, and still Lorena did not jump. After five minutes Dirk was out of film. He rushed off to find some. Before going he slung the strap of a smaller camera around my neck. 'You take it – it'll make your career, darling.'

He vanished. I stood, feeling small in the heaving, swearing crowd.

'Oh, why are we waiting—' someone sang out as a joke, others joined in more seriously. Who knew whether she could have heard or not? The brutal wind was in all directions.

I rested the camera on my chest.

'Fucking hold it up, darling, or you'll never work again,' came Dirk's shout from somewhere as he haggled for film.

A policeman with a loudhailer leant over the railing, urging the press to back off.

'You blokes drove her to this, now you're trying to finish her off. Go away for chrissake and give her some space.'

'Ooooh! Getting all New Age now, are we?' came a shout. There was a roar of laughter. The wind whipped up on the filthy marble waters of the Thames. Cars hooted in exasperation. It was always like this. If someone had a heart attack on the tube, curses rang out, newspapers were pushed brusquely aside as glarers faced down the asphyxiating victim and blamed lifestyle, chips, beer, smoking, too much enjoyment of the sexual act, for delaying their journey home.

Lorena staggered forward to the front of the lamp, her little narrow heels skittered on its curved surface.

'She's gonna *go*!'

Dirk had had no luck getting film, and he scrambled back to me, reaching for the little camera. I eagerly lifted it for him but something had caught, some part of the strap had become tangled up with my bag, and my stiff, blue hands, cramped into claws, could barely help.

'She's going!'

Lorena made as if to jump, but slipped first and so fell sideways, her body jerking like a puppet. Dirk in desperation grabbed the camera and held it up, while it was still around my neck, his cold face stuck against mine in a parody of intimacy, jerking my head sideways as he tried to focus. But he was too late. Her fall was quick. There was a fever of whirring, but Dirk had got nothing. Lorena crashed into the water, the lurid peppermint green of her coat flaring its last against the bilge-grey waters.

'You stupid bitch! You're going to get total shit for this.'

We drove back in silence. He couldn't even crash the gears,

the car being automatic. He raced out of the lift ahead of me with a look of such childish self-righteousness on his face that I thought he was about to report me for swearing. There was no one in the newsroom except Ivor, who seemed irritated that we had distracted him. Dirk dived in.

'She fucking nudged me, didn't she!'

I shook my head in disbelief. I began to tell the story but it came out all wrong. Dirk continued to curse me. Ivor stared at me with a cold, pinched mouth of authority.

I had cost them thousands of readers. They had trusted me. It was not for me to tell them how to work. I coughed and coughed as he spoke. A vicious knot of self-justification tightened in my stomach. I wanted to scream, to kick this bastard across the room and see him jackknife against a filing cabinet. I turned to walk out of the office with acid cascading inside me. What Dirk and Ivor saw, of course, was a sullen, silent departure, unleavened by tears or reasoning.

In the lift, I felt a familiar trickle between my legs. I was raw, my skin taut and splitting. I had given up all medication, even live yoghurt. My eyes stung. In the last few days I had woken to find them stuck together, a tearing feeling as I tried to open them. The lashes were crusted, and every time I went to the mirror ever more pale, thick mucus had built up.

I jabbed the button. The lift stopped and I stormed out of it, not knowing where I would go or for how long. I had gone several paces before I realized that I was not in the lobby but in the same corridor as I had been lost in before. I was so angry by then that to turn around and admit the mistake to myself, even entirely unseen, would have been impossible. I kept going, grimly, hoping a fire escape would appear. I walked and walked in the thick silence. Then I heard laughter followed by a low, strangled scream. I slowed my tread. That unmistakable voice.

'. . . oh, God, you know I feel a bit mean saying this—'

There were cries of sarcastic sympathy.

'But – oh, for chrissake keep her still, can't you! – but where does she get those *clothes* . . . and that *hair*! Why oh why doesn't Ivor rape her or something? You know, we should kick him out of the club if he doesn't stop being such a wimp!'

Several voices chimed in jovial agreement. Someone declared that they needed a piss.

'Well, do it here, then!' There was an avuncular roar of laughter that barely hid another scream. Just as I was about to open the door someone else opened it, almost casually.

Lyndi was crouched, naked, over the struggling body of a sheep. Its fleece was half pulled back, its legs stuck through with large cartoonish nails. The sheep's head thrashed from side to side as it struggled between gasps for breath. Its belly wobbled violently. The tiny woman bounced around on the flayed shining sac to the great amusement of her audience. There was a continuous noise from other animals, cats, dogs, goats in cages, and bits of straw and feed and an odour of shit. The room was full of naked, bloodstained people, all of whom I recognized, either from the staff of the *Skip* or the front pages of others. Some bore small implements, and were queuing in a spiral for their turn with the sheep. It all reminded me of a school play.

I could not hide from them. On seeing me, their expressions changed from the relaxed engaged in their hobby to ravenous hatred. I turned and hurtled back down the corridor. One face bothered me. Its owner was tall and dark-blond. Its expression managed a flash of pity for me before joining the rest.

It was only as I was running out of the building and towards the tube that the truth dawned on me. This was a *story*! I rushed home to Gabriel. He was watching the news.

'They torture sheep naked! I've seen them! They're all in on it – that's why their arms are covered in hay and stuff! There's blood everywhere and there's some famous people as well! And I think I saw Nick there too!'

My tone must have jolted Gabriel. Usually I addressed him with the oblique fearfulness usually reserved for an inadequate, aggressive parent. Gabriel turned and looked at me with pity.

'Sarah, if I might ask this rather hackneyed question, what exactly are you *on*? I know you're a bit naïve, but isn't this just a little *pathetic*?'

He did not even look at me as he spoke.

'I mean, let's be frank, you're not really a *journalist*, are you? You've been there six months, you *still* haven't had your name in the paper, and you haven't made *any* contacts. That Nick thing was a fiasco, in which you were entirely to blame for your *gaucherie*. Why don't you go and get a job as a secretary like my sister did? You can look very nice when you try, and there won't be these pressures on you which you obviously can't really handle. I do rather think you surpassed yourself at some point during your educational life and you've been struggling to . . .'

His drawl continued. I went into the bathroom and closed the door. I took off my clothes. My skin was flaking lightly, and there was a tight incipience about it, as if, whatever had happened to it, there was more to come. I ripped a torn nail from its housing and the blood seeped out like a tear. The pain was fiery for such a tiny injury. It seared with brightness against the miserable clay that was building up inside me. If I died my soul would sink like a stone.

nineteen

IT HAD OCCURRED to me that, to get anywhere, there must be pyramid-selling of the self. One must hand out carefully constructed myths and talk-ups to a small band of associates, who then each take their piece and divide it between several more who each do the same, and so on. And they are all paying each other down the line in gratification for knowing me and having been privy to such stories and ingratiations in the first place, and my fat handout at the end is a whole army of people sold on the idea of me and ready to talk me up to whoever will listen. And so one gives the impression of being popular, being known, being *in*.

The evening of my discovery of the sheep ritual, I tried to call the news desks of several dailies, but my breathless rendition of the facts got me nowhere. I was brushed off rudely. Then I began to doubt myself, and then to wonder if the whole thing was not simply a silly practical joke to accompany a promotion – perhaps I was about to be made a real reporter. But that was impossible. I was universally despised.

These thoughts ran round and round my head as I lay in bed, sleepless, the worst and most lurid paranoias and obscenities accompanying them. Scorn was a large stinking cat that followed me everywhere, linking around my ankles, tearing my flesh as it climbed onto my back and embedded its claws in my shoulders. I woke to my alarm, my mouth limed, my eyes seeping, crusted, my lungs giving forth great shots of phlegm. Gabriel, in open disgust, had moved out of the bedroom and was now sleeping on the sofa.

As I was filling the kettle, I looked through the window into the little grey yard. Someone had casually tossed a decapitated goat's head over the wall. The sight of its gaping mouth reminded me of how much I despised these animals' teeth, the prissy row between narrow, unexpressive lips. I was distracted from it by a creeping spark of itching under my arm. My greasy hair flicked up and tickled my eyes. I dug my soft nails into the stubbly flesh. My fingers were flaking in sympathy with my feet. Strangely, the skin beneath the sloughed patches was becoming whiter, purer, not the scaly red I would have expected.

My whole body was discharging gently with every breath, as if I had had my chance, my pearl of life, and wasted it; and now it was melting and running out of me before I had even understood how to use it.

I had become resigned to the patient coagulation between my legs. Today, defeated, I put on a pair of baggy jeans for work and the inevitable showdown. I dressed and left the house, leaving Gabriel asleep.

Anger rose in me as I walked down the street. I felt like someone else's voodoo doll, my temper flowering as the needles in my skull increased in size and number. As I got into the train I yanked a woman out of my way, so hard I heard her neck crack. She began to protest but saw the stare in my eyes, the height, and thought better of it.

My self-possession began to disperse as I arrived at work. I began to feel almost nervous, while buoyed up by self-justification. In the lift, the squashed body of a mosquito was stuck on the fifth-floor button, my floor. Someone must have been in such a hurry that they didn't even see it.

I walked straight across the room, expecting a shout or one-fingered beckoning. But nothing. Not a word. Heads remained down. There was even a cheery greeting, but I could not have been sure it was addressed to me.

I found my desk stacked even higher than usual with papers, about five feet or so, covered in figures and graphs. I was expected to photocopy everything for some great new story. I took the first pile, about the size and weight of a baby, carried it to the machine and thumped it down on the glass. Lifting the lid two thousand times was laborious, so I left it raised and taught myself the trick of closing my eyes just as the light went across. And so I stood passing paper back and forth, sweating more with each incandescent flash, not noticing the fine sticky black powder, the essence of basement stairwells and dead flies, that was slowly puffing out of the side of the machine and onto my jacket. In the loo, where I rushed to clean up the implacable chemical, I gazed in the mirror and I despaired at my spots, great growths like lumps of ageing tapioca bursting forth in slow motion from scarlet aureoles.

Fingers were clicked, and I was ordered first to make coffee and then to open that morning's mail while everyone was in a meeting. I had long since stopped communicating with my fellow Juniors, who could barely be seen, they had so wormed their way into the woodwork. I took the coffee jug and went to fill it. I saw that here was a chance for revenge. Joyously I locked the toilet door. On my return, another load of papers had been left on my desk. People gazed in awe at the vast pile as they passed.

I enjoyed opening the mail. Each day there was a new rush of other people's misery so great that I felt privileged in comparison. Alongside it came consumer complaints so unstintingly petty I usually presumed they were practical jokes. Biros with lids which did not match the colour of their ink were enclosed with diatribes of apocalyptic venom and threats to 'go to the television programmes'. Today, as every day that week, benefit cuts were the chief cause of pleas for help. So many people could not live on what the state gave them, so many people with so many different types of handwriting. The paper was often ludicrously small, and covered on both sides, and therefore hard to read. I thought perhaps there was a story there, Big People help the Little People, very *Skip*. But even as I stood up my phone rang and I was summoned to Lyndi's office. My heart beat faster. I went first to the bathroom, where I noticed a particularly significant subcutaneous attempt on the side of my nose. I attacked it bravely before going in to Lyndi.

They were all in there. The percolator across the room made a gentle puffing sound over the tic-tac of marbles played ferociously on the carpet by Ivor and the Aryan. The pale man who had welcomed me on my first day, but never spoken to me since, unglued his eyes from my crotch and spoke.

'I'm sorry, Sarah, but I think it's best if we let you go. After the Lorena Adams fiasco we didn't feel we could trust you with a *real story*. News comes first, Sarah, not compassionate heroics!

You could have ruined Dirk's career! We were obliged to do a very pricy deal with another paper, a very pricy deal indeed. About the weight of your salary, in fact. And, anyway, we felt that your ideas weren't really improving.'

'Yeah!' called the Aryan, his voice muffled from under the table.

Outrage filled me. I raised my voice. 'What about—'

'What about what?' they all cried in unison, glaring.

'Don't cry, Sarah, you just don't fit in!' said Lyndi, 'What with the jeans and all!'

I wasn't crying, but someone still offered me a Kleenex, which I took, bemused. I put my hand up and found the side of my nose was soaked with plasma from the spot, which was weeping implacably.

The percolator glopped away, hidden from view. It would start to smell soon, but by then I would be well gone. I had soaked my hand holding the pot while I squatted over it, but it was worth it. In the past week, with a strange and happy prescience, I had made a point of drinking only the darkest and most dehydrating drinks, and eating the most pungent vegetables and luridly enhanced ethnic foods. Perhaps this strange ritual would rid my body of its pallid secretions.

I took my bag and strode away. Pride and release buoyed me up as far as the lift, whose doors heaved shut with magnificent slowness and utter inexorability. The mosquito's legs and wings had finally succumbed to gravity, leaving the crushed torso to manage alone.

Back home, I remembered that Gabriel had gone to a party. He had reluctantly left me the address, ordering me at the same time not to hang around him, and in fact he might not be there anyway so not to expect anything. I watched television for a while and vowed not to go. But I was desperate to lose myself.

The party, in a fashionable part of west London, had been going for quite a while. There were about twenty people in an immense, obviously parental, room that could take a hundred easily. On the wall was a vast family portrait, five of them wearing flared jeans and white T-shirts *circa* 1978. A girl crawled about on the rug looking for lost beads from a broken necklace. I was instantly cornered by a baggy-eyed man in a beige leather jacket.

'You work in the media, don't you? I'm very quick to guess what people do. I'm in television. Got any charlie?'

A girl with a blonde bob swung into the room wearing a purple suede rasta cap and a short green trapeze dress which gave her the look of the abused and murdered younger sister in a low-budget Hollywood horror film.

I had met her before. She was a friend of Gabriel's. Her name was Kat and she sold little coloured bits of things and held out leaflets about world atrocities. She'd just been to South America with her boyfriend, who'd been dealing coke. He was a greying, crewcut TV producer, specializing in music festivals, named Nimrod. Every time I'd met him, whatever the weather, he sported a *boubou* with a repeating pattern of little Vaticans on it that he'd bought in Amsterdam.

Kat offered me a small pill. It bore a strong resemblance to some laxatives I had seen advertised in a railway station some months before. I declined politely, backing at the same time into a giant aluminium sculpture of a leek on which someone had hung a dog lead.

'My father was a Macedonian sailor who ran away with my mother and they had to live on sugar cane for six months. He had the biggest prick she'd ever seen . . .'

I caught the white flash of Gabriel and excused myself to find him. People swayed on the stairs and clustered on the landing. I went up another floor. Things became more exclusive. Bathroom doors slammed in my face at every step. I rounded the corner and passed a door that someone had not bothered to close. Two people leaned against the sink. They were neither tall nor handsome. She was plump, he lightly built, but every available part of them was stuck together like hairbrushes. His hips were canted forward into hers but they were not moving. They were not kissing each other but simply *looking*, their eyes locked with a power I did not know people were *allowed* to have. I stopped. I could not help it. I had never been looked at like that by a man.

Without breaking her gaze, the woman leant slightly and closed the door. I walked on, crying tears for someone I had never known. Laments at the lack of general human contact are far keener than any directed at a specific person. By the final door I had had enough of tapping politely and burst in, infuriated and miserable.

There was Gabriel, sucking the cock of a lithe, slender black man, whose silver jeans lay open, peeled back like discarded trout-skins. Had I ever actually fantasized about him, this would have been my first port of call. The man's wiry hands gripped his pale head like seasoned leather straps. They stopped in mid lurch. Gabriel unclamped and looked sideways up at me, his face impenetrable as a housefly's.

'Your roots are showing,' I said.

'Get your feet off my fucking jacket,' he snarled. It was a new one, white leather lined with yellow silk. I did not move. I wanted to curl up until my joints calcified, fused together in a ball and suffocated me.

'Gabriel, I've been sacked.'

'Good. Then you can fucking move out, preferably *asap*.'

'But—'

'Fish, get out!' he shrieked.

'Hey, relax, Nidge.' The man smiled at me as he stroked Gabriel's hair. 'Volatile, your friend, isn't he?'

There were so many things I could have done at that point: taken a photograph, thrown something, insisted upon joining in, simply watched them. But I turned and fled. I did not belong here. Here or anywhere. I had long since ceased to be able to communicate with anyone. The great mouth that whispered at my back had well and truly plugged me with its tongue.

'Everyone! This is Sarah who's depressed!'

'Hello, I'm Sarah and I'm depressed.'

'Well, hey! Let's all clap Sarah! As we *all* know, understanding you have a problem is the first step on the road to recovery!'

'Tell us about it, Sarah!'

'I've just been sacked from my job and my boyfriend finished with me and before that I discovered him with another man at a party and I've been drinking the whole time and I've got all these minor illnesses—'

'Sarah, that's terrible. You've suffered so much! Sarah, you have been so, so brave. Take her hands, Camilla, Luckie.'

'—and then I caught them all one night torturing a sheep and there were lots of famous people there naked and they all looked at me and wanted to chase me—'

'*Stop*! Stop a minute. Sarah, you do realize this is a group for *normal* people. Schizophrenics are Thursdays. It's really not fair of you to do this to us if you suffer from anything like that. Have you been hearing voices, Sarah?'

'No, no.'

'Sarah are you *sure*? You can't just tell them all to go to Lanzarote for the weekend, now, can you?'

'I'm not hearing voices, honestly, but—'

'Sarah, sorry, can I just interrupt, what sign are you – *no! No!* Let's guess everyone.'

'Scorpio, no, Aquarius, no—'

'You're all being ridiculous, she's a Virgo.'

'No, none of those actually, Taurus.'

'Oh, really! You don't look like a Taurus, oh, well . . .'

'I just can't see why I've deserved to be treated like this—'

'You need a chant, Sarah, try this one – Nyuuuuuuuuu Mah!'

'I don't want to chant, thank you.'

'Did your parents not give you enough love, Sarah?'

'I suppose so, I don't really remember.'

'That's abuse too, Sarah, it doesn't have to be sexual.'

'God, that's terrible, let me do your cards. Flicky! Put on some oil.'

'Take these drops, Sarah, moneypenny for self-worth and fraudulanium for the will to look to the future.'

'Sarah, this turquoise algae clipped gently and without harming a living being from the steppes of Tristan da Cunha will help you find your chakras. It stains your lips blue, though, so don't waste the doctor's time with stuff about heart attacks.'

'Well, Allie, not that Sarah should be taking her problems to a doctor anyway—'

'No, never!'

'But I've got discharge down to my knees and my teeth are falling out.'

'I know, let's do some prostrations!'

'I don't want to prostrate myself, thank you.'

'Have you tried not shaving? It's a great release from the everyday pressures of a male-dominated society. Ooooooh, sorry, Dominic and Sam.'

'I was given all the worst jobs to do and one day I couldn't take it any more, so I pissed in their percolator.'

'Sarah, oh, God, that's brilliant! Sarah, oh, yeah yeah yeah!'

Mawkish cheers rose up. I fled, as someone shrieked something about a tower. I received a bill the next day, which I threw in the bin.

Perhaps someone should design a twenty-second tarot card, the Lone Woman. There she would be, one hand between her legs, the other held palm out in exhausted pride, a modest roll of bank statements in one corner, a single saucepan in the other. She would represent endeavour in the face of discouragement, and self-sufficiency, a sticking out of the neck; self-doubt no more than a momentary breath of wind against one ear of corn in a vast plain.

Gabriel, in a last burst of fairness, vanished, giving me two weeks alone at the flat. And so I sat, not bothering to look for a new place, not bothering with anything. I got up, cried, squeezed my spots, drank, burnt myself cooking and sat down in the chair. Magazines, with their bright riffling tales of other people's success, made me scream, as did newspapers. The television drove me mad, and so I lived, pacing, eating whole packets of biscuits absentmindedly, standing sometimes for hours with my head resting against the door jamb. No one called. As a child I was more capable of such solitude, of seeing when the evening cartoons were and waiting patiently, all day, for them to come on.

It came to me that sanity was an egg, in my case broken but the fluids still intact, that I carried around in my cupped hands. So fragile I must have appeared to people, so easily spilled, and now my hands were shaking and I could not hold it much longer. Only madness could heat and harden it into something definable, controllable. My vision began to wobble and fade, and when I looked in the mirror, my irises had become opaque, as if injected with milk.

The smell in the flat was so strong that it was as if someone had lifted the roof and inserted its source quickly before running away. Trying to retrieve a postcard that had slid down the back of the fridge, I grabbed, sobbing, at the smeared white metal box and dragged it sideways. There was a screech as some tiny metal object trapped under one of its feet cut into the tiled floor. I reached behind it and there, deliquescent and green-grey, was my melted face, the fruit imploded, tufted madly with bright growths of white and grey fur. I put on a rubber glove and tugged at it. The surface came away and I realized that inside the pure scented façade of fruit was *meat*, meat and a mash of fish, judging by the comb-like skeletons that structured the rotting mass. This accounted for the flies that had bobbed and sailed in the air around us as we ate. Gabriel had blamed the drains.

One day when spring was well and truly upon me, I tried to call the Samaritans. The phone was dead.

I decided to kill myself. Why? My adult life so far had not been particularly fulfilled, but where was the bereavement, the terminal illness, the soulmate gone, the life's work tossed away in the wind? The truth is, that in a world where people thrived on pulling themselves together, I had been pulled apart. And the bigger truth was, *I had let it happen.* When I was a little girl, when my eyes could just see over tables and beds, and I had laughed and made things and *devised,* a big man came and selected parts of me for his consumption. When I was thirteen, young jackboots kicked open my eyes, my every sweet red opening. Now I was an adult cipher, an allower, a human convenience. *I let it happen.*

I bought a ticket and sat on a noisy little train, with too-narrow seats and irritating intimacy. I clamped my hand over my mouth, every finger dug deep into the surrounding flesh. Breathing shallowly through my nose I sat, unblinking, for over an hour.

'Jesus loves you, you've got to remember that.'

The woman leaned across to me and touched my hair, steadying herself with her other hand as the train rocked. We passed under a bridge. Her black skin shone like silver in the flashing darkness. She was smartly dressed in a fuchsia and white suit with a nipped-in waist and matching hat. Her face was so kind. I felt the familiar well of tears, as always when a stranger punctures the membrane of private misery.

She had a child with her, about five years old, an adorable

little girl, her hair braided in tiny acorns all over her head. She wore a red coat with a bright orange sweater underneath, and held a shiny little book with thick cardboard pages depicting hungry caterpillars and beneficent lions. She was turning and turning the book, her hands like leaves as they twisted back and forth. The train passed through a field of Friesian cows pushing their moist black noses through the skinny hedge. The little girl let out a shrieking cry of delight. I reached over and slapped her so hard she fell sideways against the window and remained there, staring at me with huge terrified eyes. The mother leapt up and began screaming in my face. The old man next to me grabbed my arm and shouted as he shook it. People craned over the backs of their seats, their faces striped by the bars of suitcase rests as if I were in a cage, or they were. I sprang to my feet, heaved open the carriage door and jumped.

Everything went dark. I flew and flew. I did not land. I could not open my eyes against the light or close my ears against the screaming in them. I seemed to disintegrate and then to disperse. The sound and movement stopped. I had no breath. I was bathed in silence.

I opened my eyes. A huge translucent creature was edging coyly towards me out of the darkness, its face pulsing with the circulation of its luminous blood, all mouth and the huge bulbous eyes of the deep-sea dweller. I fled upwards, the dank waters parting in a mist of light. I reached the surface. I felt a catch in my throat as I absorbed the new atmosphere on shore.

There was not a living creature anywhere, nothing but grey rocks and dull, foolish vegetation. I blinked, and I was back at the office, from where I had been sacked two weeks before.

sin-eater

twenty

WHERE WAS I? That question done to death. It was the *Skip*, but the people were different. And they were not approaching me with a mixture of firmness and pity on their faces, not at all. I appeared to have quite a prominent desk, almost a *space*. Had I died? Was this heaven or hell? Christ! Heaven a bureau, hell the same. Strangest of all was my new feeling of power, or, to be more accurate, an absence of the sense of insignificance. I felt like a balloon suddenly let go, or a once-trapped buoy flying upwards. For the first time ever, I felt what I presumed was normal, more than normal even. I looked down at my hands. They had somehow lost their fuzzy childlike outline and had developed subtle sinew. When I moved there was a sense of structure just below the surface of my skin, yet when I touched myself, discreetly as if taking a pulse, there was the same pressure, the same fading white moon.

People nervously approached my desk and put things down on it, nodding quickly and quietly as they did so, almost to themselves. It seemed a ritual deference, at the same time sincere, the kind that goes with thanking cashpoint machines.

I wondered what I looked like. I stood up to go to the

bathroom. Confidently I strode out and ran straight into the corner of my desk. Had I thought to walk through it? The force of the collision sent the upper part of my body flying forward in graceful whiplash. My recently brushed hair swung slowly, sympathetically.

'Are you all right?' came a concerned call from nearby. A man looked over, almost respectfully. I smiled. In the bathroom, I listened to a frantic spraying sound from one of the cubicles. So some things hadn't changed. There was always one who, in terror that another might smell her shit, madly sprayed great spurts of Chemellia Lovely-Home after herself. While I waited for the vile odour to clear, I dared the mirror. It was still me, Sarah Clevtoe, bending slightly to see into the little square of reflected light. But now I was dressed beautifully in a neat suit the colour of ivy. I wondered at the glossy strength of my hair. I could have laced a shoe with one strand. Or strangled somebody.

Before I had time to investigate my appearance further, several women came in, chattering. Instinctively I jumped back into a cubicle and skidded on some water, no purchase possible on the tiles. I fell back against the toilet seat, the hard edge jabbing my spine, my head pounding the toilet's ceramic upper body.

'Oh my God, are you all right?' came the chorus.

I jumped up and smiled at them. They swirled around me for a moment or two and disappeared. Something was odd. I had felt a nudge, a fast pressure against my flesh, but no more. It had been the same with the desk. I tore down my skirt and tights to look at what should now have become a red patch turning to purple. Nothing. I had felt no pain.

Almost laughing I clenched a fist and tapped my chin. Nothing. I hit harder, and harder, until the saliva clicked against my teeth and tongue and my head shot back. I felt nothing, merely a sensation of contact. I refocused and looked in the mirror. A woman was standing in the doorway, looking at me with the aggressive bemusement certain older women in offices reserve for the young and uppity.

'Oh, just a medical piece I'm working on!' I trilled. I looked down at my shoes, trying to affect gangling self-deprecation. They were very expensive, a deep red velvety suede with silver buckles.

I waited until the woman had gone and dug my nails, which were long and rock-hard, not the congealed and flaking appendages they had been before, into my face, dragging them downwards. I felt the sharp pull of skin, but it did not hurt. I frowned. It had almost been pleasurable. Was this a new layer of muscle I had discovered? Had nerves died, or overgrown? Perhaps, I thought excitedly, I had become incredibly strong! I tried, as discreetly as possible, to rip the loo door off its hinges, but more people came in and I had to leave.

I returned to my desk. For the first time in my life I had *minions*. As I sat, rummaging softly in my handbag for clues to my identity, I remembered the sweat, the soaked shirts and reeking underwear, the pain settling on my lower back as if an anvil were strapped there, my voice crushed to a tiny murmur, awareness of my increasingly useless existence like a black bag pulled over my head. All this had gone. In its place was a warm, creamy tranquillity.

My bag was full of papers. I pulled out a handful. There was a cheque for two thousand five hundred pounds. There was a piece of the headed notepaper of a Dr Timothy Jackson, with several psychiatric qualifications appended. There was also a small, thick calling card with the name of a clinic engraved on it, and a contact number. Since the clinic's *raison d'être* was not written on it, I assumed it treated sexually transmitted diseases. It appeared that I freelanced on the side, saw a shrink to reconcile myself with my decadent, high-flying lifestyle, and, perhaps as a by-product of the latter, suffered from a minor infection. So, I had become a successful citizen. Underneath all the paper I found an address book. I recognized nothing in it, but there were many hastily scribbled numbers put down with the speed of one-offs.

A pile of readers' letters appeared in my in-tray. My drawers were already stuffed with similar ones. Closer examination showed they were responses to a *Skip* campaign on behalf of the increasing number of those unable to live on welfare. There had evidently been some changes in the law. It dawned on me that time had moved quite a long way forward. It was not simply my appearance and molecular structure that had developed.

I scanned the letters, but found it impossible to understand all the painstaking calculations. They all seemed to ask, *What have we done to deserve this?* for which I had no answer. One letter caught my eye.

Dear Ms Clevtoe

I wrote to you ages ago about my problems with getting money. That's not to say 'getting' in a horrible way but I can't seem to get them down at the social to understand that I can't live on fifty quid a week. I had an accident when I was young. I've never quite got the better of life. I suppose I could join a circus, but I'm not that much of a freak! Not that disabled people are freaks but I sometimes feel like one.

Yours

I could hardly read the name. The writing was small, the words curled and crushed like little springs. The writer gave an address south of the Thames, in the dull matrix of streets named after philosophers and mathematicians, a part of the city many I had once known refused ever to visit.

A memo appeared on my desk requesting me in the deputy editor's office. Perhaps I would now discover who I was. Just as I was nearing the deputy's door I overheard a belch from the other side of it, followed by a voice saying, 'You know, Phil, I've said it before and I'll say it again, what most women need is a damn good fuck! Sort 'em out in no time!'

He looked profoundly uneasy as I breezed in.

'So it's today, isn't it, Sarah?'

'Er . . .'

He looked straight at me. He had revived from his brutish slump and was sitting up, attentive and friendly.

'Today you're interviewing Mirabelle Haight, aren't you? We need a cracking good piece, Sarah, given who she's married to, ha ha!'

Mirabelle Haight. My old university acquaintance. While still at St Drew's, Mirabelle had homed in on Kosmo Turpin, sixties relic, wealthy newspaper magnate and official Older Man. The college gossip sheet had buzzed with references to her climbing in and out of his Daimler outside the gates, and her five-day long weekends with him. And now, it seemed, her first book was just published: *Mummy, I'm Going To Be A Bit Late For Lunch, I'm Just Off To Change The World!.*

'Thanks for doing this, Sarah, we remembered you knew her so we didn't think you'd mind.'

Indeed, I relished the idea of seeing her again.

'So you're pleased with, er, my *role* here,' I ventured, making an expansive hand gesture.

He looked at me with polite incredulity. 'Of course! Sarah, what do you mean?'

I felt an urge to threaten him, to force him to tell me what I had become, but somehow I knew I should retain a superior distance.

'I just wanted to make sure everything was OK, understood, you know.'

The deputy dared a knowing, conspiratorial look which he then hastily covered up with a shy smile. Frustrated, I continued.

'Obviously, the quality of my contribution to the paper is very important to me.'

He raised his eyebrows politely. I was getting nowhere.

'Sometimes it's important to re-establish just what is expected of one, you know what I mean.'

He looked politely and slightly fearfully into his lap for a moment. I sensed a resistance to his responsibilities. He held his half-clasped fingers up before him in a praying action, partially hiding his face. His skin was pale and puffy, the black hairs unattractive against it. His knuckles were grazed.

'You don't have to worry about *that*, Sarah.'

It was no good. I simply could not suddenly demand, *Yes, but what am I actually doing here?*

'Fine!' I prepared to go. As I stood up abruptly the pinkish-grey light flashed over the surfaces of the photographs.

'Lovely children!' I said. He looked uneasy, as if he wished for multiple sets of cupped hands with which to cover these references to his family life. I left the room and ordered a taxi, which seemed a suitable thing to do.

On the way to Mirabelle Haight's, I flicked through her book. *Mummy!* was based on the theory that women can get exactly what they want if only they'd stop complaining and just get on with it. It had chapters with titles like *Once Victim, Always Victim!* and *Work Him!*

At twelve-thirty I arrived at a large white house with steps up to the front. The bell, a shining marble cap the size of half a tennis ball, was buried in a recess ringed with gleaming brass. I heard no sound, but became aware of tiny feet running towards me. There was a slow, hydraulic hiss, and a Filipino woman peeked round the huge door and let me in. After ushering me into a drawing room of sorts she scampered away. I sat, for about an hour, staring around.

The room was full of travel souvenirs, artifacts from far eastern countries, all ranged around me as if on a market stall. There were teapots and carpets and prayerstools and cowbells and pouches of every size, shape and smell. On the wall was a large yellowing mirror with a rough gold frame, whose artless rusticity was rudely broken, every four inches or so, by a full breast carved smoothly into the wood. There was a half-hearted smell of joss-stick with a hint of disinfectant. I wandered through the door. The hall stretched away behind the staircase, with no further sign of this dusty memorabilia. I advanced into the gloom. There, nestling beneath the stairs, were two little doors, one marked *Kosmo's Pot,* and the other, *Mirabelle's Little Room*. A noise sent me trotting back to the exotica.

The maid appeared again and led me up the stairs. On the way, several women passed me, chattering and joshing as if in a medieval street scene. On the upper landing, the maid indicated a choice of doors and vanished. I advanced towards one of them.

'No, no! Over here!'

The speaker, clearly able to see me, had let me walk almost into the wrong room before calling out to me from behind. I turned and there was Mirabelle Turpin, *née* Haight, fatter, but the same, with that long heaven-blonde hair and swimming-pool eyes, her clothes a silky sweep of beige. Small clutch bags lay around her like misshapen eggs recently laid.

'How sweet – you turned up on time! We were having lunch, I'm afraid.'

She did not even get up, but remained on the sofa, a bulging pink pinstripe. There was a large portrait of her and her husband on the wall behind her. The room was painted navy blue, a colour that had always made me want to curl up and wait for death. I greeted her, and put my tape-recorder on the table, next to the one that was already there. I tried an admiring tone.

'Your book's all over the shops.'

'No! Put the tape on first, and mine too, please!' Her voice jumped up sharply to a childlike sound at the end of the sentence, although her face wore a smile of ineffable superiority.

'You've got a lot of interviews today. All those people I saw coming down the stairs!'

'Oh, no, they look after Pulchinella.'

There was no sign that a child lived in this house, except for a framed photograph on a side table, of a little girl looking faintly trussed in christening robes.

'Now, we *know* each other, don't we?' said Mirabelle.

'We most certainly do!' I said with false brightness, drawing arcs on my pad while looking at her out of one eye.

'Of course, I remember you!' she added generously, 'You used to get drunk a lot and do daring things on ropes in the Dickens garden, didn't you?'

I raised my eyebrows. Perhaps this was meant as a put-down. Complacency should be a crime, I thought. The air around her was rich with self-satisfaction.

The conversation began with her house. I admired it in the requisite way.

'Oh, it's just a little place. But, Sarah, where do you live?'

'In Kensington.'

'Yes yes, but where's *home*?'

Then we talked about babies.

'You know, it was so lovely being pregnant. I had three adorable nurses all running around for me. I could never remember their names, so I called them Tracy, Sharon and India. The other two never forgave India for getting the posh name, and it just made them all the nicer to me in the hope that I'd rechristen them! But you know what those girls are like, I'm sure, Sarah.'

Then we discussed men.

'I suspect you're still single, aren't you, Sarah? Yes! I thought so! I always knew all those silly students with Megadeth posters on their walls and stripy sweaters weren't really for me. And then I met Kosmo and it was all lovely.'

Abruptly her voice took on a sermonizing tone, as if giving a prepared speech.

'You know, Sarah, I always knew I'd succeed! Funny, isn't it! You've read my book, of course. While I was beavering away at it, half the people I knew at university were still dropping acid in Goa! You know what I mean!'

The book was cleverly aimed at women who were like her, or, more importantly, women who wanted to be like her without really knowing why, who felt that feminism had very little to offer women who jolly well got on with things.

'I'd *never* call myself a feminist! All that silly graffiti about rape in the library loos, and all those *demos*. What a waste of time! I always knew that all I had to do was *be* and everything would come out right!'

I sat quiet throughout. Once upon a time I would have felt threatened by such a person, but now she seemed to me no more than something under a microscope, a pale, curling, transparent parasite.

'You know, Sarah, I'm *terribly* glad I got married. I mean I always seemed to have quite a strong effect on men. The weak ones flocked to me quite fascinated. I needed more than that. Kosmo's quite tough, as you might imagine. I don't think many other women could handle him, to be honest.'

Suddenly she fixed me with a stare.

'It's funny, you never really *featured* in college, did you?'

I retained my razor-cut smile.

Just then, the tiny maid popped her head round the door and, almost with a curtsy, dragged in a couple of huge black bin-liners. She could have fitted inside one of them easily.

'Madam, would you like me to throw them away or shall I take them to the Sue Ryder?'

Mirabelle beckoned and the woman dragged the sacks across the room towards us.

'I'm having one of my clear-outs. You can't keep every piece of clothing you've ever bought!' Mirabelle sighed and dipped into one of the bags. She pulled out a long, pale grey silk knitted cardigan bearing a well-known label.

'You know, Sarah, that would look great on you. Would you like to try it on?'

I looked at her. 'Grey's not really my colour. I suppose I could dye it green.'

'You're not bloody dyeing that! It cost two hundred and seventy pounds!'

She looked at me, her face flickering for a moment with pettish outrage, before tossing it back in the bag.

'Thank you, Magdalena.'

The woman looked expectant.

'Oh, God, chuck them in the bin. I need you to do the kitchen cupboards this morning.'

The maid struggled out, the bags seething over the carpet.

My hostess eyed me suddenly, and leant forward with a ghastly complicity.

'So, Sarah, are you seeing anyone from college these days?'

I still had no idea who I saw these days, if anyone at all.

'Oh, a few.'

'Still seeing your great dark man?'

I looked at her.

'What do you mean?'

'Oh come on, Sarah, if we didn't know *you*, we still knew all about that! You always looked so tough in your leathers and things and we thought you had him at one point, but then suddenly you looked a bit lonely and we thought, well well well, got a bit out of her depth, then, didn't she? Rather a case of the social bends!'

She gave a smile of such savage complacency that I wanted to kill her. It was not the first time in my life I had felt this way about a person. The difference was that now it seemed possible.

I stood up and went over to where she was sitting. I turned off the tape-recorders, jumped on her and kissed her on the mouth. Her face smelt of powder, her breath of vitamin pills tempered by raw onion and coffee. Around her neck was a thin warm worm of silver, a relic of travels in the East, which I toyed with for a moment while she clawed at me. She started screaming, so I slapped her roughly. I felt nothing. I looked up and caught sight of us both in a mirror, a huge Floretian special from an upmarket department store. We made an absurd sight. She struggled. I clamped my hand over her face and stared at her. Suddenly I was bored.

I had hoped the interview would culminate in some smart Socratic dialogue, with Mirabelle flummoxed by my wit, charmed by my insights, and finally, resolving to mend her absurd ways and turn to a path of unassuming sweetness and spiritual curiosity. But instead I made my delicate hand into a fist and punched her in the mouth. I was shocked by my own action. It seemed wrong. I had meant to spread peace and love, but it did not seem appropriate. Her split lip bloomed with blood. She was strong from all those hours spent at the gym, but she may as well have been grappling with a steam-roller. I grasped a handful of her hair and curled it round my fingers in a way that seemed somehow familiar. Her head turned and for a moment she relaxed, clearly hoping I would let go, but being violent to this woman felt like a long-dormant *hobby*. I boxed her ears with my knuckles. The fat pearl studs in them shuddered.

To kick her would have been uncouth. This was an intimate punishment, almost like sex. I licked a finger and straightened out her eyebrows. Suddenly I had the thought that it would be fun to black her eye, but did not know how to go about it. Were you supposed to hit the eye itself, or would a blow to the nose have the same effect? I decided to *nut* her instead. Afterwards I let my head lean against hers for a minute, bumping slightly with her struggles, our hair combined in a shining whorl against the back of the sofa.

Blood from a lip sometimes has aesthetic resonance. Blood from the nose is only gauche. It mixed with her tears and nasal mucus, softly marbling as it ran down her chin.

'You poor thing!' I smiled. I tucked her fallen hair back behind her ears like a nurse or a lover. Then I tore open her silk shirt to reveal her breasts, safely cupped in Swiss silk jersey, pristine, no lace. I kissed them curiously. A copy of *Mummy!* lay next to her on the sofa. I threw it across the room. Its pages split apart and it flapped like a shot gamebird as it fell to earth. I got off her and picked up my things, leaving her curled up among the cushions. I trotted down the stairs two at a time. Outside in the street, a young boy had bedded down on the two enormous sacks of clothing. I smiled at him. I half expected the police, summoned by some secret alarm. But they did not appear.

I set out to discover where I lived. I knew the address from the first page of my address book, but not where it was. When I repeated it to the cab-driver, he looked impressed. The cab shot through the gentle dullness of Maida Vale and the litter-strewn sidestreets of Kilburn; past the filthy Cottage, onwards and upwards. So I was rich! We were entering a region of London so bijou that the cab could barely work its way down the narrow streets.

'This is as far as I go, love, I don't want to risk another respray,' said the driver, indicating the width of the lane that led, apparently, to my home. I paid and took my bag and walked, the path twisting, the signs becoming ever more stylized and tipped with more and more gilt. Occasionally I had to turn sideways along the period walls, ducking to avoid hitting my head on the traditional lamp-posts. Up and up.

The tiny road seemed to stretch out and curl upwards for ever, past doors that were not mine. Entrances became shinier, the brass of locks and letterboxes covering ever more of their surface area. The sound of traffic faded. Soon, all that remained of city sounds was the expensive scrape of my shoes and my bag rubbing softly against the wall. I stopped. My front door. Inside and up again, the stair carpet as thick at the top as at the bottom. My flat. The door opened with an expensive ratcheted clunk. I wondered at the extreme cleanliness of the place, and presumed there was a person who *did*. This, I realized, would have been my first experience of such a person. My mother's domestic rituals had extended so far into her day that there would have been no room for the clumsy ministrations of an outsider. I ran to the bedroom and looked in the wardrobe. I was single! I relaxed.

The answering machine was flashing a message. I played it

while looking round the kitchen. The voice was urgent yet ingratiating, and mentioned that there was something on offer I might like. On the table lay special subscription offers for Amnesty and Greenpeace, and a petition about local noise levels. I was momentarily disappointed in myself, such civic normality. Then I noticed more papers, shuffled together. Receipts, the same headed notepaper, and several more glossy appointment cards from the clinic. What did I freelance in, exactly? Perhaps fashion journalism. But, then, why was everyone so deferential at work? Certainly my clothes were exquisite, at least compared with what I had worn in my previous life. Was I a model? It occurred to me that I had simply sailed gently across one social margin and was nothing more mysterious than a high-class prostitute, taking calls and hopping into cabs. And yes, here was a cab account bill with a letter attached, all on embossed paper, the universal braille-signal of quality, discreetly stating the address (not mine), to which it should be sent. The perfect day job to keep my contacts up to scratch. I laughed at the possibility. The phone rang.

'Sarah, listen. I'm really sorry but they want to do a couple of those shots again.'

I found myself sighing theatrically.

'Look, I'm sorry, OK, but you know I'll see you right, and they don't mind setting it up again and of course you'll get more, it's just that the angle wasn't quite right . . .'

His voice tailed off.

'I want double the money or nothing.' I hung up. A model, then, perhaps nude, perhaps not. Whatever I was, people were paying me handsomely.

I scrutinized the clinic appointment cards and wondered,

concerned, what was wrong with me. I did not feel remotely ill. On the contrary, I was buzzing with strength. Perhaps they were simply alternative therapies, cloud chambers or sacred dung-massages. I looked inside the fridge. It was full of little pouting displays of raw fish and ready-chopped vegetables. In the freezer was bottle upon bottle of vodka. I looked in vain for a little beige bowl, encrusted with pinkish-brown leavings, but no. I had no pet.

I ran to the sitting-room window. The view! I was at the top of a hill, looking down through a vast cleft that split the buildings as if specially for me. The lights of the city flickered on the plain below. I turned to look round the room. Pale shapes shone out of the darkness. I turned on the light.

The room was filled with bones and fossils, arranged with a naturalist's loving care, tempered by that of the aesthete. On the coffee table was a pair of huge shoulder blades, perhaps from a cow, like cavemen's clubs, monumental. Along the mantelpiece lay a row of vertebrae, arranged at all angles, so that they appeared anthropomorphic, squat dancers from one side, faces from the other. On the wall huge ribs fanned out in an undulating curve. Where had I collected all this? Abattoirs? Fields? Abroad? There was no sinister vibration, more a strange feeling of safety, of shared warmth. In pride of place, on its own stand, sat a fat skull, perhaps that of a lion, partially inlaid with silver. In the middle of the floor sat a vast ammonite, which should have been in a museum. The carpet was a deep greyish brown.

I flopped onto the sofa, which was a soft lilac suede. There was no television. I had not yet discovered any books. I sawed briefly at my hand with a small jawbone that lay nearby, but still no pain. The phone rang again. A slight American accent.

'Sarah! Darling! I've got my Black and Decker in one hand and a bottle of Wild Turkey in the other. Just say the word and I'll come straight over and kick the shit out of you.'

'Oh, boring!' I yawned. 'We did that last time. Can't you think of something more original?'

He sounded genuinely crestfallen. 'But I thought – I thought we had something going there.'

'Yeah, you thought . . .'

I discovered a hitherto unrealized talent for silences. Neither of us spoke for several seconds.

'I'm sorry you feel that way, Sarah. All those great times we had. I kind of wanted it to be, you know, you and me.'

'Well, it isn't, I'm afraid.'

'OK, Sarah. I respect that. I'm going to miss you.'

He really seemed to mean it.

I went to bed quietly. I dreamed I was standing in a forest, looking passively down as tiny arrows sailed up to meet my flesh. The tips bent like lead as they rebounded and scattered to earth. Then I was motionless, looking into summer light, and suddenly the point of a great trembling crossbow was hovering in the air before my face.

twenty-one

I AWOKE AND SAT UP quickly. Confused sensation washed through my head. I looked at the clock. Below the digital display flashed the words 'Day off! Enjoy!' I smiled and fell back, raggedly. As a sad teenager, I had found it comforting that even the most poised and privileged people were, at some time each day, lying as messily horizontal as I was.

The light moved slowly round the room as I lay. The sheets were the colour of a deep fresh bruise, with a soft bloom on them like the skin during a blush, or the head of a penis.

I broke the surface of my consciousness and sat up again. I looked down at myself, my breasts, my stomach, my thighs softly moulded in the morning sun. The light caught my pubic hairs and tiny filaments of gold flashed among them as I breathed. I tugged idly at them. They were as defiantly strong as those on my head.

I entered the bathroom, which was done in shades of silver, with crimson floor tiles, each decorated, in darker red, with a Chinese dragon. The shower rose was huge, about a foot across, shiny and old-fashioned-looking, as if come upon in a market and lovingly adopted, at no matter what cost to the temper. I pulled the thick, curved lever in the wall and waited for the dribbles and hissing, feeble mist. A moment's wait and then a missile of water tore into my scalp. Rich mineral steam cleaned my throat. Looking up, I noticed several smaller implements attached to the showerhead, all on the same ribbed silver hoses that hung around it like the arms of a chandelier. I pulled down a small flat attachment with an intense configuration of holes in it and ran it all over my body, the jet cutting a visible track in my flesh. The soles of my feet, my coccyx, the back of my neck all sang with relief in its path. My nipples sprang to life as if pushed from inside. Laughing at my predictability, I moved the jet down my stomach and down through my hair, parting it. The water drove into my clitoris, firing thousands of times a second like the frantic needle of a sewing machine. I bent and parted my labia to watch. To my amazement the excited knot of flesh was not flattened by the deluge but remained thrust forward, implacable.

Once dry, I threw on a white cotton dress, grabbed a carton of Ribena from the fridge, and ventured out into the street. My calves tightened as I descended the steep dark little path to the main road and burst out into a bright noise of traffic, of delivery vans, of laden families arguing. As I negotiated the pushchairs, dogs and bags I experienced a sense of absolute removal. I could almost hear the hydraulic wheeze as my eyes and neck swivelled. People stared at me, but then I was tall, perhaps attractive.

A group of teenagers came towards me, types I might once have shied away from. I looked at their clothes and laughed aloud. Flares and long, pointed collars were back, and more heinously than before. They giggled. One glare from me stopped them short. A chic woman in her forties overtook me, dressed in a designer version of the same outfit. Her hair was a burning cap of red, her soft green leather bag bouncing soundlessly at her hip. Her feet were tiny, made more so by the clumping high heels that cramped them.

'How *wonderful*!' I said. 'Where *did* you get those *incredibly flappy trousers*?'

She turned to me, ready to scorn a lumpish eccentric. My eyes locked into hers.

'You mean, *whose* are they?' she responded.

'Well, I presume they're yours, unless you whipped them off somebody else!' I rejoined, jovially. Some people do not enjoy surreal chat, and she turned back to her original path, mouthing something.

'Excuse me,' I began to call out, when my eye fell on a little girl making her way between the bumpers of the large cars at the side of the steep, winding high street. She had split from her long, straggling family and was capering on her own. I noticed her because she had a look I found familiar, an insane curiosity. The rest of her brothers and sisters trotted carefully along behind their parents in ordered trajectory while she tacked and vectored, mouthing secret codes, mantras, who knew what.

As I drew closer, I saw that she was staring intently at her distorted reflection in a car bumper, moving her head up and down, back and forth, her image rippling in alien mugshots as she pulled face after face into the curved chrome. She wore a yellow dress, overdone, cake-like, and her hair was braided carefully, but she seemed to know these were no more than trappings of parental pride. They had no relevance to the game she was playing now. I slowed right down. The sun leapt up at me from the shining metal. The little girl's forehead stretched until it was almost square, the rest of her face cramped, effete; then her eyes burst into saucers, like those on hideous postcards where a little peasant child cries tears like cauliflowers over a donkey that has accidentally shed its load of Christmas presents in the dusty lane; then her mouth became huge, a toad's. Sucking intently at my Ribena, I bent to join her, reminding myself of those pictures I used to stick on my wall once upon a time, women's faces, already mutant before being touched up for the camera. The little girl giggled. I became so absorbed that it was only when someone shouted that I realized she had left my side and run out into the road. I sprang out after her, scooped her up and landed nearly at the other side, narrowly missed by a huge estate car. The driver cursed me. I carried her back across to the sound of clapping, her mother chattering and shouting. I held her daughter out to her and stepped back into the road.

No one, least of all me, had heard the bus as it freewheeled down the hill, the driver eager to end his early shift. It cut me down like a blade of grass. The front wheel ran over three-quarters of my body and bounced down again, dragging me along by my dress. There were screams and a silence. I stared at the underside of the bus for a moment and then tried to get up.

'Oh, Christ, she's moving! It's all right, dear, don't worry, someone's gone for an ambulance!'

My dress was caught under the wheel, pulled sideways, revealing my legs and knickers. I yanked at it. The bright space between the bus and the road darkened with legs and tentative faces. There was a click of a camera and a teenage boy giggled.

I spoke. 'Does anyone have a knife or something?'

'Oh God! She's trying to commit suicide because of the pain!' someone shrieked.

'No, no, it's my dress. It's caught,' I replied irritably.

After frantic discussion someone produced one. I hacked at the cloth and snaked out from under the bus, dusting myself down. There was a purple patch on the shiny grey ground where the wheel had burst my Ribena carton. A huge arc had gone from my dress. I looked around defiantly. Several women rushed up to me.

'I'm a trained nurse – she must be concussed – sit down, dear, while the ambulance comes!'

'I'm fine, honestly. I'll just have to go home and change this bloody thing!' I heard a siren. I did not want to waste time. I turned and walked briskly away. Several people were screaming at the bus-driver, who had become violently self-justifying in his terror.

'There, what did I tell you?' he shouted, pointing. 'She's fine, she's absolutely fucking fine!'

Several people were staring at me. I vanished back up the little lane and went home to change. When I emerged, reshowered, I had put on a sober suit and tucked my hair in a hat. I did not wish to be recognized and asked to bless people's rings.

I walked up to the big park on the hill. It was a huge place, with slopes and lakes and copses and winding paths and a corner for every narcotic and sexual predilection. I walked to the biggest space I could find and kept on going, upwards, to a great shoulder of land from where I could see far out across the city, the sky a limitless cathedral etched with radiance. I stood still for a long time, the sun at my back. The longer I stood the more I felt I was watching myself from above, a small figure in black among the rippling pools of green. Alone, alone. But, after a while, all the light and air and the innocent colours became a menace. These were not my worlds, these worlds of the dissolved, the integrated, the chemically purified. I had no idea who I really was, but I knew I belonged below, in the world of darkness, ingestion, excretion, of entrails and smears.

Instinctively I headed for a dim-looking little copse that protruded from a much larger group of trees. I hurried down the hill, cutting through a group of tourists with their ludicrous pastels and white legs. I picked up speed as the hill got steeper and thundered through the undergrowth into a glowing ante-chamber, dim on the ground, but with the sun tearing through the leaves onto my face with the intensity of stained glass. I flung myself down on my back.

I was free to play, to splay. I kicked my feet up into the air, hands grasping the tough little plants around me. There was a harsh animal scent from the bush beside my head. I turned to the side to look. Used condoms, cigarette packets, beer cans, clothes; the bright colours dulled as they retreated into the mushy pile of leaves and sticks, time taking everything back to brown.

I closed my eyes and writhed ecstatically, the enforced sophistication of my newfound daily life rattling and falling off me like cheap jewellery. There was a heavy tread, a filmic crack of twigs, and I sensed a new presence in my light. I opened my eyes to find a huge cliché of a man, in a donkey jacket and combat trousers, grinning down at me.

''Avin' fun there, dear? 'Owsabout if I join you, then?'

He stood for a moment, hoping to enjoy the spectacle of my pleading. I looked up at him. He smelt of beer, ketchup and feet.

'Be my guest!' I said pleasantly with a smile.

His expression turned to rage. 'You fuckin' stupid bitch! Don't lip me arahnd!'

He kicked me in the leg. I thought of the bruise it would once have left, a scatter of blues and turquoises like one of Monet's waterlilies. He got down on one knee, pulled up my shirt and grasped one of my breasts, forcing it until the white flesh squeezed between his fingers like blancmange. Then he went for my skirt. I lay still, looking at him with an expression of amused irony. He fumbled, one hand out in preparation for a clawing defence that never came.

'Dear oh dear, what do they teach you in schools these days?' I said, affectionately. In reply, he punched me repeatedly around the face, swearing. I closed my eyes and waited for him to stop. He yanked my skirt up and forced my legs apart. He did not bother to pull my knickers off, merely yanking them to the side.

'That's what he did in that film. Jack Nicholson, wasn't it?' I said.

'Fuckin' shut up!' he screamed, grabbing both my hands in one of his.

'Oh, come on! You can do better than that! I think they do it on a table or something.'

He twisted my hands, evidently thinking he was hurting me. I waited patiently while he unzipped his filthy trousers and pulled out his penis. It was huge by any standards, with a disproportionately large head and glinting eye.

'I'm gonna fuck you so 'ard you're gonna wish you've never been born.'

With vicious speed he rammed the heel of his slabby hand into my mouth, the fingers digging into the soft skin below my eyes. I was rewarded with a kaleidoscope of dancing rhomboids, orange, silver and brown.

He came forward from his knees and thrust straight into me, his breath suffocating. I politely turned away but he cracked my neck back with a trill of clicks in the vertebrae. He kissed me, his tongue's acrid residue piling up against my teeth. He must have weighed fifteen stone at least. After about ten seconds he gave three great roaring gasps, pulled out of me and shot his semen all over my face, the small amount belying the flourish with which he performed the action. He sat back on his heels.

'Kinell!' He looked at me.

'Feel better now?' I asked, sitting up, wiping away the hot fluid as I did so. He stared at me. There was no blood on my face, no swelling. My skin was still the same uniform rosy putty of the North European Caucasian. And I was smiling.

'The Yorkshire Ripper, insiders say, used quite literally to fuck his victims' brains out. Now there's a thought,' I said, eyebrows raised, picking a sliver of mud from under my nail.

'Yeah, well.'

'Have you ever done that?'

'Done wot?' he said, petulantly pulling out a crushed packet of cigarettes.

'Slashed up a woman and fucked the wounds, your own personally customized vaginas?'

'You swallowed a dictionary or wot?'

There was a pause.

'Christ I'd never do a fing like that. Shit! Whacha think I am?'

He looked aggressive again.

'Relax! I was only asking!'

''Scuse me, but who the fuck are you, anyway? Seriously, who the fuck are you?'

He looked bemused as I rearranged my clothing and settled in the grass. I wished he could have told me.

'Aha!' I said. 'Perhaps I'm a casting director auditioning actors for a great new film!'

His face lit up greedily.

'Or a bored housewife looking for a bit of rough trade! How many times could you manage to do that for me in a day. Five? Ten? But I mean seriously brutally, no messing around.'

'Well, wait a minute, I mean, don't get too 'asty, will you? Fuck!'

I sat up and stared at him. 'You mean you couldn't manage it?'

His face looked even more unintelligent than before. I wondered what brought him to the park.

'Do you do this a lot?'

'Do wot?'

'Approach single women in parks and rape them? And in the *morning* too!'

'But you were lying on yer fuckin' back in the bushes. That says cunt to me!'

'There *is* a case for eugenics,' I mused. And then regretted it. For this was a human being, after all, a tree of cells and motor functions, a carrier of hopeful genes. Perhaps, like a latter-day St Francis of Assisi or Siddarthan guru, I could tame his urges and stroke them into oblivion.

But I didn't want to. My mind displayed a scene of him leaping on me with a knife, the knife bending and withering and he, having exhausted the use of penis, fist and weapon, falling to his knees and begging forgiveness.

I picked a lush spearlike nettle and ran the tip idly up and down my face.

'Careful, it's a stinger!' he said, almost concerned. 'Don't wanna spoil your career.'

'Such botanical knowledge in one so city-bound!' I replied. 'Are you sure that's what it is?'

He crawled over to the nettle patch and poked his fat, grubby hand into the thrusting plants, snapped off a stem and pushed the leaves into his own face. He cursed as his skin began to blister. 'Bloody Norah!'

Their diet of human secretion and moral darkness had given these plants exactly what they needed. Those were no ordinary nettle stings, the little measle of welts that goes down in an hour or two. These stings were the size of fifty-pence pieces, and increasing by what I could see, thickly white through the intense red of the skin around them. The man looked at his hands in horror and began to whimper.

'I must tell you that I'm fighting an urge to come over and pop you like a piece of bubblewrap,' I told him, playfully.

'I carnandle it.' He was shaking. 'Are you from Mars or wot?' One of his eyes was so swollen it could barely open. It was time to go.

'Well, I'll be off now!' I said, briskly adjusting my clothes. He didn't hear me. He was frantically touching his face and poking the fat, taut, burning sacs of skin as they multiplied.

I made my way out of the little copse and back into the sun. Back across the brow of land, along the little paths. At one point there was a shriek and a cricket ball, with the full force of an eager amateur bat, stung me full on the cheek. It bounced off and fell to the ground. Lost in thought, I wandered on until footsteps thundered up to me.

'Oh shit, oh shit, are you all right?' A ginger-headed student in a yellow sweatshirt appeared beside me and looked at me in horror.

'What?' I said.

'Sorry,' he said lamely. He hunted around for his ball. There was a silence when he found it, torn and flattened. I walked on.

I had been sitting in a little café, all fine lines and invisibly clean glass, for twenty minutes when I looked in my diary and saw I had a meeting in the middle of town.

Down and down the vast hill and round Regent's Park and down through the neat construction of streets where doctors worked. The more vulgar doorways were decorated with plaques of shining metal, some an arm's length wide to accommodate the qualifications. The most illustrious establishments, however, had none, so that the passer-by had no inkling of the worlds behind them, and only the most select and unusual clients even knew which ones to enter. It was through such a door that I led myself, after applying my finger to one of three oval buttons, brassy, liplike, *designed*. I took a rattling but highly polished lift to an area made infinitely airy by the gigantic sash windows that lined it. I had never seen such windows. From ceiling to floor they ran. As I looked, one of the lower sashes began to rise, majestically, inexorably. The distant sound of traffic poured upwards and inwards like a swarm of bees.

'Miss Clevtoe. Come this way.'

A young man, clean and reasonable, indicated a waiting room.

'Er, who am I seeing today?' I ventured.

He looked gravely surprised.

'Why, Dr Jackson, Miss Clevtoe, the same as usual.'

It was the psychiatrist whose headed notepaper I had in my bag. So this was where successful women came to weep over their failed relationships, and their desperation for babies there was no time to have. Women who felt that children had been slaughtered by their not having them, and how up there in the air just above their heads waited two or three sad-faced little souls, philosophical with disappointment, wanting desperately to enter the sweet pullulating corals inside them and fuse with them. This was where rich women came to align and realign the miseries of their lives in near-infinite permutations, like a child playing with a Rubik's cube.

I wondered how much we were all paying for this. Given the premises, a lot, my bourgeois self assumed. I waited, surrounded by magazines. Flipping through them, I saw that nothing much had changed. Pictures were bigger, weirder, but still surrounded, supported, by women's bodies and faces. The bodies were, if anything, more exaggerated. They were either prepubescent sticks or impossible contraptions of enormous breasts and male swimmers' shoulders coupled with tiny waists, minuscule bottoms and infinitely long skinny legs, botched photofits all of them. My name was called.

I walked down the corridor. Everything was silent. A door lay open. I entered a large room whose walls were lined with bookshelves. Some held books, while the majority supported glass cases containing china babies wearing every type of national, historical and professional costume. I caught sight of a Tyrolean yodeller, a young Fagin and even a little doctor. All had pale complexions and over-rosy lips like tiny bows.

'Sarah!'

A blond man in a white coat jumped gracefully to his feet and rushed towards me, his leather chair spinning with the force of his leaving it. He took both my hands in his.

'SarahSarahSarah! I can never quite believe it when you come back like this! Sit down sit down! Have a cup of tea! Me! Anything!'

His gold-and-pink looks were the type favoured by casting directors searching for romantic interest of the officer class. His effusive manner was glossy, convincing, especially when he ran his hand through his thick corn-coloured hair. I sat and smiled. He was trembling slightly, as if he had come upon something marvellous.

'Now then, my dear! Today I thought we'd start with some more tests. As usual, being of my own design, they're quite interesting and I think it would benefit us both for you to try them. Do you want to come through?'

I got up and followed him through a padded door into the next room. He shut the door and suddenly turned to me with deep intensity, his eyes blue fire.

'Sarah, I know I say this every time, but you could be the best thing that's ever happened to me. I mean that. I'm so glad I found you, Sarah. Oh, God!'

His voice and whole body lurched with the final expostulation. I half expected him to produce a ring. His palms were slightly sweaty, but then he looked the energetic type. He indicated a long table covered with objects and a chair.

'Ok, Sarah. First of all. Come over here, come over here. Look!'

His voice had wound itself higher and tighter, like an uncle trying to cajole his little niece into peering through binoculars at a distant, brown bird.

Laid out before me were two vast trays, one piled high with cigarette butts. There was a rank, chemical aftersmell.

'Sarah. I want you to pick these up one by one and put them over there on the other tray.'

I looked at him. My new self was more fastidious than the old. I frowned.

'Sarah, you agreed. You agreed we would do whatever I asked, it's in our contract. This is *my therapy* and you agreed to it!'

His voice had changed. Evidently I *had* agreed to this, and I was apparently desperate for a cure for *something*. So I began, pointing my nails as if trying to pluck out a nipple hair, bestial, unwanted. The smell coursed into my nostrils. I affected an air of gentle puzzlement, eyes wide. After a few minutes, like every repetitive task, this one took on an organic rhythm of its own. There being no real load to carry, I was obliged to go with the weight of my own hand, back and forth, dipping and rising, derrick-like. I became intoxicated with the task, forgetting the smell. I was woken by a shout like a great bell.

'Stop now, Sarah!' bellowed Dr Jackson. I had forgotten his presence entirely. He had been ticking off on a clipboard.

'OK, next test. Sarah, I want you to take your shoes off and put them back on again, but when you put them back on I want you to put them on the wrong feet. Then I want you to walk up and down until I tell you to stop.'

I could not help my look.

'What are you, stupid?' he shouted. I looked down and swapped over the shoes as I was told to. I moved, my walk spoiled, my clothes jerking slightly as I tried to retain my dignity. Suddenly I became aware of my feet the way I never had been, as if they were someone else's that I had borrowed. It made me feel as if it was my feet themselves that were wrong, that I should change *them*. I walked up and down, only then noticing the soundless dry atmosphere of the room. There was no echo, no comforting reminder of existence. I could almost hear my heart above my tread on the thick carpet. Patiently I put my head down, and again the task became part of a greater act of balance. I imagined that I was a cow pushing a beam round and round over endless grain.

'Sarah, stop now!'

But I wanted to walk. I could feel my shoulders elongating downwards to the ground, my hips canting backwards, huge plates of muscle pooling and re-forming.

'Sarah, *stop*! Last one before the chat.'

I did not speak.

'Sarah! Are you awake? What's got into you today? See that box over there. I want you to put your hand in it.'

I was becoming bored and irritated. Why had I opted for such a ridiculous therapeutic treatment? Perhaps this man was about to announce that I was a rare Eternal Salamander, only two thousand of us born each century. I walked back to the table and pushed my hand through a piece of slit black gossamer into a soft mass of fibres. I turned to Dr Jackson for guidance.

'Hold it there until I tell you.'

I waited a minute, perhaps two.

'OK! Take it out!'

I pulled out my hand. It was glistening brown with ants, hot little garden ants with their hourglass bodies and nodding heads chugging over and over each other against my skin. Perhaps they were biting me. I looked at him. He looked quizzical, slightly infuriated.

'Extraordinary, truly extraordinary.'

The bronze glove swelled and rippled.

'You're a funny one, aren't you.'

He leant against the corner of the table and sighed down at himself. Then raised his head with gusto.

'Right. Talkies!'

I wondered what he meant me to do with the ants. He seemed to have forgotten them. I wiped them off against my skirt. For the rest of the day, one or two would appear from my clothing and then disappear, as if colonizing quietly, or considering it.

He led me over to the window and indicated a leather couch. He began to pace.

'Now where did we get to last time . . . Ah! I know! That autumn afternoon you were going to tell me about.'

He sighed again and tugged at his upper chest hair with a clenched fist. As if a button had been pressed, I began to talk about my early childhood.

'The light had the softness of a mid to late afternoon in early

November, relaxing the eye as the throat in turn accepted sharper and sharper cold. Nature flared through the swelling mist with every dying berry and leaf. I threw my ball for our puppy one last time, the sheened scarlet plastic glowing against the powdery light. My throw was crazed. The ball sailed over the hedge and onto the path.

'Billy was still scared to go far from the house. He suddenly became very interested in a clump of grass, shining in the dew. He sniffed at it intensely, eyes closed, ears covered in burrs. I reached up to undo the gate. I could see the ball, bright among the dying nettles by the wall. I was scared to put my hand between the poisonous spears. Suddenly there was a grown-up behind me, a large one with a deep voice. He had an enormous dog with him that towered over me. It shoved its shining nose through the hedge and sniffed at Billy. It could have picked him up in its mouth. The man bent down and touched me swiftly. There was a sound of Boys on the path. He fled. Later, the tea was hot and comforting in my mouth. And that's all I can remember.'

There was a silence. I did not want to look at Dr Jackson. He was moving strangely, as if marking out dance steps.

'Go on.'

'It was summer, I was older, and my parents were out shopping, leaving me in the garden. Billy lay on his side, his almost hairless stomach pink and patched with black. The grass was sucked of its moisture in this extreme June and was itchy to sit on. Beneath it, tiny daisies fought for life. There was no breeze to flap my comics and I pored over them, sucking a long, green frozen tube of ice from a transparent plastic wrapper. I was surrounded by the smell of roses. There were hardly any clouds. Plants waved, not with wind but as if desperately searching for it.

'After a time, I went to the garage and found some bamboo poles and some bricks. I constructed five jumps on the lawn. I put Billy's collar and lead on him and pulled him across the jumps. The heat was a thick glass bell around me. I jumped with Billy until he became reluctant and tried to slip his collar. I stood still in exasperation. A shadow flickered over the sun. The man appeared again. Later, I lay down and examined the glistening trace of his semen in the grass. That's all.'

I felt nothing as I spoke. Dr Jackson was edging towards the door of his lab.

'I'm still listening,' he called, propping the thick door open with a thick metal wedge.

'This goes further back. I was four. I loved the darkness, I loved sound in the darkness, which is unusual. Usually the cover of night invites silence, a merging, a sidling into a slyer dimension where even the breath must be censored. But not me then. Night was just a colour like the rest, just an atmosphere to play in.

'I grabbed my toy telephone and pulled it down the path on its string. The wheels skidded on the compacted mud, the bell whizzed sporadically. I slowed down, aware of the lights of my parents' house at my back. Their neighbours were out, and as I passed their house the light gradually faded, leaving only soft sheened outlines in the black. Darkness took me under its arm.

'The phone stopped ringing. I jerked the string again. I was walking so slowly now that the little bell barely sounded. The wheels halted. I stopped. There was a darker shape against the black wall. A voice called my name. I went towards the speaker.

His voice said, "Why don't you answer that phone, Sarah?" I wasn't that young, I knew it wasn't real. "It's not a real phone," I said, reassuringly. "Oh, really?" came the voice again. The man scooped me up in his arms and explored me, all the time whispering warmth and confusing comfort. I remember being put down suddenly, his feet disappearing. I turned round, still gripping the string, and skidded on the phone in my small red three-buckled shoe and onto my knee, and that pain, the sharp, surface pain that is kitsch in its incongruous brightness, threw me back into the conscious world. I scrambled up and ran, still holding the string. I tore along, dragging the toy on its back, the scraping noise white, violent, drowning the sound of the bell which continued to ring.'

There was a silence from the lab.

'You know, Sarah,' the doctor called, returning, 'you really ought to write down some of these little stories, they're quite amusing!'

He reappeared in the doorway, his erect penis stretching up and out before him. From this distance it appeared incongruously dark, bronzed, as if a transplant. As he came nearer I realized it was teeming with ants from the box on the table. I looked on. Dr Jackson sat down, as if this was normal, as if this happened every week.

'Do you know, Sarah, there is nothing more I wish for than to really hurt you, to break you and re-form you. How long is it since you felt any pain?'

His face was flushed. He sat still for a minute and then, with lightning speed, picked up a paperknife and stuck it into my hand.

'Sarah, you're a sado-masochist, aren't you? Hell, why

glamorize? A masochist! You're my discovery. I could really use you for a lot of things. Stick with me and you could be in every textbook in the land.'

Dr Jackson looked down at himself. The ants were evidently starting to bite, for he was sucking in his breath and chewing his lip. His penis twitched under its crawling carapace. A dangerous helplessness came into his eyes. I expected him to ejaculate there and then, or force me to do something, but he did not. His voice trembled slightly. 'OK, you can go now, Sarah, I'll let these little bastards finish me off. Shall I write another cheque or would you prefer banker's order?'

We discussed how I was to be paid, and I turned and left. I suspected, however, that today something was a little different from usual. The ants were clearly nothing new, but the whining screams that increased in volume and intensity as I pushed the carved malachite button on the lift told another story. The ancient safety gate clattered shut and I was ushered down to the sound of the young man running to his master's aid.

twenty-two

I HAD ONE MORE appointment at what I presumed was the clinic, which was a short journey from one of the huge arterial roads that feed London to the West. I took a taxi past exhaust-blackened suburbs and superstores to a business park.

The building was huge, seemingly windowless. The door was small, wooden with glass panels, casual, like the back door of a semi left permanently ajar for children and dogs to run through. I knocked. A woman answered without a word and took me down a corridor and left me. I waited.

'Miss Clevtoe!'

There was a modest thundering in the corridor and a group of people scudded into view.

'Miss Clevtoe! Thank you for joining us.' A very glamorous woman stepped forward from the group and smiled at me.

'Miss Clevtoe I'd like you to meet, er, Professors Vitalo and Benn who are going to be with us today.'

'Sarah, if I may call you that,' the first professor said with theatrical obsequiousness, 'I feel so privileged to meet you and take part in what they're doing here. Thank you! I mean, thank you for helping us to, er, push back the boundaries of science!'

They all laughed heartily.

'So! What are we going to do to Miss Clevtoe today?'

A tall man stepped forward, smiling.

'OK, Miss C, stand just there so our guests can get a good look at you. Take your jacket off, please. Sam, could you pass those notes over to me. First, I'll recap. Week one. We did electric shocks. That was quite an interesting session from everyone's point of view. The boys upstairs definitely got what they wanted – mind you, the hardware's pretty impressive. She took the strongest current we could get without bringing in a supplementary generator.'

'What about using the mains?'

'Oh, yeah, yeah, we got a couple of wet-finger-in-the-socket shots. She took it like a rock, didn't you dear? Week two was injections, cyanide, strychnine, all the old favourites plus phenol, of course. But our little wonder didn't do a thing, so only science benefited that time, ha ha! Here, look at the figures.'

He held a paper over to the professor and the woman. To my pride, they gasped.

'Week three, sound. We did everything, highs that could shatter cast iron, and lows that could make your teeth samba out of your mouth and your bones turn to gravy. Not a sausage.'

The professor looked at me with wonder in his eyes, almost love. 'Last week we did pressures. That was a great one, the best yet. We took her to a car-assembly plant and had her get in the chassis mould and sit under the compressor. I must say you were lucky not to have been in on that one, the bill was a killer! It'll put the plant out of action for one hell of a while. I must say, little Miss Pounds-per-Square-Inch – pounds and pounds if I may be so bold – ' There was a general snigger. ' – the genetics boys are going to have fun with you.'

So, I was involved in scientific experiments. It all seemed so obvious that I wondered why it had taken so long for me to work it out. It dawned on me that I had become a fairly important person. I demanded a cup of tea. It came in seconds. While I was drinking it, the second professor, a squat woman, walked up to me.

'Do you mind?' she asked. She put out a stubby hand and gripped mine for a moment, then she began to stroke it.

'It's like any other skin!' she mused. 'There are muscles, veins beneath!'

'She's not an *android*, Professor Benn, she's *real*!' called the glamorous woman, condescendingly. 'This isn't *Star Trek* or something!'

I smiled benignly. There was a sound of sucked biro being pulled out of mouth.

'You, Sarah, are a marvel, are you not?' called a bearded man, hitherto quiet.

'It seems philosophically interesting to be here,' I rejoined. 'I've often wondered—'

I was cut short by backs departing and an arm taking me firmly down another corridor. Twenty minutes later we passed through two enormous steel doors bearing red, yellow and black images of skulls, lightning, tents and tanks, like stickers on a child's wardrobe. We had entered an enormous hangar. In the middle I could just see a small illuminated stage with a backdrop.

'So this is the laboratory?' I asked. There were distinct sniggers.

'Wake up, darling,' someone mumbled. 'Christ, what did you give her? Doesn't she even remember last week?'

My companions left me and began to climb a spiral staircase to a viewing balcony forty or fifty feet above. Below the balcony there was no light, or at least the blinding lamps that illuminated the little stage did not allow me to see what lay beneath. A man in a white uniform appeared, and led me over the linoleum to the platform.

'OK, love. The usual, then.'

'What?' I asked.

'Would you mind, you know, stripping off?' he asked, repeating in surprise what was obviously a formality. I supposed not. He led me to stand while he smeared a cold, pale gel over my chest. He then grabbed a handful of wires with suction pads on the ends and began to stick them on me.

'What's this for?' I asked, as the skinny strands of covered wire began to populate my flesh.

He looked surprised that I had asked. 'We always monitor you during the, er, *testing,* don't we?' he replied. 'You know the score. If you run into any problems here's a buzzer that connects to the control room.'

'Yes, yes, but what are you, er, *testing* this time?'

'Ballistics,' he replied. 'They'll probably call the film *War Baby* or something corny like that.'

Before I had a chance to reply, his two-way radio shrieked at him.

'Can you do something about her hair, Joanne says, oh, for fucksake, Joanne, it looks fine from here – just fluff it up a bit, will you, just to keep her happy,' the voice added in a long-suffering whisper. 'She'll be wanting to *tong* it next!'

The man in white pulled a brush from his top pocket and performed flicking actions as I sat.

'Her nose, Mel, her nose, it's a bit shiny still. Thanks, mate, but you know what she's like. The punters ought to be fucking grateful for what they're getting, but oh, no, it's got to be *perfect*. Christ!'

The attendant patted me with powder and left me. I sat back on the padded platform that had been provided for me. For the first time I felt uneasy. Not because of what would be done to me but because of my position at the centre of someone else's universe. With every small grey rubber patch and wire that led from me to consoles, screens, hands, and ultimately others' minds, a tiny duct seemed to open in me, deflating, depressurizing. I sat and waited.

A voice echoed from a Tannoy. 'OK, Miss Clevtoe. Old-fashioned rifles!'

There was a rush of clicks. I stood as if it were expected of me. The arc lights sang as they were turned up. I began to sweat slightly. My eyes fought against the brightness. I suddenly noticed dark stains on the floor below me. Before I could really register them, ten sharp reports sounded in quick succession. Ten times I felt the flicker like an insect's wing as the bullets crashed and crumpled, falling useless to the felt below my feet. My body hairs waved as the bullets fell, like bleached summer grasses in the August heat. There were shouts from the balcony behind the glass. Above the balcony I caught sight of another viewing window, the room behind it bathed in red. Objects moved, heads turned.

'Pump-action shotguns, Miss C!'

There was a whistle, and three masked men broke out of the

darkness and ran towards me, the shiny fabric of their clothes whizzing as they raced over the lino. When they were six feet away they began to fire. It seemed such a waste as they jerked out their armouries on me; I experienced no more than a light brushing sensation. I lay back on the platform and stared upwards as the bullets charged between my thighs, only to deform, fall and join the increasing pile below me.

'Perfect!' I heard someone shout. I opened my eyes. High above me winked a remote-controlled camera that for a moment seemed to nod and smile with my movements as if trained in conversation. I looked straight into the lens. I barely heard the next reminding shout, or felt the shells that pounded my flesh.

'Open wider, please!' The voice was hoarse.

A screaming bolt of metal thrust into my vagina and stopped dead. For the first time since my new incarnation I felt a sensation, definitely a sensation. I felt a desire, even a love, the whole equation of my life filling out as I lay. I looked down at myself, the white-hot silvered cylinder buried among the crisp chaos of my pubic hair. I stood and pulled the missile down and out of myself and began to walk back towards the balcony. The electrodes tore off me like leaves.

'We need you for another ten minutes, do you mind?'

I ignored the voice and carried on.

'I order you to stop, Miss Clevtoe! This is extremely irregular!'

I marched under the lights, up the spiral stairs and through the door. There was a pungent smell in the observation room. My audience was frozen in the midst of intense sexual activity, skirts ridden up, trousers collapsed around ankles like paper bags. I tossed the dense, heavy tube of metal at them and turned away, shielding my face from the explosion.

Naked I walked, along roads and roaring underpasses, ignoring the hooting horns and bellows from lorry cabs, until I found a taxi. When I got home, the flat was warm, scented. I tried to sit for a while but could not.

Slowly and sadly I took a bottle of vodka from the fridge and walked to the bathroom. I stared into the big, round mirror and put one hand on my breast, with its baked smell from the long day. I squeezed the unstructured flesh, held in place only by a lucky bell of skin and muscle. I closed my eyes. Images came at me out of the past.

Soft pastel colours came to me, peaches, apricots, corals. After a while they took on a sheen, a white glow in a low light, the sheen of chintz. I imagined my parents' lounge, years ago.

I picked up the vodka and poured it over my head. The biting liquid ran into my eyes, my mouth, and down the narrow écru waste of my body to my vulva. I felt no pain from the clear alcohol, only sensation, like sparks on the dull surface of a dying star.

My mind's eye found soft surfaces, cushions, yielding velours, all rippling with the same exaggerated auburn hues. The soft gilt of a framed painting came into view, two gigantic nudes the colour of catfood. It was the reproduction Renoir I had always stared at in wonder, trying to compare those women's bodies with my own.

I reached down to a trolley by the basin and picked up a block of wood and some sandpaper. With it I began to rub my body in circular sweeps. If I strained, I could just feel a tingle. In my mind, a smell rose up, of lurid sauces, something battered, hot in a tinfoil tray. A Chinese takeaway from the local in the square.

I pushed the trolley into the bedroom. From it I picked up two toothed metal clamps the size of a large dog's jaws, and snapped them shut on each breast. My flesh bulged. Above the bed was a thin, strong metal rail screwed to the wall. I knelt on the pillows, turned my back to it and knotted my hair around the rail. The knot held as I leant forward and let my hair take my weight. I spread my knees and pulled from under the pillow a long thick white rod of bone, a femur, with its shining bulbous head. Leaning forward on my hair, I pushed it into my vagina. The bone glistened in the light as I pushed it in and out. My scalp tingled faintly.

I urged my memories forth. My mind's eye registered the whole room, dried grasses in a vase, the puppy curled next to me. Suddenly, making me gasp and work the bone faster, a large hand, brawny, docile, appeared from the huge figure beside me and clasped my tiny fingers firmly. Programmes flashed on the screen in front of us. Where were my parents? The puppy slept on, and the hand remained, clasped over mine, squeezing gently but barely moving, a safe hand, a protecting hand. I leant towards him and felt the coarse wool of a sweater against my ear. The hand was so firm it did not need to promise, to affirm, to prove it was warm and large and loving, never leaving me. Never, ever, leaving. Gradually I felt the big body turn. The other huge hand came to rest on my knee, splayed wide. Then it began to move upwards, walking finger by finger, trembling as it palped, like a soft, benign, enormous insect.

I was gasping, my vagina gripping at the bone's sheeny head. Simultaneously, as his massive finger reached my tiny labia, his chest hot and damp through the rough wool, I imagined a pressure on my temple, lips pressing, a tiny spontaneous sound as his mouth touched my skin for barely half a second. A kiss of love.

My body surged inside and I coughed out a cry as I came, blood staining the hot gush as I pulled the bone out and fell back against the wall, staring with lost eyes, my mouth void. I saw the blood and cried. I had secretly hoped, however irrationally, that there was something living inside me, something that needed me. The feeling evaporated as my juices dried, and I slept as a machine sleeps, extinguished.

The day before was already distant as I dressed for work in the morning. By the time I was out of the door, the memory had fled down its perspective to a point of infinite distance.

No one bothered me at the office, and before I had time to become bored, a memo announced an editorial meeting. Now I would learn about what was really going on in the world. The reporters looked slightly worried when I sat among them, as this was evidently unusual behaviour. I was the only woman there. I smiled to reassure them as they talked. The usual ideas were walked around the circle, this time with a stronger hard-luck element. The Boom had certainly fizzled out. Homelessness, repossessions, pollution, motorway tolls, it was all there. Someone mentioned Mauves, a prominent merchant bank said to be funding the government.

'They're not still in, are they?' I asked. There was a round of laughter. Mrs Thatcher, however, had evidently gone, sneezed out of the club. Somehow, I felt she had not left the offices of the *Skip*, and that we were all breathing the air she breathed still, along with that of Jesus and Oliver Cromwell.

Someone sketched out a detailed process by which party funds travelled from one place to another. God, another bloody boring conspiracy theory, I thought.

'. . . of course, we know who's behind it all, don't we? Alexander Pulver.'

The name cut through my musings like a laser. Alex Pulver! Instantly my little finger flew to my mouth and I began chewing and sucking the nail, frowning as I did so.

'What's he up to?' I snapped. They looked surprised.

'He's their head of PR. He's fucking powerful, but then his family have a history of donation to political parties.'

I felt my eyes grow wider and rounder until they were like those of a dog, glazed and fixed on a distant movement. My memories reared and bounced. I remembered my confusion, the indignity of hard knees thrust between my legs. I chewed the skin around my thumbnail. They were all looking at me expectantly.

'Yeah, yeah, carry on.'

'OK. In the light of the government's Moral War, there's some stuff here I wish we could print, but . . .'

There was a knowing laugh. This had obviously become a regular feature of the meetings.

'Right. Without mentioning any names. The MP for Shovelworth, dog-fighting ring based at his mansion. The MP for Crabley Wood, circulates paedophile literature – God, this one's a real nasty, someone's got a regular feed of small boys from a home he donates to and another bloke's been shelling out thousands in shut-ups about his predilection for little—'

'Stop!' I said, 'How do you know all this is true? And if it is true why don't you fucking print it?'

There was a heavy silence.

'Sarah, the legal implications—'

'So? If it's true it can only do good, can't it?'

'There are other considerations of which you are obviously aware . . .'

They all looked at each other, and then at me. I obviously looked dangerous.

'Bullshit! God, I'd like to talk to those bastards.'

'Gatecrash Pulver's wedding and you'll meet them all, I'm sure.'

Alex's wedding. The soft wink of sunlight through the birches as the guests tread softly over the grass. A strong quartet playing merrily, the chink of bottle on flute, the creamy rush of bubbles. The belches barely restrained below innocent pearls.

There was a rustle. People were looking at me. I had picked up a glass paperweight, *A Souvenir of Mexico*, it said, and was squeezing it in my hands. As I passed it back and forth it became squashy, like jelly. I felt my face twist. As I squeezed the humour it softened further until it oozed between my fingers. Suddenly there was a sharpness in my hands. The glass had almost dissolved and the tiny scorpion that had been trapped inside was revealed, hard in my palm. My eyes were swimming. They were all looking warily at me. I got up and left.

I thought over Alex's forthcoming wedding. The memories burst forth, foul blooms on my consciousness. The expression of assumption he always wore, the blanking out of all kindness as he turned to join his friends, locking the obsidian fortress of the eternal 'we', on whose walls no grip can be found by the outsider. 'We' was a word I barely ever used.

My mind became weevilled with remembrance. I had to lead it somewhere else, entertain it, train it, even. Back at my desk, I looked through all the letters that had come about lost benefits. The holes in the social net had grown and more and more people were falling through it. I came across the letter with the illegible name which had struck me previously. I decided to visit the writer, and do the story myself.

It was a sunny day. I crossed the river slowly, the cab pushing patiently through accidents and roadworks. South of the Thames there was an indefinable feeling of social sepulchre, but also the gentle warmth of a seaside town. It had a security about it, as if I could hide out for a while in one of these endlessly similar streets, to emerge rejuvenated, remastered.

Clutching the letter, I found the street, the house, its bell. Today my mind was not on charity, on kindness. I wanted ideas to run with, a cause to take up for my own benefit. I was desperate to silence the voices that called to me from inside.

There was a sound on the stairs and the door opened. A white, scarred face looked up at me, one eye socket slightly flattened on the eyebrow, and containing an obviously glass eye. The man wore a stained blue sweatshirt bearing the name of a football team. One arm hung by his side and he held a stick in his hand. His expression was distant as he let me in, but perhaps that was simply his eye. I apologized for turning up unannounced, but he had left no phone number. I followed him up the stairs. He was small, with mousy hair and a cast-down, tired face. But there was a power in him, even with the limp, as if he could literally pull himself out of his body and swing up, strong as a monkey, onto some higher plane.

His flat was like so many London flats hastily converted to multiply the living space in what was once comfortable bourgeois living accommodation. It had poky rooms with high ceilings, and unpainted hollow doors with splinters flaking off the edges and squeaky push-down handles. His kitchen and sitting room were all one. There was a smell of baked beans. The carpet was a worn dark turquoise, with freestyle swirls of white and korma yellow, the table a flaking laminate. The walls, which were painted a dull white like a student room, were covered in Blu-Tack stains and fading sports posters. There were copies of the *Skip* lying everywhere, some extremely faded.

He passed me a chipped cup of tea, so dark it seemed made from rusty nails, and a small plate with two stale digestives. I sat down. The armchair was scratchy, ludicrous, saffron-coloured in fifties style, with a high back, and flaps at the side like great blinkers, designed to destroy casual conversation.

'Thank you for coming to see me, Miss Clevtoe.'

It seemed over-formal to address me this way, but perhaps my new existence had brought with it a corresponding demeanour. I realized I still did not know his name. I was suddenly embarrassed to ask.

'It's nice to see big people like the *Skip* taking notice of little people like me.'

His one good eye accompanied his small smile. I should not have expected him to grin, unless in a modest self-deprecating fashion. Here was someone who had obviously lived alone for a long time. And yet there was something slightly incongruous in his manner, like a thin discoloured ring on a tree stump. He sat with his mug of tea and looked at me for a while, expectantly.

I remembered why I was there, but did not want to raise his hopes. I asked him to explain his problems. He went into a brief, seemingly well-rehearsed spiel about his situation. It was all too believable. He was quite willing to appear in the paper.

'The problem is, Miss Clevtoe, what loses me a lot of sympathy is that I can actually walk, you know, perambulate, and so I don't even get what I need to live on. Look.'

And he showed me his most recent benefit cheque, as if I might not believe him. He got up and moved stiffly across the room to the window. Every so often he would shoot a quick glance at me. His face was suddenly bathed in sunlight through the net curtain. His scars made abstract lacework down one side of his face.

'It's funny, you know. I had a lot going for me as a sportsman once upon a time. I was a fucking good bowler, and I could kick a ball around too. My parents, they're just ordinary people, but they really wanted me to be something. All the other kids were pissing around, hanging round the estate and Mum and Dad thought, no, let's get something better for our son. They wanted more for me than that.'

He added quickly, 'So Miss Clevtoe, tell me about your life, then, now that you've got so successful?'

There was something strangely personal in his tone. His plimsolls had holes.

'Oh, I've done this and that. I work pretty hard, you know!'

'Ooh! I bet you do!' He was suddenly aggressive, his eyes flicking over my clothes.

'Look. Sorry, you're right. It was a crappy thing to say, but it's you I'm here to talk about, not me.'

For a moment I could not tell which of his eyes was glass, he looked so detached.

A hammer lay on the rickety side table.

'Do you have anyone to help you with your DIY? A neighbour or someone like that?'

'DIY? Why would I do DIY? Oh, that, yeah, sometimes someone comes in—' his voice trailed off, boredly.

His hand suddenly passed over his face and squeezed it down the middle, down the bridge of his nose. He seemed in pain.

'Are you all right?'

What do you suggest? What do you offer to someone in this situation? Aspirin, a drink, love? He barely registered my words.

'Look, tell me, because we'll have to use it in the article, how did you get like this? What happened to you?'

'HOW THE FUCK DO YOU THINK IT HAPPENED, SARAH CLEVTOE, PUPIL AT WHALEY SCHOOL, INHABITANT OF SEDGEBOURNE?'

With these spat words he picked up the hammer in his good hand and ran at me with it. The narrow armchair had me trapped within its rigid form. He brought the hammer down with practised aim straight onto my head. Once, twice and on, faster and faster.

His other arm swung helplessly with his movements, the thumb and forefinger flipping up and lightly touching my breast as he smashed at me. His eyes were closed, his lips pressed together. He breathed through his nose, I could feel droplets of liquid on my face. Then he began to get tired and opened his mouth to pant. He backed away with a drunken movement, threw down the hammer and fell into the other armchair, his hand across his face. All I could hear were the cars in the street and his breathing. I waited patiently for him to see me, but he would not uncover his eyes. His lips began to move.

'I've done the bitch at last, done the cow, I've done her. I've done her. Just look after me now, just take me away. JUST TAKE ME AWAY!'

He got up, still with his eyes partly covered and averted, and went to the window. Throwing the nylon net to the side he threw the catch and began grappling with the sash window with his one good arm. It was painful to watch, as he edged each side up a quarter of an inch and then the other, his dead arm mocking in its uselessness.

'I've done the bitch. I've smashed her. I've done it.' He had the window up five inches when I said quietly, 'Ben. Please don't.'

He turned and froze. He looked first at the hammer and then at my face. He rubbed his good eye and shook his head.

'Have I died? Sarah Clevtoe, have I died? Tell me, or am I so bloody useless I can't even kill a bitch who ruined my whole life? Tell me, Sarah Clevtoe. I've been looking for you for a long time, you know. And now I can't even get rid of you.'

He began to shake and then to cry. I sat in the chair and watched him. He looked up at me briefly and then down again.

And then I did something I had never before done in my whole life, and that was to go and put my arms around someone without fear, without supplication, without helplessness or obsessive lonely desire. I knelt by his chair and reached out to him.

'You destroyed my fucking life. I wish you'd killed me. My dad got cancer and my mum's in a home now. She hardly speaks or anything.'

'Do you know what they did to *me*?'

'Who?'

'Them, those boys, Alex and the band and all that lot.'

'You screwed the whole bloody lot of them, that's what I heard. They all came round to your house the whole time, and then they used to come back and brag about it and draw pictures of you and everything.' He wriggled for a moment in my grasp, turning his head away with disgust. I pushed my face into his hair. It had an animal smell. I rested my head against his, and calmly told the story of my life, as far as I knew. He listened. When I had finished he spoke about his own, the endless round of letters, claims, operations, physiotherapies, car journeys, waiting rooms full of posters, special forms to fill in, incomprehensible demands from the local council, the fading of his parents. When he finished he seemed to relax for a minute. We sat in silence. A delivery van hummed outside. A dog barked. Ben thought for a minute, then stood and began to talk again.

'I don't know if I can forgive you, Sarah, not yet.'

He paced up and down.

'But those bastards! I wanted to say to Dad, "It's a horrible place they're all stuck-up cunts let me make my own way," but they'd worked so hard and I just couldn't let them down like that. Toffee-nosed wankers, bloody arseholes. I could hardly see to write my exams I got such fucking headaches, and that was two years later. I mean, it's all the same blokes now, isn't it? All that lot, they're running the government, they're running the fucking establishment, it's all the same fucking people! God I'd like to bomb those cunts out of the fucking universe.'

'Well,' I said, 'why don't we?'

twenty-three

AS IT HAPPENED, we decided to poison them instead.

I rushed back to the office and fabricated a suitable excuse to set the single Junior on to researching the Pulver wedding, the guests and security. There was a look of bewilderment on the editor's face that I was involving myself in such a project. He had the air of being about to comment, but did not.

Flushed with excitement, I plotted. With some difficulty, given the exquisite contents of my wardrobe, I cobbled together a poor-yet-presentable outfit and went to offer myself to Alex's caterers as a temporary employee, having pleaded investigative journalism as the purpose of my short leave.

As a tall person, I played awkward-but-efficient, giving my potential employers a feeling of power tempered by slight mystification about someone who they felt might have been designed for higher things had she not contained some production-line fault. I displayed eagerness and organization, a willingness to put on an ill-fitting uniform, an appropriate accent, and legs suitable to be shown off at the very brink of vulgarity.

I was hired for several weddings, at the first four of which I acquitted myself beautifully. I learned to sail my tray of eats into the most close-knit and confidential groups of guests, and beguile them utterly with my gentle humour. As I gained their confidence my wit would become a little more outrageous, a little more directed, and they would stuff more and more of the salmon bites and their gaze would begin to follow me as I tacked on through the crowds.

My employers loved me. They loved me to the extent of allowing me to help with the preparation of the food itself, which became a source of irritation to some of my co-workers. However, I won them over too with my total humility and willingness to accept their every suggestion as superior to my own. I became a bundle of self-deprecation:

'Hello, Sarah, it's a nice day today, isn't it?'

'Well, huh! Dunno about that – maybe it'd be even nicer for you all if I'd just stayed in bed.'

'Sarah, don't be silly!'

'On a day like this, I'll be going to work, and every time I get to the ticket machine, it changes to "Exact money only", every single time! And then the other day I was waiting at the bus stop when a dog came and pissed all over my ankle!'

For good measure, I sometimes talked about myself in the third person: 'Well, huh, of course guess who's at the end of the queue but Sarah, and just as she's getting to the hatch the woman puts up the "position closed" sign and says, "Sorry, love, come back the Thursday after next."'

Sometimes I indulged them with amusing tales of my stupidity as a child.

'Do you know, until quite recently I used to think egress meant female eagle! And that the wait button at pelican crossings was just for kids to teach them how to cross the road and so I'd be standing there for hours waiting for the lights to change, and that the Rambo films were about Rimbaud, you know, the French poet, and I was amazed when all the boys at school were so keen to go.'

The expressions I received at the latter example made me realize I was sailing extremely close to the wind. After that, if I felt such a remark coming on, I would swear instead, 'Well, of course, look at those coffee ads, you only have to deconstruct the fucking pile of shit what a load of wankers they are, don't you reckon?'

Ben went to the library for pharmacopoeias. I knew I had to atone for what I had done to him. Sex was out of the question – he had not been able to obtain an erection since my attack on him, and he was too proud to accept money from me. I resorted to sending him anonymous gifts through the post. Although neither could have said it out loud, all we wanted was to stand under a great roaring cataract of unconditional love until we were washed clean of our misery and self-hatred.

The Pulver wedding party was the last of an intense season of work for the catering company, and the largest. It was being held in the grounds of a once-great family home that had been turned into a hotel and conference centre. Alex was marrying the daughter of a coat-hanger baron, who had insisted that every guest be given a pair of padded, monogrammed samples to take home. There was a full-size and functional merry-go-round made of ice, and a walk-in model of Trafalgar Square, with column and lions made from great heaps of Twiglets, all constructed by some specially flown-in Chinese bridge-makers, and a champagne fountain for paddling in.

We were cooking on-site, in our own marquee which was

shaped like a chef's hat, soaking, basting and slicing from five o'clock in the morning. One of the company's specialities was deep-fried sweetbreads handed out as an *amuse-gueule,* and it became my job to hurl the little bits of natural punctuation into a crackling vat of oil. Although by then I had performed the action hundreds of times, I was still always shocked by the hissing scream of departing liquids as they hit the surface of the thickly bubbling oil. I became quite obsessed with the task, and demanded to do it with a vigour I barely comprehended.

People began to arrive. This was one of those weddings where the parents have rewarded themselves by inviting ninety per cent of the guests. Tycoons, grandees, mandarins and their ladies were all out in force. The string quartet played, the grass was soft and springy underfoot. Fingers flashed with rings. The sun caressed the brim of every hat and the bright bone in every smile.

The shout came and I began tossing things into oil. The gas roared beneath the two-foot-wide-pan, deep with golden liquid. I worked joyously, with the same fervour as when I shuffled through leaves in the park. With particular violence I hurled forth one lump of flesh. There was an odd clang against the side of the pan. One of my rings had flown off with it. Without thinking, I plunged my hand straight into the oil to retrieve it. The woman working next to me screamed, and the supervisor came running over with a look of horror. I was still fishing around as he grabbed my arm. He looked at me and frowned.

'It's really not that hot!' I exclaimed brightly, wiping my hand. The sweetbread crumbled in my palm.

Later, when I had prepared a tray and was about to do my rounds, I crudely wiped my brow and dismayed the assistant chef by swigging from an open bottle of bleach instead of the flask of water standing next to it. I really had not noticed. I was starting to get strange looks but I didn't care.

'How long do you give this marriage, then?' someone said. Almost instantaneously the receiving line was called, and two hours passed as the guests queued patiently. I regaled them with caviar thins and raunchy, sailor-like sayings, which soon had the little knots of people looking out for me.

Some of them looked like decent, friendly, accommodating people, and I felt a tiny flicker of doubt, but then a whole vanguard of shrieking, bellowing monsters arrived, picking their noses and farting, and I became fixed in my resolve. One can perhaps forgive a personal affront, but not a general one.

Alex's new wife was tanned, boxy and organized-looking, with a well-practised eye-smile which made her face, when it relaxed, a network of caramel and white stripes like a tie-dyed scarf. I recognized Kev and Keef and handed them their sausages with equanimity. They had grown fatter, their suits more expensive and better fitting. I felt serene. There was to be no vengeful showdown, no war of wit, no rabbit punch after a sexual lure into the bushes. They all smiled at me, and I grinned back and tossed my hair. Exhausted, watchful girlfriends kissed and hooted.

And there was Radger, grey-haired, clutching his champagne as if it were a pint, his hand clawed round the delicate flute, held close to his chest. He had evidently had a few. As I looked at him I imagined I could see another pathetic, ageing man, whose hand once twined my hair in an ancient grip. I returned quickly to the kitchen tent.

The five hundred guests were to be seated at five long tables, ranged in rows on the huge lawn. The white cloths and silver put out a blinding radiance, like the mad refulgence of light-bulbs before they die from a surfeit of power.

The baron had spared no expense and our suppliers had done their best. A clear pale green soup made of rare cave lichens flown in from the Himalayas; then, to be eaten with bread made from the ground bones of the white tiger, dishes of baked eyeballs of salmon, the soft humours congealed and opaque; pungent roes, eaten with specially made spoons, their tiny cupped ends like crochet hooks; the brains of small forest creatures lightly poached on beds of chicory.

Voices burst immoderately forth from the feast. I trundled up and down, waiting nervously for the *tour de force,* ten oxen, each stuffed with a calf that was stuffed with a lamb which contained a swan stuffed with a pheasant with a quail inside it, the whole basted in a sauce the colour of mahogany. Twenty decorated shire horses, pulling cantilevered cranes, lifted gigantic silver lids from the immense serving dishes.

Each ox and its contents contained enough poison to kill about twelve thousand people. It was an ideal substance, one that through the action of heat gave off a gas deadly to humans, one whose molecules gripped all living flesh, never letting go. I had felt as if I were in a fairy tale as I opened the little bag Ben had given me and placed the grey lumps inside the quails' tiny carcasses.

The guests were dead even before they had swallowed their first mouthfuls. I was not sorry to miss the speeches. The deaths were quick but agonizing, enforcing paralysis and helpless expulsion on the victim with the rush of a blowtorch. The string quartet, who had become tired and were sneaking in cover versions of Beatles songs, threw down their instruments and ran. There was silence.

I left my post and walked up and down the tables. The guests sat in various frozen poses of shock, every one of them finally freed from the grip of social rules and acceptabilities. One women, in a coral-coloured suit, her face squeezed in horrified bemusement at the ejaculations of her body, resembled a huge prawn, the two long curled plumes in her matching hat sticking out at mad angles.

A single cloud passed briefly, dusting the upturned, twisted faces. I laughed out loud as the shadow ran over the scene, pulled up one of the musicians' footstools and began to eat. Doves cooed in the trees.

'Hey!'

Ben had been waiting outside the gate for an opportunity to walk in. He had resolutely refused to dress for the occasion, and I had had to ban him for appearance's sake. Now he had managed to find some champagne, and held an open bottle in each hand. He sashayed over to the table and dumped them with a flourish.

I should have kept my wits about me as I tore at some bird's breast in its velvety gravy. I should have calmed his excitement and reminded him of what we had done. Before I could stop him he pulled off a slab of meat, toasted me with it, and forced it into his mouth.

I screamed to him and ran, tipping over the little stool. His vomit sprayed. He stiffened, his eyes fixed on mine. I forced my hand into his mouth and yanked at the meat, still barely chewed. His teeth clamped down on my fingers. His body shuddered, his damaged arm swayed, he barely made a sound.

He fell back against the table like a shop dummy. Ben was dead. I looked at him for a moment and returned to my seat.

I picked up the stool and arranged it in a space between guests. Stretching my legs straight out in front of me I rested one elbow and began to eat. Every so often the silence was broken by a body slipping sideways and falling stiffly to the ground with the thump of a cricket bat tossed on a lawn.

Slowly the sun moved round, glittering down through the birch trees. Chewing hard, I looked up for a moment at the tall white trunks and delicate structure of branches around them, and then at the sea of corpses that lay around me.

I ate an entire ox and began another. Darkness fell. I was not afraid. Patiently I cut the cooked flesh.